To Bobbi ~
Enjoyed meeting
you at the
hideo Spa!

The Secret at the Breakers Hotel

A Palm Beach Mystery

CAROLYN CAIN

Carolyn Cain

Pittsburgh, PA

ISBN 1-56315-287-8

Paperback Fiction
©Copyright 2002 Carolyn Cain
All rights reserved
First Printing—2002
Library of Congress #2001095143

Request for information should be addressed to:

SterlingHouse Publisher, Inc.
7436 Washington Avenue
Suite 200
Pittsburgh, PA 15218
www.sterlinghousepublisher.com

Cover Designer: Jeffrey S. Butler —SterlingHouse Publisher
Book Designer: Bernadette E. Kazmarski

This publication includes images from (Corel Draw 8) or
(Adobe 6.5) which are protected by the copyright laws of the
U.S., Canada and elsewhere.

All rights reserved. No part of this publication may be repro-
duced, stored in a retrieval system, or transmitted in any form or
by any means—electronic, mechanical, photocopy, recording or
any other, except for brief quotations in printed reviews—
without prior permission of the publisher.

This is a work of fiction. Names, characters, places and incidents
either are the product of the author's imagination or are used
fictitiously. Any resemblance to actual events or persons, living
or dead, is entirely coincidental.

Printed in The United States of America

Acknowledgements

I wish to thank the following people for their help and support in the long gestation period of this book.

First, Jan Fogt and Cricket Pechstein, the Rat Pack, for friendship beyond words.

Second, David Hagberg, whose writing skills are so bountiful he can afford to share.

Third, the members of the Mystery Writers of America, a group of writers whose generosity is exceeded only by their talent, especially Barbara Parker for her encouragement and Diane Vogt for her friendship.

Fourth, the members of my many writing groups, including but not limited to Marie Ziobro, Sandi Haddad, Trish Doberganes, Marilyn Ivison, Anna Caulfield, and the Vero Beach Bunch, Sharon Townley, June Holland, Sue Mather, Emily Cole, Jane Huber and John Mackie.

Also, Kathy Mutch, who was there at the beginning, and Pam Macaluso, who showed me what it was to want to be published.

Fifth, to James Ponce and James Jennings Sheeran, whose stories about Palm Beach past and present set my imagination on fire and fueled my desire to set books there.

Sixth, to the residents of Palm Beach, whose gifts to charity, lavish galas, commitment to style and dedication to leaving a wake of beauty have resulted in a society so much larger than life that it was irresistible to this writer.

And finally, to the Town of Palm Beach, a town with a personality so distinct this book could have not been set anywhere else.

Dedication

With love and gratitude to Sam,

Beth and Richard

Chapter One

Money can't buy happiness and don't let anyone tell you it can.

I was sitting on a patio overlooking the sapphire water of the Atlantic Ocean while beside me my friend of forty years snuffled into a lace hanky. Although I wasn't yet quite sure what the problem was, having just been summoned to her Palm Beach mansion by a tearful phone call, I was pretty sure the love of money would somehow be at the root of those pitiful tears.

LaLa's fair hair fluttered in the sea breeze. "Wally," she hiccuped, "I think Booth is having an affair."

Aha, I thought. *How do you tell your best friend her husband is a stinker? You don't.* "Nonsense," I lied. "Booth loves you."

The truth was, I had known both LaLa and Booth Ewen since we were students at the Palm Beach Day School, and Booth had always been a shit. But LaLa was an angel and angels don't grow on trees, so from the moment they married right out of high school I had kept my opinion to myself. If you don't appreciate the enormity of that gesture, it's because you don't know me. My husband would be the first to tell you that Wally Tupper rarely has an opinion she doesn't like— and express. Some people call it obnoxious. I prefer to think of it as honesty.

But I reached down for whatever sensitivity I had in me, patted LaLa on the shoulder, and tried to figure out what was the right thing. "Is there anything I can do?" I asked. Helpful wasn't my normal mode either, but I'd seen it work for others.

LaLa glared at me with eyes the color of cornflowers and pursed up a pink little mouth. "Hell yes," she snapped. "Follow him and find out."

Now, we live in Palm Beach. There's a certain segment of the population here that makes a social life out of going to parties where they do nothing but talk about all the other people at the party. I'm not one of them. I hate parties, and I really hate gossip. I don't follow people, as a rule.

"First off," I started, "that's a very unusual request."

Her hair drooped in a momentary doldrum. Real people on this earthly plane are always disappointing LaLa. She prefers to communicate with those in another world. Today, however, they apparently weren't home. "My spirit guide is on vacation," she said. "I'm not in touch with my inner self. I need your help. Didn't you go to police school, or something?"

"One criminal justice course."

"Same thing. How hard can it be?" She stood up, glided to a pool side table and picked up a cell phone.

While she was dialing, I sat in the sun of the balmy South Florida November day and thought about how my life might have turned out differently. I was blessed with the curse of a family fortune, and with no need to earn a living, I have approached life as one long series of learning experiences. What I'm ever going to do with all I've learned I don't know, but I figure I'll be the savviest octogenarian on my block some day.

LaLa was referring to my somewhat unusual college career. Since I didn't really need a degree, I just went wherever my interests took me, including one trip to Manhattan to attend John Jay School of Criminal Justice.

I went to seventeen colleges in all, changed majors every time, and only quit going because I married Pitt Wesson, a man who wanted a career as a banker. Pitt asked me to use the drama courses I had taken at Yale to play the role of the wife of a corporate banker on the fast track. I acted the part because I didn't really have anything better to do.

When LaLa finished talking, she sat back down beside me, her dress billowing around her pale legs. I said LaLa was an angel, and it always seems as if her clothes and hair are trying to get back up to Heaven. Her hair is spun gold and her clothes seem to be made of gossamer and are always ruffling or swirling around her. Right now, though, she was firmly grounded in a wicker chair with the telephone clutched in her lap. "He's gone to the Breakers," she said.

The Breakers is one of the center rings of Palm Beach Society. The one hundred-year-old hotel is a big part of Palm Beach history, and locals go there all the time for meetings, lunch and society galas: It has quite the upper crust cachet. "So what?" I said, then asked, "Who was that on the phone?"

"When Booth left earlier today, he told me he was going to Miami on business." She smiled one of those don't-believe-it smiles. "But his chauffeur says he's waiting for him outside the Breakers." She shook her head in disbelief. "Bastard. Who does he think pays the help, anyway?"

LaLa stood up, her hands floating into the air as if to cause me to levitate. "So. Get going."

"LaLa..."

"It's not like you're going out of your way," she argued. "We're meeting Peep for lunch at the Beach Club anyway; it's right there."

I was stumped for a comeback. LaLa and I had to tell our best friend some very bad news passed along via the well-developed and well-tended Palm Beach grapevine. It was not going to be a pleasant lunch. I gave her a baleful stare and a nod of surrender.

"Fine," she said. "I'll meet you in the restaurant at one o'clock—it's almost that now. You bring me some information about what my husband is up to. Shoo."

I shooed.

I hopped into my red 1962 Corvair convertible and pulled out onto North Ocean Boulevard. Turning south, I putted toward the Breakers but on impulse, passed it by and continued south to Barton Avenue, where we live.

If Booth were at the Breakers, he'd be there for another five minutes, I figured. I wanted to pick up my morning edition of *The Palm Beach Tattler*, the daily newspaper that enthusiastically records the comings and goings of the town of Palm Beach. The newspaper would help break the bad news at lunch—as if this day weren't bad news already.

I turned right and then, in the center of the block, pulled into our driveway. I pushed the garage door button and, leaving the car running, ran to the kitchen door, which is never locked, and opened it. As I grabbed the paper off the kitchen counter, I gave a yoo-hoo to Petal, our live-in housekeeper and one of my few concessions to life among the monied. If I didn't yoo-hoo, Petal would call the police. She's a little on the nervous side, but I think if I were a thief I certainly wouldn't be targeting my somewhat modest—relatively speaking—home on Barton Avenue.

Barton is a small, quiet street tucked in the middle of some of the most expensive homes in the world. Our little island town is less than four square miles and has a summer population of only about ten thousand, but they say we house more than twenty-five percent of the world's wealth during the winter season.

My husband and I live on Barton because that's where my parents lived and that's the house that became mine when they disappeared on a flight through the Bermuda Triangle in 1945. Pitt has lobbied since we married to move to one of the larger, oceanfront homes that are the hallmark of life in Palm Beach. He's now the president of the Palm Tree Bank, and he thinks it's important for him to host the right kind of parties in the right kind of house. But it's my house, and that's that.

I can walk east a few blocks to the Atlantic Ocean or west a few blocks to Lake Worth, which separates Palm Beach from the real world. I can walk a few blocks south and be in the center of town, which is made up mostly of immaculately maintained Mediterranean buildings from the 1920s, when Palm Beach came into full flower as the premier winter resort for the wealthy.

Back in my car, I drove east on Barton and then turned north on South County. When I reached the Breakers entrance, I turned right into a palm-lined mini-boulevard. Ahead of me loomed the imposing concrete Italian Renaissance presence of the hotel. The dozen or so parking spaces allotted to those who eschew valet parking were full, so I pulled to a stop under the *porte cochere* and waited the few seconds it took a valet to reach my car and whisk it away.

I clutched the newspaper as if I could wring all those words right out of it. What remained of my tattered good mood seemed to disappear around the corner with my Corvair. My anger with Booth and my hunger were running neck and neck in a contest to bug the hell out of me. In spite of the fact that the opulent hotel lobby teemed with slim women who would gag on a grape and spit up on their designer dresses if you forced a Swedish meatball down their throats, I was so hungry I would have snagged a passing cheeseburger and devoured it right there in front of Calvin Klein himself.

One o'clock was early for a two-martini Palm Beach lunch, but late for my stomach. The whiny little piece of gut had made short work of my six o'clock toast and was now grumbling so loudly I was sure it could be heard by the busy Friday check-in crowd. It didn't do to have your body parts making noises in the lobby of The Breakers. The patrician hotel prided itself on its Old Money grandeur, and I was pretty sure hotel staff would tell me I could take my bodily functions and check them into the newer and flashier Ritz Carleton down the street, where they allowed that sort of thing.

But I've been a resident of Palm Beach for all of my fifty-two years, and I no longer worry about what's allowed. I leave that to my more society-conscious friends, two of whom I was meeting for lunch, which was why the trip to the Breakers was planned in the first place and why I couldn't eat when I damn well pleased.

I dodged a flying wedge of tourists, almost tripping on a woman with too-black hair and too little spandex. She had a Yorkie the size of a healthy rat tucked under her arm, and they both glared at me. I spotted Booth Ewen about thirty feet away toward the south end of the hotel lobby. He was crouched behind a fresh cut flower arrangement the size of a vintage Volkswagen. I tried to get his attention, but he darted from behind the flowers and disappeared around an Italianate column.

I knew he had seen me, and it looked for all the world as if he were trying to hide from me. I circled the lobby. If he was trying to hide, he was doing a good job of it.

I took a moment to ponder why I was playing Sam Spade, detective, and came up with the world's oldest reason: Like Eve, I guess I was just curious. If LaLa was headed for hurt, I wanted to head it off. It's my nature to plunge in without too much thought. It's gotten me in trouble before.

At the moment, however, I was too hungry to worry about it, and I headed toward the Tapestry Bar, across the lobby and through the broad hallway on the north side of the Mediterranean Courtyard. There, I ran smack dab back into the tourists.

"Henry Flagler built his first hotel, the Royal Poinciana, just across the island," said a familiar voice. Reginald Wert, unofficial Palm Beach historian, was leading the tour group through the hotel. "Then, one hundred years ago, the Standard Oil millionaire built what was to be his grandest resort for the wealthy–the Breakers." Reggie turned and beckoned to the dozen tourists, their wrinkled clothes and openmouthed stares distinguishing them from the immaculate aplomb of the hotel guests. "Step lively," he said, backing down the corridor, hunching over in his too-large hotel blazer, as he fluffed his hands to bring them along. "We have a lot to see."

He spotted me and beamed in my direction. Putting the tourists on hold with upheld palms, he sidled over.

"Major debacle in the holiday ambiance department," he said out of the side of a silver mustache that matched his neatly trimmed hair. "There's been a scheduling snafu."

The Breakers always pulls out all the stops when it comes to Christmas ambiance, with choirs of angels singing from every rafter during the season. From somewhere across the lobby, I could faintly hear "Silver Bells" being sung in four-part harmony. "I hear Christmas carols," I said. I sniffed. For the first time since I walked in, the full sensual force of the Breakers' holiday experience hit my nostrils: evergreen and bayberry. "I smell Christmas scent." Fresh green garland was draped on every arched window and around every doorway. "I see Christmas decorations. The halls of the Breakers are decked, Reggie. What's the problem?"

Reggie put his hand on his hip and lifted a padded shoulder in mock indignity. "Somebody scheduled the Don We Now Carolers at the same time as the Sons of the Beaches Barbershop Quartet." He raised an eyebrow. "You just missed them, but darling, for a few minutes, we had both of them singing at the same time and the guests were beginning to twitch."

"Seems like there'd be room for both of them, somewhere, in the hotel," I said. It was a big hotel.

"My dear. You have no idea." Reggie pranced his fingers around in the air. "They were circling each other like tomcats around a Siamese bitch in heat. Every time the Carolers hit a high note, the quartet tried to throw them off by pumping up the harmony. Of course, the Carolers had to retaliate, which they did, thank you very much, by hitting high notes out of the Sons of the Beaches' key and the result was a caterwauling that sent the French crystal chandeliers to trembling."

"I gather the quartet won." I didn't see any sign of the Don We Now Carolers, a segment of the Gay Men's Chorus and a very popular entertainment around town.

"Management promised a showcase event for the Carolers on a peak night; it smoothed their ruffled feathers."

I squinted down at him. Reggie knew almost everybody who was anybody in Palm Beach. "I was sort of looking for Booth Ewen," I said. "You seen him?"

He inclined his head and jerked it toward the lobby. "Yes, certainly did. As I was rounding up the group, he broke through us almost at a run and headed down the south hall." He looked at me with a question in his eyes. "You would have thought the IRS was on his tail. Why?"

I knew I couldn't fool Reggie, but I owed it to LaLa not to blab. "Oh, you know," I said, putting the most innocent look on my face I could muster. "Just curious."

"Right," he said. With a wink and a nod, Reggie turned and strode to a spot behind a fringed brocade sofa near the center of the 200-foot Italianate lobby. The gaggle of neck-craning, swivel-headed gawkers pushed past me to follow their leader, quacking excitedly among themselves, none of them looking and walking in the same direction at the same time. The woman whose size-eleven Nike cross-trainers had tripped me in the lobby now trod on my heel, glared at me and flounced off, her red and purple flowered T-shirt and gold spandex shorts bouncing in time to the four-part harmony of "Sleigh Ride."

"Oh, one more thing," Reggie called out as he herded them down the hall. "When I first saw him, Booth was talking to someone. A woman." He glanced down at his group and stage whispered over their heads. "An outsider," he said.

I felt some small twinge of kinship with the tourists, who were about as out of place in the Breakers as the Muscogee ducks in the ponds of the golf course surrounding it. It was always the same. Like birds, the tourists migrated south in the winter, although most of them spent less on their two-week vacations than some of the Breakers' clientele spent in one night at the hotel. Armed with their Yankee rudeness and their awful accents, the tourists would drink too many Harvey Wallbangers and eat too many gator bits and then go home and tell everybody how tacky Florida was, except for Palm Beach. And those Palm Beach people, they would say after visiting Worth Avenue, could learn a thing or two about bargains if they just went to the fashion district in New York.

I could identify with not fitting in, because I'm five foot seven inches of gawk and totally without social grace. It came on me slowly over my childhood, as I realized with dawning appreciation for my limitations, that I would never be perfect. When I was fifteen, I thought I might become Miss America. But I gave that up when I realized that since my mouth rarely checked with my brain before speaking, those tough impromptu questions would be murder. When I was seventeen, I thought I might become a high-fashion model. But when I turned eighteen, my butt and bosoms blossomed into melon-like fullness. Oh, well, I thought, I didn't like wearing high heels anyway.

So, although I'm the kind of person who is just grateful for a day when my cuticles are soft and my skin doesn't flake in public, I resigned myself to living in a town where women hire people to put their makeup on for them.

I have learned to compensate. I have brains, which keep me busy. I have a sense of humor, which keeps me sane.

I also have money. Lots and lots of money, which goes a long way toward making me feel better on a bad hair day.

But my most precious asset is my nanny, Erma. It was Erma, just nineteen years old and fresh off the migrant truck from Alabama, who was hired as my live-in nanny when I was an infant.

My parents' disappearance set off a struggle among my various distant relatives as to who would have baby Wallis Tupper living with them. Mostly, I was unaware of all of this until I got to be around seven. But Erma was not. Raised on a farm by people who had no money but heaps and heaps of family values, Erma marched herself into a judge's office and told him she wasn't letting this baby—that's me—fall into the hands of people who only wanted her for her money.

The judge agreed, and named Erma as my legal guardian until someone could prove to him they had my best interests at heart or until I was old enough to decide for myself. It wouldn't happen that way today, but it was wartime and people were a whole lot less bureaucratic about what happened to orphan children.

So Erma, who later married and had a family, raised me as one of her own, with one exception. "Some day," she would say to me, "you'll have lots of money. And I'm going to prepare you for that."

What she did was make me into a sort of a Southern Dorothy dropped into a wealthier Oz. At least Dorothy could click her heels and get out of Oz. Instead, my good witch tried to teach me how to recognize the flying monkeys when they were dressed to the nines in designer duds.

From his post, Reggie pointed out heirloom tapestry wall hangings and thick, medallion-patterned carpet over Tennessee marble floors. I glanced at my Timex and quickened my steps. I didn't need any tour guide to tell me about Palm Beach. Anyone who knew Palm Beach would be looking not at the pattern on the carpeting but for the dirt swept under the rug.

It was my problem that I was getting ready to lift up the corner of my best friend's carpet.

Chapter Two

I WANTED IN THE WORST way to be sitting at the bar sipping something cool, but the tourists were between it and me. They were listening openmouthed to Reggie— himself a relic of some stature in the Historical Society of Palm Beach—as he regaled them with Breakers lore. Their eyes blinked wide open with astonishment as he swung his arm around toward a six-foot vertical chessboard made of glass and told them about the eleven thousand dollar price tag. Their heads cocked with interest as he related the story of the Breakers Babies, born while the hotel had been converted to a hospital during World War II.

I sized up my possibilities. Going through them was out of the question. Their elbows were all akimbo and it was risking rib damage to try to make a dash into their midst. Going around them was my only chance, so I fixed my eyes on the bar and set out.

"And in 1925," Reggie was saying, "the Breakers burned for the third time." I tried to scoot around him as he continued his story about the 1926 rebuilding of the hotel. "So they asked, just how fireproof can you build this building?" he said jovially. The tourists laughed, their eyes cutting back and forth nervously, their noses sniffing for smoke.

Reggie snagged me by my arm as I passed by.

"Tell your husband I'm still on the trail of his genealogical information," he said. "You sure you don't want me to do yours, too?"

My husband had recently decided he wanted to find some highborn branches in his family tree, and had asked Reggie to help him find them. I, on the other hand, have no interest in digging into—or up—my family history. "Nope," I said, extricating my arm and crab-walking toward my goal. "With apologies to your historic sensibilities, Reggie, there's no point wasting time on a family tree for me."

He pursed his lips in resignation. "Very well. Tell Pitt I'll let him know when I find something interesting."

It hit me at that moment that I didn't have much of a story to tell LaLa. I hated the prospect of more tears, and I got an idea for a plan that might keep LaLa dry-eyed, at least through lunch.

Reggie, a single gentleman in a world where the single man always gets invited to dinner, did not lack for a social life. But his one true love was genealogy, the search for the ultimate family tree. He loved to poke into people's families more than he loved life itself. I decided to let that love do a little work for LaLa, even though it was a move I felt I would later regret.

"I'll make you a deal, Reggie," I said.

He put his group on idle and gave me his attention. "What kind of a deal?" he asked.

I smiled, smug. "I'll let you do a genealogy on me if you'll watch out for Booth Ewen and let me know who you see him with."

Reggie considered this for a minute, just to put on a bit of a show. The other love of Reggie's life was the Breakers, and he kept a sharp eye on the comings and goings in the hotel. This was something he would have done anyway. But he might be afraid that to agree to snoop on command would somehow be unseemly.

I sweetened the pot. "It'd be a real mystery, you know. It would be quite the search; a real feather in the cap of any genealogist who could find out about my family tree."

He was melting. "Do you have a birth certificate?" he asked weakly.

I had won. "Nope. Don't know where I was born, only that I was born in 1944. You'd really have to dig."

He made a big show of giving in. "All right," he sighed dramatically. "Since it's you, I'll do your searches—both of them."

He turned back to his group, but flung a parting shot over his shoulder: "If you were born in 1944 in Palm Beach, *you* could be a Breakers Baby, you know."

Not wanting to step on his own exit line, he grandly but silently waved the group on down the hall.

I turned back toward the bar and heaved my butt up onto the nearest stool. I'm not much of a drinker but the soothing ambiance of the Tapestry Bar always makes me want to take it up full-time just so I can spend more time there. The room is a collection of mismatched furniture pieces covered in fabric of turquoise, coral and royal blue that somehow blends into a cozy nest. The bar itself is solid mahogany, polished to a gleam. Behind the bar is a mirror, so if you want, you can discreetly see what is going on behind you. I watched gratefully as the last of Reggie's group disappeared down the hall.

Artie Marsh, the day bartender, stepped up to the other side of the bar in front of me. "Drink, Ms. Tupper?" Artie was twenty-something, ebony-eyed and alert in the way of good professional bartenders anywhere. He waited while I debated with myself. I don't like to dull my senses in the middle of the day, but if ever there was going to be a day when I wished to be senseless, it looked like this might be it.

"Wine, I guess. Something light, please."

He set a cocktail napkin in front of me, swooped a glass from beneath the bar, then poured a golden liquid into the glass and set it on the cocktail napkin. "Try that, madam," he said, with a flourish and a half bow.

I did. It was soft with an oaky undertaste. "Good," I said. "Thanks."

He nodded his satisfaction and stepped back, returning the bottle to wherever he had gotten it. I looked in the mirror. The only light in the room came from indirect sunlight through the heavily draped windows overlooking the courtyard and the glow of a dozen antique lamps. At the end of the bar, two waiters in identical vests and white shirts chatted in low tones. One watched an affectionate couple nuzzling near the chess set. The other looked at a well-lubricated party of senior citizens cutting up at a wrought-iron conversation group in the corner.

"Artie?" He nodded and hopped back towards me.

"You seen Booth Ewen?" I asked, more out of necessity to pass the time than any premonition LaLa's husband had been in the bar that morning.

"Yep," he said, surprising me. "He was here a few minutes ago." He grinned and lifted two eyebrows quickly, Groucho Marx style.

I didn't say anything for a second. Frankly, I was taken aback. I'm no private eye, though I am a little nosy about what makes people tick. "Was he alone?" I ventured.

"Yes, ma'am, he was."

I know Artie, have known him since he started working at the Tapestry Bar five years ago. He is the perfect bartender, which means he knows when to talk and when not to. He was holding something back.

"Did you speak to him?"

He sensed a game starting and dipped a chin coquettishly. "Yes, ma'am, briefly."

Artie's animated antics kept customers amused, me included. In his off hours, he was a popular leading man at the Royal Poinciana Playhouse. "Did he tell you where he was headed?"

He hung his head in mock shame. "I'm sorry to say he didn't."

I waggled a finger at him. "Tsk. Tsk."

"All he said, Ms. Tupper, was he had to meet somebody. I got the impression his meeting was here in the hotel because he looked at his watch and said, 'she's late.' Then he gulped down his drink and took off."

"Hmm," I said. "Speaking of late, I'm supposed to be meeting Mrs. Fenton here. Have you seen her?"

He nodded toward the hotel entrance. "Coming in now." He grabbed a highball glass, filled it with ice, reached for the Stoli bottle and poured Peep Fenton's drink before she had made it halfway through the lobby. I said Artie was a good bartender, with a good memory for the regulars. That's what Peep would order the minute she hit the brass rail.

"Let me ask you something," I said, remembering why LaLa and I were meeting Peep for lunch today. "Do you think money can buy forgiveness?"

Artie thought a minute, started to lean his elbows on the bar but thought better of it, and shook his head. "I've seen money buy a lot of things I didn't know were for sale," he said. "What's your point?"

I looked him in the eye. In Palm Beach, the help frequently are thought of as invisible. Therefore, they know everything that goes on.

"Can money buy forgiveness for murder?" I asked.

Artie shot a glance over my left shoulder. "This is Palm Beach, Ms. Tupper. Some say here, money can buy anything."

I turned to greet Peep Fenton, whose day was about to be ruined if Artie was wrong.

If 33480 were in the dictionary, it would have Peep's picture under it. That's the Palm Beach zip code. Peep was undisputed Queen of Palm Beach society. She got there by having the fortunes of an oil baron and a Virginia tobacco family or two in the bank. She also had eight generations of patrician Virginia blood in her veins. The fortune was a requirement to rule Palm Beach Society. The blue blood was not, but it helped.

I worried today that the capricious fates who had dealt my friend her good fortune were preparing to take it away. These were the same fates, mind you, who bestowed upon Peep the shallowness of character to believe that these things were important.

Five foot, short of the barstool even in three-inch heels, Peep gave a practiced hop up into the seat, wiggled to fit her fanny to the chair, and took a deep swallow of the drink Artie had set out for her. She set the glass on the napkin and gave him an appreciative smile. Then she rummaged for a compact in her purse, held up the tiny gold mirror and fluffed a curl of perfectly coifed red hair.

"Hello," I said. "You're late."

"No, I'm not," she said, snapping the compact closed. "I'm right on time. You're not supposed to arrive on the exact hour, you know."

I didn't know, but I knew better than to argue with one of Peep's rules. She had a raft of them, and she lived by them. She lived by the rules because she was skilled at the game, and her skill had made her a winner in the quest for the prize. There never has been any secret to what the prize is in Palm Beach Society: It's power. Women can get power in a variety of ways, but for the most part, in Palm Beach, they got it the old fashioned way: They earned it.

It was pretty clear cut. If you wanted to be top bitch in Palm Beach, you guarded the biggest pile of bones. In recent years, that translated to some twenty to thirty million bones, or dollars, that go to charity in Palm Beach, raised mostly through the half-century old tradition of the charity gala.

The women who head up the charity balls have the power—and the bigger the gala, the more money raised, the greater the power. Peep had chaired the most prestigious gala in town for a dozen years. It was the coveted position in town and some women would have done anything to get there. Anything.

Not to carry this dog analogy too far, because it never amused Peep, one stays top dog in a pack only as long as the others respect her. Let that dog falter, even slightly, and they'll turn on her and rip her to shreds. Another will be ready to take her place as she slinks away licking her wounds.

"Okay," I said. "You're not late. But drink up, 'cause LaLa's been waiting at the Beach Club for fifteen minutes."

We finished our drinks and walked back through the lobby and out the south door toward the parking lot between the hotel and the

Beach Club restaurant. Peep trailed behind me, putting up a low-pitched protest the whole way.

"I don't know why we have to eat here. I don't like it here. It's too big. Why couldn't we go to Ta-Boo? They would put us by the fireplace on a day like this."

"Because it's too nice a day to be stuck in some dreary, dark room watching people watch other people, that's why." I held my face up to the sun, enjoying the warmth, and kept walking.

Peep continued to grumble under her breath. I wanted to have patience with her, knowing what was coming, but patience isn't my strong suit. "Grumbling doesn't work with me, Peep, you know that. I know it annoys you to go to places where you can't be seen with the right people. But it annoys me when you worry about such petty things."

She stopped. I turned around. She waited until I was watching to stomp a foot in protest. "It's cold," she said. "And slow down."

I waited for her to catch up. "A breeze blowing in from the ocean isn't exactly a blizzard, Peep. Honestly. There may not be enough money in Palm Beach to buy God's favor when it comes to the weather, but that doesn't stop people in this town from trying."

She took her time reaching me. "I don't know what you mean, and I don't know why we are meeting here to plan the Garden Club Christmas Gala. The Garden Club meets at the Four Arts Building."

I dredged up some compassion and smiled down at her. "You know," I said, walking slowly so she could keep up, "I wouldn't even belong to the Garden Club if you weren't gala chairman. You know what Pitt says about the Palm Beach Garden Club."

"I know what your banker husband says." Peep stepped up on the curb in front of the restaurant and held one finger up in the air, statue-like. "What good is a Gaahden Club in a town that thinks money grows on trees," she mimicked.

I laughed. Peep was a born mimic and could nail Pitt's Boston accent every time. But she had already lost interest in the routine and was rooting around in her Gucci bag, spilling used tissues and breath mints onto the sidewalk. The doorman gave her a dirty look for the mess he would have to pick up. I returned his glare, then bent down and picked up Peep's car keys where they had fallen, waggled the leather piece with the jaguar on it so she would notice and stuffed them into the mink-lined pocket of her jacket.

We walked into the cavernous restaurant. LaLa waved at us from a table across the room. Peep pranced ahead of me, and I followed the sound of her heels clicking on tile as I looked out at the sunny

Florida day. The ocean sparkled outside a wide wall of windows to the east. Tourists frolicked in the pool to the south.

"Hello, dears." LaLa floated a hand in our direction as we sat down. She and Peep kissed in each other's general direction. She winked at me and mouthed, "Later," which I took to mean she didn't want to discuss Booth in front of Peep.

I had known Peep and LaLa since we all were in grade school. We had grown up, gone to college and married, but our basic relationship never changed. I was always in the middle as Peep spun in the vortex of the chaos that was her life and LaLa tried to hover in the quiet air above hers. As we learned each other's vulnerabilities, we developed a triumvirate in which two of us would always be protecting the third from attack. It was why I couldn't say no when they needed me—because they had always been there when I needed them.

A waitress came up to the table. "Just coffee, please," I told her, giving Peep a don't-you-dare look as she opened her mouth to speak. Peep drank too much and it worried me.

"Stoli on the rocks," Peep said. "What in heaven's name is going on, LaLa?" Peep looked around the room as she spoke. "You made it sound like such an emergency. I thought this was supposed to be a Garden Club meeting."

LaLa fluttered a hand in Peep's direction and settled a pitying gaze on her briefly before turning to me and giving me a here-I-go look. She took a deep breath. "No meeting, sweetie. No members."

Peep fumbled for a Dunhill in a leather bag tucked into a side pocket of her purse. She frowned, flicked a gold lighter and inhaled. Then she looked up, green eyes flashing a warning. "Don't tell anyone I'm smoking."

I shook my head. "Peep, it's no secret that you smoke. Just because you pretend you don't doesn't mean everybody doesn't know you do."

Peep took a deep drag and huffed out a stream of smoke. "Oh, Wally, you always tell me what everybody knows. As if I don't know what everybody knows. And you exaggerate. Not everybody knows I smoke. Mitchell doesn't know."

I flapped a hand in front of my nose, dispersing the smoke. "You have a highly developed sense of fantasy, Peep, especially about your own life and surroundings. You have been married to Mitch for six months now. Of course he knows you smoke."

LaLa leaned toward me, slim fingers picking at a yeast roll. "Wally, don't tease her."

"Oh, it's just sport, LaLa." Peep was busily brushing an imaginary ash from her Chanel winter white cashmere sweater. "She doesn't listen to me, anyway," I pointed out.

Peep flicked an ash into the ashtray, then looked up, aware of the silence. "I do, too, listen. What did you say, LaLa?"

"I said they've quit. Every one of them." There were tears welling up in LaLa's eyes. But then, LaLa cried when the Chamber of Commerce called the police to pick up a treed raccoon.

"What do you mean, quit?" Peep snapped her head toward me. "What does she mean, Wally?"

I shrugged my answer. "She means we are the only ones who agreed to come today. Or at least that's how I translate it." I wasn't really ready to give her the rest of the bad news yet—at least not until I had eaten my lunch. If Peep threw some sort of fit, I might be able to handle it on a full stomach.

"Oh, like I don't speak English," Peep said, rolling her eyes. "I understood what she said. I just don't know what she meant." She paused while the waitress delivered the coffee and her drink. "What does this mean to me, this thing you said about no members?"

"I mean," LaLa said, "that they have all quit the club. The Garden Club. I mean, Peep, that you are now chairman of a Palm Beach garden club that, for the first time since 1928, has only three members. And here we sit."

The waitress returned to take our order. Peep sat, stunned. I ordered her a salad and me a burger and when the waitress had moved on, I said, "I love Palm Beach. It's like watching an ant farm."

Peep had decided not to hear the bad news. She gave a dismissive wave of her hand. "This is not happening. People don't quit the Palm Beach Garden Club." She turned to me and in her best dinner party conversation tone, changed the subject. "Who has ants?"

"Word is, there's talk of starting another club." LaLa lifted a piece of roll to her mouth and popped it in.

Peep frowned and shook her head, still in denial. "The Palm Beach Garden Club has been the most prestigious garden club south of Newport since the turn of the century. No one who is anyone would start a new club when they could belong to this one."

I was curious how this was going to play out. LaLa had told me on the telephone the day before what was happening and why, but I still wondered how a full-scale mutiny by the thirty or so members of the garden club was going to be handled, tactically speaking. "Now let me get this straight, LaLa," I said. "They have started their own garden club. Even though they live in Palm Beach and this is the Palm Beach Garden Club? I suppose they plan to have their own gala, as well."

"That's right," LaLa said, leaning back to allow the waitress to put a bubbling dish of cheese-drenched portobello mushrooms in front of her.

The pursuit of wealth and social prestige are taken very seriously here. "Subtlety is not something Palm Beach values, is it?"

"Not high on the list," LaLa said.

"Well." Peep's brow wrinkled. She crossed her arms in punctuation. "Well, well. Probably they'll come to their senses before anybody realizes and will be back at the next meeting."

LaLa gave me a meaningful look. "Did you bring it?"

I nodded. "Yep." I reached down for my canvas bag, dug my arm in and pulled out the newspaper I had brought with me. I opened it to the page I wanted and gave Peep a sympathetic smile. "Listen to this."

The Beach Session
by Rezna Van Daly
Society Editor, The Palm Beach Tattler

Palm Beach Ladies who lunch have something new to chew on. The Palm Beach Garden Club Gala—oldest and most prestigious gala in town—is in trouble. Word on Worth Avenue is the gala has been canceled. Some say there isn't enough membership left in the garden club to throw a tete-a-tete, much less a gala. Perk up those Cartier-clad ears and listen, darlings, for the crumpling of this gala will mean the toppling of the crown of our reigning queen of Society. Did her fall from the heights start a year ago when other heads rolled? Stay tuned for more about this.

Peep opened and closed her mouth, but no words came out. LaLa reached over and touched her hand.

"It's okay if there's no gala. That might not be such a bad thing," I said, nodding my agreement and waving a French fry at Peep. "One less charity ball in this town would not be a disaster. I don't know why this bothers anybody. It's just an old garden club and I hardly ever came to meetings anyway. Why do we care?"

"You know very well that if I cancel the gala I might as well pack up and move. You aren't anybody in this town unless you run a gala. You know that." Peep's hands were trembling as she pulled another cigarette from her case.

"It's silly, that's what I know." I crammed the French fry in my mouth and punished it for the frailties of the human ego.

Peep stared down her nose at us, her chin pointed at the sun shining high in the Florida sky. Then she sat straight up, picked up a fork and aimed it at a radicchio leaf as if it were Hitler's spawn. Slowly, her eyes narrowed. "Silly, is it? I'll show you what's silly. I'll show them. Nothing is canceled. There's going to be a gala. The best damn gala in town. I'll kill somebody if I have to, to make it happen."

I gulped. "I wouldn't say that too loudly, if I were you, Peep."

I stuffed the last bite of my burger into my mouth and looked at my friend. I really had no reason to think Peep had murdered her first husband. Why most of the town thought so was beyond me. It had been an accident. One that could have happened anywhere.

But it hadn't happened anywhere. And it hadn't happened any time. It had happened one year ago right smack in the middle of the Garden Club Gala, which was always held at Peep and Eaton Mellon's estate, and which was always highlighted by an extravagant display of Christmas lights and animated decorations. For a dozen years, Peep had imported a host of electricians to put on a show that made the Garden Club Gala the talk of the town for weeks.

Last year, a life-size, animated Santa Claus waved from a full-size sleigh, complete with prancing reindeer which drew it around a mile-long track. On a nearby stage, a dozen tiny elves did a little dance while they made toys. Over the years, guests had been encouraged to bring real toys to be given to needy children, and last year was no exception, with hundreds of goodies piled around the elf tree.

That night, with hundreds of people spilling in and out of the house and onto the loggias and lawns, one unfortunate matron suffered bad timing on her trip out to the tableau. She stumbled, literally, on Eaton's head, which had rolled down the hill from where his body still lay on the tracks. Bloodcurdling screams later, people stopped admiring the ingenuity of it all and started commenting on the killer potential of the knife-sharp sleigh runners.

The medical examiner confirmed Eaton had died from the fatal misfortune of being separated from his head. The police said in public it appeared to have been an accident but in private they asked a lot of people if they had seen Peep out by the tracks. And they had never closed the case.

Nobody had the nerve to call her a murderer to her face, so Peep kept her social position but became the topic of whispered conversations at parties around town for months. Finally, the gossip had dwindled down to the odd look here and there.

Until now.

"It seems," I said, "that someone has convinced the police to re-open the case of Eaton's death. And there's a rumor floating around they are going to arrest you for his murder."

Chapter Three

THE THING ABOUT MONEY IS you can love it or you can hate it, but you can't get away from it. If somebody tells you smoking is bad for you, you'll believe it when you see enough people hacking up chunks of their lungs. If somebody tells you speeding is bad for you, you'll believe it when you see enough mangled bodies wrapped around trees. But if somebody tells you money is bad for you, you're going to think they're crazy, because there's nothing you can see that makes you think it's true.

After lunch, having sent LaLa to see after Peep with promises to both of them to stop by later and talk, I decided to pop in on my husband and fill him in on my morning. He's president of the Palm Tree Bank on Worth Avenue, the ritziest street east of Rodeo Drive in Beverly Hills.

If you don't have two thousand dollars to spend on an Hermes scarf, you probably don't shop seriously on Worth Avenue, home to Cartier and Tiffany, to Chanel and Armani.

You could call the Breakers the pulse of Palm Beach and Town Hall the brains; Worth Avenue would be the open palm of welcome.

You have money to spend? Right this way. Step into the cool, clean stores of Worth Avenue. There's even a dog bar in case Fido gets thirsty on his way to get his new jeweled collar.

Worth Avenue grew to its present gilded status because near the east end of the avenue is the Everglades Club, unarguably the most exclusive club in a town that cherishes its exclusivity. The Everglades was opened by architect Addison Mizner and sewing machine scion Paris Singer in the twenties. Singer knew how to position himself at the top of the social heap: He determined that membership in the club had to be personally approved by him every year. He was a very popular guy, and the Everglades Club flourished.

I drove up and down the four blocks of Worth Avenue, from ocean to lake, searching for a parking place. Some days during the season you can barely get from one end of the street to the other for the limos waiting outside the stores. Pitt's bank has an underground parking garage but you have to stop and get a ticket and I just didn't want to fool with it.

Several circled blocks later, I lucked into a parking space on Co-coanut Row, just off the avenue, and walked east a block to the Palm Tree bank. Inside, as always, the bank lobby was as clean and fresh as a newly minted bill. The polished marble floors reflected the crystal chandeliers and the smiles of the tellers who waited in eager antici-pation of helping their next customer. Pitt insisted on the smiles, just as he insisted on the lively classical music. He wanted his customers to have the total sensory banking experience.

"Ambiance," he said. "That will make the difference in how people choose a bank." He even asked me one time if I thought the smell of new money could be replicated in an air freshener.

I waved at his most recent secretary, who looked all of sixteen, and went on past her desk as she looked through me, which people seem to do more and more as I get older. I opened the heavy cypress door to his office. He was on the phone, but pointed to a chair, which I ignored in favor of his private bathroom.

When I came out, he was off the phone. My long, lean husband folded his hands as if in prayer, rested his chin on his hands, and gave me the full attention of dark brown eyes that could charm the fleas off a dog.

"What's up?" he asked.

"LaLa thinks Booth is cheating on her and there are rumors Tony is going to arrest Peep for killing Eaton." I flopped into the chair in front of his desk. "And Reggie hasn't found anything on your geneal-ogy yet but thinks I might be a Breakers Baby. What's up with you?"

"I need you to pick something up for me, as long as you're here," he said. Then, "What's a Breakers Baby?"

I snorted at his sense of priority. "Born at the Breakers. I'm serious about the other."

He shrugged. "If you want to find out if Peep's going to be arrested, go ask your friend the chief of police, he'll certainly know. Maybe he won't tell you, though."

"I didn't think of that," I said. I'd known Palm Beach Police Chief Tony Taranto for years. Even if he didn't tell me, I thought I could read him well enough to find out what I wanted to know. "I could ask him about Booth, too."

"I can't believe you agreed to that." Pitt rummaged around in his desk drawer, pulled up a receipt of some kind and extended his hand over the desk. "Here."

I took it. "What's this?"

"It's the receipt for that Laura Woodward oil painting I bought. My secretary said the Fuzzy Bunny gallery called to tell me they've finished the new frame. Would you pick it up?"

"Sure." It was just down the street.

He gave me a questioning glance. "You're really going to spy on Booth Ewen?"

I shook my head. "I'm sure there's nothing to it." I backed toward the door. "I'm sure the whole thing will just die out." I made a quick exit from his office rather than to try to explain what was obviously temporary insanity. I crossed my fingers and wished to be right and for LaLa to call me tomorrow or the next day. I hoped she'd laugh and tell me how silly she'd been and how there was a logical explanation for it all. Hey, call me a cock-eyed optimist.

I walked east on Worth Avenue towards the Fuzzy Bunny Gallery, one of those precious little art shops that makes a business out of searching out collectible art for people who buy paintings for investments, not pleasure. The gallery advertised itself as "the gallery that shows tomorrow's artists today," but for what they paid for a Worth Avenue address, they could have supported an entire colony of artists who were starving today waiting for tomorrow's prices.

As I neared the storefront, a thirty-something woman stepped outside and turned, holding up her hands in a frame shape toward the gallery window. As I got closer, I could see she was working on a window display of postmodern abstract works that could have been painted by a blind poodle with brushes tied to its feet. Each work had beside it a tiny placard with a discreetly printed price of astronomical proportions.

She nodded her satisfaction to no one in particular, although a couple of businessmen slowed their steps to admire her, rather than the window display. She was sleek and well tended, more carefully crafted than the works in the window. Her straight blonde hair was cut and colored to be seductive without approaching brassy. Her mini-skirt was fitted so that the silk would drape but not cling. Her Italian leather pumps were vamped especially low, showing extra toe cleavage. She had even features, young skin and a movie star smile. She was a real dish, as they say. I had long ago gotten over my urge to exterminate such physically perfect women and learned that, like roaches, there would always be more of them breeding in dark corners.

Flashing a 75-watt smile at the businessmen after a quick glance to see if they were anybody, she stepped back inside the shop. I followed her.

"Hello," I called to her back.

She spun on her heel, eyes hard, smile guarded. "Yes?"

"I'm picking up a painting for Pitt Wesson." I poked around in my bag for the receipt, found it, and waved it in her direction.

She looked at it as if I had pulled a pair of underwear out of the bag. "And you are...?"

"His wife," I finished for her, trying not to get an attitude. Pitt tells me when people don't treat me the way I think they should, I get an attitude. He could be right.

Her eyes softened right before my very own. They might as well have changed colors, it made so much difference in her face. Her stance morphed from defensive to deferential. Her shoulders melted from stiff to relaxed, slightly forward. She held out a bejeweled hand.

"Mrs. Wesson. How lovely to meet you. I'm Verity DeVale."

"Tupper," I said. "Wally Tupper." I shook her hand and tried to hand her the receipt, but she bobbled her head and raised her palms towards me.

"I'll get your painting, Wally," she said. "I'll be right back." She indicated a table in the corner with a bucket and some glasses on it. "Please help yourself to champagne." She smiled so wide it had to hurt and disappeared behind one of the display walls.

Verity DeVale was the newest trophy wife of Palm Beach mogul Thornton DeVale. Her name had made the rounds of the clubs after their shamelessly overblown wedding at his oceanfront villa about a month before. Thornton DeVale had been trying to buy his way into Palm Beach society for a decade now. It was working, although I didn't particularly care for him. I thought him so shallow you could practically see his skull. Probably she didn't care about that, or that he was short, bald and soft. He was also endlessly socially ambitious and wealthy enough to be able to do something about it. The grapevine said she was exactly what he deserved.

I didn't have to wait long. She reappeared momentarily carrying a wrapped painting, one Pitt had bought at an auction and decided to have reframed at the Fuzzy Bunny, which DeVale had bought as a toy for his new wife.

"Can I carry it to your car for you?" she offered. We were now the best of friends, apparently. "I'd be happy to do that."

"No thanks," I said, taking the painting from her. She followed me to the front of the store. "I'm parked just around the corner."

She gave me a pert tilt of the head. "I'm so sorry you had to regret our Artists for Aids benefit tonight. It will be a wonderful auction."

I remembered then that we had gotten an invitation to a benefit art auction at the gallery that night. Since bankers are one of the last bastions of uptight intolerance, Pitt had refused to go, lest he be seen talking to someone with an alternative life style. Those are my words, not his. Pitt, like some other Palm Beach residents, has not embraced political correctness with open arms. But a lot of other Palm Beach partygoers would reach for their cocktails with one hand and their checkbooks with the other that night. "We're busy," I said. "So sorry."

I wasn't of course. I hate the foo-foo social gatherings where people go to ostensibly raise money for good causes but could just as easily have stayed home and written a check. Pitt loved them though, said I was missing the point that a great deal of money went to good causes, and usually we went.

Her eyes flickered with displeasure, then recovered. "Next time." A phone rang in the back of the store. "Excuse me," she said, and walked away.

She disappeared behind the wall again and I put down the painting to get out my car keys. A piece of pottery in the back corner caught my eye, so I leaned the painting against a display stand and walked back to take a look.

I heard her on the phone.

"Ms. Van Daly," she said, apparently speaking to the society columnist who had ruined Peep's morning, "thank you for returning my call. I'm confirming that you'll be attending our Artists for Aids auction tonight. I hope you're bringing a photographer with you."

There was a moment of silence. "Um-hmm," she said. "I see. Well, if you change your mind...." Another silence. "I see."

If she had been talking on an old-fashioned phone, I'm sure she would have slammed it down. But what I heard was something that sounded like a portable phone hitting a pile of boxes.

"Great," she said. "That's just great. They can't come." That last part was delivered falsetto, apparently mocking Rezna Van Daly's British accent, acquired during a stint as a reporter in London but not lost in fifty years back in the States.

To my surprise, a voice answered her, a very soft female voice. "I'm sorry, Verity, I know you wanted them to."

Verity spoke with a controlled, patronizing tone. "Yes, Darla, I did want them to come. I needed them to put my picture in the paper. How am I going to get known around this town if I can't get my picture in the paper? That's the whole idea of running this stupid gallery."

"Why can't they come?" asked the soft voice.

"Because," Verity said, her effort to rein in her emotions and remain patient evident in her voice, "they are going to Cocktails for Cancer, which is a bigger event. It's probably where that cow married to Pitt Wesson is going."

My ears perked up. The woman had just called me a cow. Obviously she thought I had left. I heard Soft Voice speak, but couldn't make out what she said.

"Yes, I know she's in the Old Guard, Darla. Thank you sooo much for pointing that out to me." I heard the sound of boxes being moved around. She was probably looking for the phone. "Don't you understand that's the problem? Why don't people like Wally Tupper or Peep Fenton invite me to their parties? Thornton has just as much money as they do."

The Old Guard is what Palm Beach society calls people who have old money and old blood. I could have told her Pitt does the inviting to our parties, but I'm sure it wouldn't have mattered. This was one mad little social butterfly. I decided to back quietly out of the gallery before she came out and saw me.

She must have found what she was looking for: I heard the sound of a phone being put on the receiver. "Darla, darling," Verity said. "Remember our little talk about how I wanted to run a really prestigious charity benefit?"

"Yes," answered Soft Voice.

"Well," Verity said, "after this month, I may have myself a gala to run."

"Which one?"

I was almost at the door when I heard her answer. "The Palm Beach Garden Club." I stopped. I waited.

"Just as you suggested, I had Thornton put the pressure on the vice mayor to have the police arrest Peep Fenton for that horrible episode at her house last year. And then I spread around at a few meetings that it was going to happen. And mentioned it to Rezna." I heard a chair scrape the floor.

"I'm going to run that Garden Club gala if it's the last thing I do," she was saying as I grabbed my painting and darted out the door.

As much as I could with the painting in my arms, I ran to my car, my heart pounding. I put the painting in the trunk, got in the car and sat, trying to decide what to do next. I have to admit, I hadn't cared whether Peep chaired the gala. It was important to her, not to me. But what Verity DeVale was trying to do made the hair on the back of my neck stand up. I knew such things went on, I just had never been so close to it.

Besides, the woman called me a cow. That was just mean. I've been accused of being insensitive, and it may be true, but I've never been mean. She'd have to pay for that.

I started the car and drove north to Brazilian Avenue, turned east and passed the Brazilian Court, that now-famous hotel where one of the young Kennedys died of a drug overdose, on my way back to South County Road.

I found a parking place right in front of the police station, built in the '80s to match the 1920s Spanish style architecture that prevails here. I marched past the bench made of hand-painted Spanish tiles and up the steps edged to match.

Brown and tan uniformed officers were coming and going around the building, each with a smile on his or her face. Well, they should smile—it's a great place to be a cop. There are about seventy of them, and their duties range from free visits to residents to help them with their home security—theft and burglary are our major crimes—to selling tickets to the well-attended Fraternal Order of Police fund-raiser ball. They also enforce town ordinances such as the one that bans topless jogging, the one that bans skateboarding and the one that bans surfing on public beaches. They may also have to stop by and remind a resident that a city ordinance outlaws tennis ball machines during certain hours.

I checked with the desk officer, who called Tony's secretary and found out he was free to see me. When I got to his office, his secretary opened his door, gave him a saucy shake of big hair, and announced me. As I walked in, she reluctantly backed out and closed the door behind me.

He got up from his desk, came over and took my hands.

He kissed me on the cheek. "Hi, Wally."

"Hi, Tony."

"Sit down." He led me to a grouping of soft, floral-patterned chairs, and indicated one. He sat in another.

When I sat, he leaned forward, forearms on knees. "Haven't seen you in a while."

Tony Taranto was an attractive man. His body was hard and compact and his face, if not classically handsome, was appealing. His eyes were always smiling. We had dated in high school, had smooched a little on the beach. He was headed to Florida State, where he was a football hero and then, diploma in hand, a Marine in Viet Nam. We drifted apart, and I didn't see him again until he returned to Palm Beach a few months ago, a retired FBI agent and a recent widower with a grown son who had a life of his own.

I still liked him.

"I know. You'll have to come to dinner. Pitt wants to meet you."

"Love to. Are you here to report a crime?"

I shook my head. "Not exactly. I'm here to be nosy."

"Shoot." He leaned back, elbows wide, his fingertips loosely laced over his chest. He was wearing a Ralph Lauren sports shirt, cotton slacks, Italian loafers with no socks. The Palm Beach uniform, it takes you anywhere while the sun is up.

"The rumor mill has it that you are going to arrest Peep Fenton—Peep Mellon—Peep Lee—for murder."

He nodded. "I know who you mean. I didn't recognize her new married name at first but they filled me in about Eaton's death."

He leaned forward again. "Y'know," he said, "if I were going to arrest her, I wouldn't tell you."

"I know. But I'd be able to tell from the way you didn't tell me."

He laughed. "Still right to the point, eh, Wally? Yeah, you might have figured it out. But the truth is, I have no plans to arrest Peep. I've reviewed the files on Eaton's death, and despite the fact that there's been some pressure to do so, there's no evidence that I could take to the DA and expect any sort of prosecution to be forthcoming."

He gave me a sharp look. "Do you know something about it that you want to tell me?"

I shook my head emphatically. "Absolutely not. I was inside her house, just like everybody else."

"Well," he said. "Maybe not everybody. But the fact remains, I have nothing to base a case on, so there isn't one. At present."

"Thanks, Tony." I stood up, turned and walked to the door. "I'll call you about dinner." I started to ask him if he knew anything about Booth, but I decided against it, right then.

He followed me, opened the door for me. "Wally?" he said.

"Yes?"

"If I ever do find out you know something, I'll arrest you as an accessory. You know that. As much as I love you, I love this job, too, and I won't give it up to keep an old friendship. Understood?"

His secretary gave me a smug look as I nodded and walked out of his office.

I remembered then that Tony had always been a stickler for the rules, even in high school, when a lot of kids were into breaking them. I wouldn't want to have to test his ethics.

It was getting near the cocktail hour. I decided to stop by Peep's house first, then circle back to see LaLa, who lived next door to her on North Ocean Boulevard.

The sun was hitting the horizon as I announced myself at the gate at Peep's, then drove around the circular drive. The lawn in the center of the circle was where Eaton had died. Every time I came there I tried so hard not to think about it that I succeeded in conjuring up the very image I wanted to avoid. I stopped at the family door, which is offset to the side of the house. The main entrance is for guests. I rang the bell and Peep opened the door herself. "Come on in," she said. "I'm fixing drinks for Mitch and myself. Want one?"

I shrugged. "Why not?" A few more days like this and I would be the one with the drinking problem. I followed her to a butler's pantry that opened to the kitchen. I could hear the television news from the study on the far side of the living room. The family area of the house occupied about a fourth of it. The rest was made up of a ballroom, guest suites and servants quarters. It was close to being the largest estate in Palm Beach—it had been, at one time.

She walked up to the bar, picked up a vodka she already had going, and took a slug. She put the drink down, retrieved her Dunhills from the pocket of her pants, lit one with the gold lighter, and took a deep drag. Absently, she stirred her vodka around the rocks with the index finger of her left hand.

"What can I get you?" she asked.

I peered down at the selection in the well-stocked bar. "Chivas," I said. She reached for the bottle and I thought better of it. "Let me fix it."

She nodded her acquiescence. "Servants' night off," she explained. "I can fix my own, and you always make them too heavy, anyway."

She peered around the corner of the alcove toward where the television was on. "Mitch will be calling for his drink in a minute," she said.

I took a sip. "I have good news."

She opened her mouth, but before she could ask the question, a booming voice came from the back of the living room. "Where's my drink, sugar?"

Peep took a gulp of vodka from the glass, topped it off from the Stoli bottle, poured a straight Wild Turkey in another glass. Then she turned on the tap at the wet bar, took one last drag, drowned the cigarette and threw it down the drain. "Coming, Mitch," she called. "Come on," she said to me.

I followed her through their living room to the study behind it. There, Mitchell Fenton had draped his six-foot-plus frame across an easy chair and was leaned back, a fire roaring in the fireplace and NBC news on the wide screen TV.

"Ah, Wally," he boomed. "Come in and enjoy a drink with us." Peep had said she loved Mitchell's voice, which had only one volume—loud—but it made me uncomfortable.

I didn't know Mitch well, despite the fact he had been in the class that had graduated ahead of us at Palm Beach High School. He had gone on to law school at the University of Florida, married one of our high school classmates. By the time Pitt and I returned to Palm Beach, Mitch and Desdemona were in a social set we rarely mixed with.

Mitch patted his stomach and motioned to Peep to bring his drink. As she handed him the glass, he reached out and grabbed her around the knees, yanked her into his lap and kissed her wetly, groping at whatever part of her body he could reach without releasing his bourbon. Her drink spilled on her cashmere sweater, but she gave a delighted little squeal and giggled. "Mitch, we have company."

"Aw, Peep, Wally knows we're newlyweds," he said, giving me a wink. "And I don't make any bones about loving Palm Beach's prettiest girl."

Peep blushed and looked at me with dewy eyes. "You know, Mitch could have had any of those young things that flirted with him at Au Bar, but he picked me. Aren't I lucky?"

My skin felt prickly. I sat down on an ottoman stuffed within an inch of its life. "Sure are," I said.

Mitch nodded. "I don't regret it, either. Look at that little figure. She's got a better figure than some women half her age, and if she wants to tint her hair a little, well...a girl's gotta do what a girl's gotta do to keep her man, now, doesn't she?"

Peep nodded back at him as he continued. "Desdemona had let her thighs thicken up so I could barely stand to touch her," he said, "but my Peep knows how to please her man. And of course she knows her way around Palm Beach society. Thanks to my sweetums, I'm finally playing golf at the Everglades."

I chugged my drink. "I just wanted to tell you..."

Peep interrupted me. "Mitch, I have a problem."

"What is it, Baby Doodles? Somebody identify your accent as Georgia instead of Virginia, again?"

"Seriously," she said.

He gave her an attentive attorney look. "What is it, sweetums?"

"Everyone but me, LaLa and Wally have left the Garden Club," she said. "Wally says it's because of Eaton." She drew her lips in tightly and looked into the fire. "They say Tony is being pressured to arrest me. Arrest me!"

"I...," I started.

"Remember, I told you the Lord will deal with people who say cruel things, Peep. It's not our place on Earth to judge them."

"Or them me, Mitchell. Or them me." Peep had her bottom lip poked out. I wanted to get a word in but they weren't paying any attention to me.

He said, "They judged me when I had Desdemona put away, didn't they, Peep? But I did it for her own good. If a person cannot control her emotions in public, then she must be put away. I forgave them for what they said about me."

Peep sipped her vodka. "People told me I shouldn't marry you, Mitch. That if you would put your wife of twenty years in a mental institution and then divorce her, you would do the same to me. But they don't know you like I do, Mitch. Must I forgive them for their cruelty in my hour of need?"

"They know not what they do, Peep. Desdemona had lost her grasp on reality. And it was a rest home, not a mental institution." He handed her his glass. "Go get me another Turkey, Baby Doodles."

She headed toward the bar, remembering me. "Want another one?"

"No," I said. "But wait a minute." I turned to Mitch. "It's not true," I said. "I talked to Tony. He has no plans to arrest her, but somebody put the pressure on him to do it."

Peep turned back around. "Who?"

"Verity DeVale," I said. "I overheard her telling somebody she had Thornton put the pressure on."

Peep slumped into a chair, her errand forgotten. She reached for a cigarette in her pocket, then remembered where she was. "Why?"

"She wants to run the gala, I think. That's what she said."

Mitch got up, took his glass from Peep's hand, apparently deciding he was going to have to make his own if he wanted another drink any time soon. "As long as there's no truth to it, there's no harm done," he said on his way out of the room.

Peep looked at me with eyes filled with misery. "You know that's not true. The harm is already done. To the gala."

I nodded in understanding. "No one would blame you for canceling it."

She sat up straight. "The hell I will. I'm more determined than ever this will be the best gala ever. How about a membership tea? We'll get all new members. Then we'll have some sort of television interview, talking about the food pantries that won't get stocked and the babies who will go hungry if we don't have this gala. We'll ask for help in getting the invitations out and a florist...I wish we had some sort of newsworthy event to announce." She glared at me. "Think."

"I think," I said, standing up, "you're nuts to try to have a gala under these circumstances. But if that's what it's going to take to put Verity DeVale in her place, then that's what it's going to take. I'm in."

"Tell LaLa the battle cry has been sounded, and oh, yes. Go tell Rezna to put it in the paper."

I made my exit, got back in my car and drove the short distance to LaLa's house. The sun had slipped below the horizon by the time I pulled into her driveway. I noticed as I parked that Booth's Range Rover was not anywhere to be seen.

The maid sent me to the patio where I had started my day. There LaLa sat in the evening breeze, looking up at the clouds floating in the moonlight.

I told her about Peep's plan, but her attention wasn't with me and when I had finished she stood up and said, "Come with me. I need to talk to you." I followed her down the stairs and around the corner. She didn't speak, but walked into a brushy area on the estate she and Booth had purchased twenty years ago. Flush with professional success, he had decided they must live in a home designed by architect Marion Wyeth—deemed by those in the know to be second in prestige only to the homes designed by Addison Mizner. Booth had justified his preference for second best by spreading the word at parties that unairconditioned Mizner homes were simply too primitive to be considered. Booth bought the 22,000-square-foot estate, which sat on a four-acre lot, and paved most of it over to accommodate tennis courts, swimming pools and parking.

The Florida brush to the northwest of the main house served mainly to separate the house from North Ocean Boulevard. From there, Peep's estate was located immediately north on a sharp curve in one of the two main north-south roads in Palm Beach. The undeveloped section in the curve where the Ewen lot met the property line to Peep's estate was a buffer against traffic noise and tourist invasion.

Here LaLa had stumbled upon resting bodies and floating souls. She had brought me here before, and we had talked endlessly about how the burial ground had gotten there. We had decided it was Indian—probably Tequesta. There also was a small cemetery, apparently a makeshift one for those who did not survive the frequent shipwrecks on the Florida barrier islands in the seventeenth and eighteenth centuries.

LaLa came out here often to talk to the spirits.

Now, she stopped at the edge of the burial ground. I sank down on a log and scratched a mosquito bite. "If you keep on calling the dead, eventually someone you don't want to talk to is going to answer the phone," I said.

"Shh," she whispered. I stayed quiet, but with difficulty. It was spooky out there. The tombstones cast shadows in the night glow of the full moon and the palmettos rustled in the wind.

"I pity the dead," she said.

I didn't know what to say to that, so I didn't say anything. For a minute. Then I had to ask, "Why?"

"Because," she said, "I fear confinement more than any earthly experience." She fluttered her hands as if to free herself; her clothing rippled around her. "And they are eternally confined."

LaLa wore loose clothing, she avoided elevators and small rooms, and she despised being cooped up—even in her own home—when Florida's rainfall turned to storms. I could see why a coffin wouldn't be her favorite place to be. *On the other hand,* I thought, *you are dead.*

"Do you suppose," she asked, "that when people die their spirits feel free despite the fact their bodies are imprisoned beneath the earth?"

"I don't know," I said truthfully. Why did LaLa always bring up things that made my head hurt? "Isn't that supposed to be the way it works?"

She sat next to me on the log and put her head in her hands.

"What's wrong, LaLa?" I asked. "Why are we out here?"

"Velma said coming here helps free me from the chains that bind my earthly thinking," she said, looking at me with sad eyes.

Velma was her psychic, a medium who lives in Cassadaga, a little enclave of such people just north of Orlando. "Velma's not here right now, LaLa, but I am. Can I help?"

She looked out toward the ocean. "The tarot cards are an anchor for me when I can't talk to my spirit guide. They are a beacon for me when I'm in danger of losing my way. Only with the cards do I feel hopeful that I might sometime envision a light at the end of the day-to-day troubles of my life."

My shoulders sagged. I seldom heard my happy friend sound so sad, although frankly I didn't have a clue what she had just said. "What's wrong?"

"I cast the cards over and over again when I got home. Again and again the Death card came up."

I don't know much about New Age wa-wa, but this didn't sound good. "What does that mean?"

She looked toward the cemetery, at the tombstone she had erected in memory of all those whose bodies had been buried in this spot so long ago.

"Can you hear them?" she asked. "All the souls?"

A little shiver went up my spine in the 70-degree evening.

"The souls?"

"Death," she said. "They're all speaking to me of death."

Chapter Four

IN MY BED THAT NIGHT, I woke up clutching at the air around me. Although I seldom remember my dreams, this one stayed with me and I wished it hadn't. In the dream, I was chasing Booth Ewen down a long tunnel when suddenly he turned on me and his face turned into a bare skull, complete with grinning teeth that kept snapping at me. I woke up when the skull vomited up Peep's first husband Hank's head.

"Mufump," Pitt said, as I got out of bed. "Rfrgg."

I tiptoed out of the room, knowing I wouldn't sleep again, and spent the rest of the night in a fetal position on the sofa in our family room, watching a Jerry Lewis movie and hugging my dogs.

Early the next morning, Pitt stopped in to kiss me good-bye on his way to play golf, gave me an odd look, and left.

I stayed on the couch watching movie after movie on HBO, until the disturbing dream stopped continuously replaying in my mind. I'm not one to have bad dreams; I don't usually think about them when I do. But this one got to me.

Sometime after two o'clock I decided I deserved some comfort food, so I ate a big pile of bacon and eggs and a biscuit slathered with butter. Okay, two biscuits. That made me feel better, so I finally showered and dressed, then headed downtown.

I found Rezna Van Daly hunched over her computer keyboard in a cubbyhole amidst the warren of nooks and crannies that were the offices of *The Palm Beach Tattler*.

Her fingers pounded the keys with the strength of five or six decades of writing on manual typewriters, unwilling, as were many old-timers, to admit that some light-fingered wussie could produce the same hard-bitten copy by fluttering her fingers over an ergonomic keyboard.

Rezna looked up at me with a face dry and wrinkled as a page from Gutenberg's Bible; sharp blue eyes scrutinized me from beneath a hat that had been in style during the Eisenhower administration.

"Wallis," she cackled. "Do come sit beside me and see if you can not say something nice about someone." Alice Roosevelt Longworth had been one of Rezna's closest friends during the days Rezna had covered White House social events. Rezna also had known my parents and was one of the few people in the world I allowed to call me Wallis because she had been best friends with my namesake, Wallis Warfield Simpson, before, during and after that Wallis' marriage to the former King of England. Supposedly, Rezna had been a young favorite at court while the Prince of Wales was romancing the divorced matron from Baltimore. Lured by the opulence, I supposed, Rezna had returned to Palm Beach in the early '60s to chronicle the comings and goings of the Palm Beach golden for the *Tattler*. Now, no one gets anywhere in this town without Rezna's say-so.

I picked up a stack of mail—about a dozen international newspapers and magazines—and moved it to an open spot on the floor so I could sit on the ripped leather chair that was the only extra seat in the office.

After indulging me in a couple of minutes of chitchat, Rezna pointed at me with a crooked finger. "Come to ask me to watch Booth Ewen for you?" She laughed herself into a lung-wrenching smoker's cough, despite the fact she had quit on doctor's orders several years back.

"You must have been talking to Reggie." I shook my head in wonder that the woman always knew everything about what was going on in Palm Beach. "No, that's not why I'm here."

Rezna shook pointy shoulders in mock glee and rubbed gnarly hands together. "I won't tell you what I know, then."

"Well," I said, "If you know anything that would make LaLa feel better...."

"Not my job to make people feel better," she said sadly. "I can only tell them what's going on."

"So?" I said. "What's going on?"

She looked me in the eye and gave one shake of her head. "I don't know much about Booth Ewen, to tell the truth. He's not been worth watching. A desperate wannabe who snared himself a sweet Palm Beach deal. But...," she stopped for a moment, grabbed a stub of a pencil from the depths of papers stacked on her desk, made a quick note and looked back up at me, "but he has been going in and out of a lot of banks lately. Makes me wonder what the sonofabitch is up to."

"Hmm." I said. "That's it?"

"That's it," she said. "Oh, by the way. When I spoke to Reggie he told me he was going to do your family tree and you could be a Breakers Baby. The Breakers is presenting all the Breakers Babies at a New Year's Eve party, if they can find them. You're one?"

I hesitated. "That's wishful thinking on Reggie's part, Rezna. I've always wanted to be free of Palm Beach, not more a part of it." I have always avoided discussions about my family. Such discussions were painful in their fruitlessness. My parents had disappeared. There were no close relatives. That was that. I was already regretting my impulsive agreement with Reggie, but since I had started it... "Why, do you know anything about it?"

She reached down into a drawer and pulled out a ruffled sepia photo of two women, one a teenager, one older by a few years, giggling together in a carefree moment of youth. "I wish for her sake I did, dear."

I leaned over and picked up the photo. "My mother?"

She looked thoughtful. "That was taken just before I left for London. Before your mother married. Before you were born. We didn't keep in touch after that. I was too busy being a war correspondent. I didn't even know she was gone—or that you existed—until I got back to the states after the war."

I handed her back the picture and admitted for the first time, "I wonder about them."

She nodded. "If I'd known...." Then she slammed the drawer shut. "What else do you want today, Wallis?"

"A little bit of help for the Garden Club Gala," I said, relieved and disappointed that the subject was closed. "Peep Fenton really needs it."

Rezna wrinkled her nose and wheeled around to her computer. She typed about three more words and then turned back to me.

"Very well," she said. "I suppose I owe it to her mother." Rezna had been friends for years with Peep's mother. "You want me to print something?"

"Yes," I answered. "We're thinking of having a membership tea, get a few new members."

Rezna started flipping through a Rolodex the size of a truck wheel. "Screw that. If Peep Fenton wants people to come to the gala, she's going to have to have something they can't say no to...here it is."

She pulled out a card, then flipped through and found two more. Five minutes later she had made two phone calls and had handed two cards to me.

"Go see these people," she commanded. "They'll help you get this thing going pronto. And leave the rest to me."

She swung around to the computer and resumed her assault on the keyboard.

I looked at the cards in my hand. One was for the CEO of Old Money, a publishing company which, the card indicated, specialized in financial publishing; books on financial theory, investing, the economy and so on. On the card, Rezna had scribbled "invitations" next to the Palm Beach address and under it an address in a new patio home community and the notation "Five o'clock."

The second was a four-color card for Montreaux Florists in West Palm Beach. Under the owner's name she had scribbled an address in a West Palm Beach residential area.

Not for the first time, I wondered from just what channels Rezna's information came.

I was walking back to my car when I heard someone call my name. I turned to see a woman timidly waving a hand at me from the doorway of the Paramount Building, which I had just exited.

She was a little bit shorter and a lot heavier than average, and I couldn't place her age except to guess she might have been between thirty and sixty. Some women are just like that, with skin that doesn't wrinkle up. And some women—especially in Palm Beach—purchase that ageless look from surgeons, hair stylists and skin care specialists.

But this didn't appear to be so in her case. If she'd had facial surgery, it wasn't very successful, because her piggy little nose looked like the class project in plastic surgery school. Her blonde hair was too close to platinum to be stylish in the '90s. She wore a St. John knit outfit I had seen the week before on Worth Avenue but on her it stretched in all the wrong directions.

She approached me with an Armani bag clutched between hands she held close to her ample middle.

"Wally Tupper?" she asked.

"Yes?" I stopped beside my car, wary.

She came up to me and held out a hand. "I'm Darla," she said. "Darla Dugan."

I stepped back a step. "I'm sorry. Have we met?"

She smiled ruefully. "No, of course not. But I heard...I read that you might need some help with the Garden Club Gala and I...I wanted to help."

"Sounds like we're going to need it. Thanks."

She held out her card. "Whatever I can do."

The address on her card was a ritzy apartment complex overlooking Lake Worth. She was speaking to me as I read the card and I suddenly realized I had heard that soft voice before. "Excuse me," I said, "were you by any chance at the Fuzzy Bunny Gallery yesterday?"

She ducked her head. "Yes, I was. That's where Verity and I came up with the idea to help Mrs. Fenton with the gala."

Sure you did, I thought. I wondered what Verity DeVale's mousy little handmaiden would say if she knew I had overheard that snippy bitch's vow to unseat Peep as gala chairman.

She had been sent, I had no doubt, to ensure she and Verity were invited to the ball, if there was one. I stuck the card in my pocket, thinking I'd be polite but make sure these two didn't get within a mile of the gala. "Thanks again."

As if she had read my mind, she put a hand on my arm and said, "Verity isn't always the nicest person. But if you ask her to participate, she might be easier to deal with."

Surprised, I looked at her a little more closely. She seemed to be telling me to keep my enemy close to my side. She might be right.

"I'll keep you posted," I said. "We'll let you know."

She nodded her satisfaction with that answer and backed off, watching me get in my car. She stood on the sidewalk, waving the tips of her fingers, as I drove away.

I looked at the cards Rezna had given me. One of them had a time on it, so I decided that was where I would go next. It wasn't quite five o'clock but I didn't subscribe to Peep's theories about being on time if you're late, so I would be early.

I took South County to Phipps Estates, a patio home subdivision being built amidst a flurry of money and controversy. Several vintage

Palm Beach homes had been torn down to make room for it, which angered the preservationists. Multimillion dollar homes were squeezed just feet from each other on small lots, which angered the environmentalists. About the only people who weren't angry were the tax collectors.

At the little stucco gate house, I gave my name to the security guard, who checked his list and let me in with directions to follow Ficus Lane all the way to the left. It wouldn't have been difficult to find the address, since only a small portion of the estate had been built out and only about a half dozen homes were occupied.

The stucco home was virtually unadorned. In the front, minuscule builder's landscaping looked lost against the vast reach of concrete blocking. One forlorn tree struggled to decorate the area. A million dollars doesn't buy what it used to. I got out of my car, walked the few steps to the door, and rang the doorbell. Nobody answered it right away, so I knocked. Still no answer.

I wasn't that early, and I was expected. Why didn't she answer the door? Annoyed, I tried the door handle. It turned, and the door opened. "Hello?" I called. No answer. I walked down a plushly carpeted hallway.

In the living room, I saw a woman in her thirties with short, tightly curled hair and skin the color of cafe latte slumped in an overstuffed chair in front of a blaring television set tuned to the Weather Channel. Her head was drooped over as if she had fallen asleep while watching. In one hand dangled a lit cigarette, and in the other hand, on top of her tucked-under legs, sat a sweating glass of something the color of spun gold.

"Hello?" I said again. From the kitchen I could smell smoke, and as I walked in to check it out, the smoke alarm began to shriek. I turned off the oven, put the blackened remains of a formerly frozen dinner in the sink, and looked through the pass-through to the living room.

The smoke alarm had done its job, and she was brushing off her lap where, apparently, she had spilled her drink when jolted awake.

She looked up at me, sheepish. "Sorry," she called out over the shrieks. "You must be Wally."

After I had waved the smoke alarm into silence, I walked back into the living room to make sure she had not dropped the cigarette. She had the same thought, and was on her knees groping around under the chair, stockinged feet poking out from under a slim, tailored suit skirt. "Here it is," she said.

She got up somewhat unsteadily and sat back in the chair, mashing the cigarette down into an overflowing ashtray. "Have a seat."

I sat on a baby-butt soft leather couch. The sofa and chair set from Roche-Boisbois looked new and had cost her a pretty penny, but on the leather chair she occupied there were a couple of cigarette burns.

"Sunny and fair," said the weather man.

She reached for the remote and clicked him away. "Ha," she said, "as if they couldn't just record that and replay it every damn day down here."

I glanced at the card. "Ms. Jackson?"

"Vanessa, please," she said. "And I really apologize for this. I just got some bad news and....it was just the straw on the camel's back." She swept the room with her arm, as if there were a camel standing there.

"No problem," I said. "Maybe you'd rather I come back at a better time?"

She squinched her eyes shut. "There is no better time. There hasn't been a better time for a couple of months."

"Can I help?" I couldn't think of anything else to say.

"Bring back my husband," she said. She tucked her feet underneath her and took a deep breath. "Explain to me how come it is that when they tell you that you can have it all, they fail to mention that it's a big fat lie...that if you do get it all, you'll just have to worry about losing it."

"I'm sorry." I really was sorry—sorry that I was stuck in this woman's unhappy life and didn't have a clue what to do to make things better for her. Damn Rezna, anyway, for getting me into this. I don't like to get involved in people's lives. The next thing you know, they'll want to get involved in yours, and I'd just as soon they didn't.

"No," she said. "I'm sorry. Sorry I never had time to have children. Sorry my husband was jealous because his business failed and my career took off. Sorry he slept with his secretary in retaliation. Sorry they're both on a beach in California and I'm stuck here in hot as hell Florida running a magazine. Sorry I let a crooked investor get his mitts on my life savings. Sorry the cat ran away because he was pissed that I left him alone for eighteen hours a day."

She leaned back and closed her eyes. "Sorry that I'm drinking my life away," she said softly.

"It is hot," I agreed. "But it's only November. It'll get worse."

She glared at me.

At a loss for anything else to do, I went to the kitchen, got us both a glass of ice water and came back in. "You told Rezna you wanted to help with the Garden Club Gala?" I said, handing her one of the glasses.

She nodded, sipped the water. "I thought it would get my mind off all this."

"Well," I said, thinking I would like to get my own mind off all this. "Let's get to it."

She sat up, gave me a grateful look. "Okay. Let's."

I left about a half hour later, after we had agreed Old Money would pay to have the invitations printed and addressed within the week and she would call me to arrange to get the guest list.

I handed her my card as I left. "Next time," I said, "call somebody before you set yourself on fire."

She looked at the ground and closed the door behind me.

I drove west across the Flagler Memorial Bridge hoping that the next volunteer to want to help the Garden Club would be a more cheerful one. The address I sought was just up Flagler Drive in the Old Northwood section of West Palm Beach, which has become quite trendy among the "too cool for Palm Beach" set. There was a heavy renovation effort to restore some of the fifty-year-old homes, and the stucco Spanish house at the address Rezna had given me was one of those that had recently been redone. The outside of the tiny house was immaculate, with an etched glass art door and windows looking onto a postage stamp size front porch. The landscaping was first class. A four-story banyan tree anchored the yard and was surrounded by citrus trees, ferns, flowers and date palms.

I walked up the steps to the door and rang the doorbell. It was answered immediately by a striking young man with neat blond hair and a buff bod barely covered by short cutoffs and a sleeveless T-shirt.

"Oh," he said, his face registering disappointment.

I looked at the card. "Mr. Montreaux? I'm Wally Tupper. Rezna Van Daly sent me."

"Oh, yes," he said. "I'm so sorry. I was expecting someone else. Please come in. And my name is Digby."

The polished wood floor was covered by an Oriental carpet. The home felt warm and inviting. A giant spray of freesia sat in the middle of a table in the foyer. The sweet smell hung in the hallway.

"You've done a nice job on the restoration," I said. "I'm glad to see people bringing this neighborhood back."

"Thank you," he said, obviously pleased. "We're going to be on the tour this year. Come on back to the sitting room." I followed him to the back of the house.

"I'm having a glass of wine," he said. "Can I get you one? Chateau Margaux '78."

That didn't mean anything to me, but I said yes, and he brought it to me in Waterford crystal. We had just started to talk about the flowers he had agreed to do for the gala when I heard the front door open. He looked up.

"Excuse me," he said, and walked toward the front of the house.

I heard voices, male voices. At first they were just a murmur, but they got louder.

"You're going back to work, Raymond?" Digby said.

"Yes," was the answer.

"Again?" Digby had a little whine in his voice.

"Yes." Raymond sounded annoyed.

"You aren't going to help with the party at all?"

"Nope," was the answer, defiantly.

"We have fifty of our best friends coming here tomorrow night and you don't plan to do a thing to help?" Digby was sounding pathetic.

"Now you have it," came the answer, patronizing.

There was silence for a moment. I wondered what I should do. I didn't know, so I did nothing.

"You never do anything around the house," Digby said. "I've made a showplace out of our home and you haven't lifted a finger. All you do is work. I think you'd rather be at that bank than here with me. As a matter of fact, I think you go to work at the bank to get away from me. You work all hours. Some days you work around the clock. I know something's wrong."

The response came quickly. "Stop it, Digs. You're imagining things. Anyway, you knew when we moved in together I didn't do housework. Somebody has to make the money in this household and it looks like that's me. So just stop whining."

I heard heels tapping and they were coming my way. I tried to arrange my face in an I-didn't-hear-a-thing look.

Raymond stopped when he hit the doorway. "Oh. I'm sorry." He was tall and slim, and groomed to a fair-the-well from his Armani suit to his buffed fingernails. He had that elegant, assured look of good-looking young men who move comfortably in boardroom circles.

I stood up, acutely aware that my own cuticles needed attention. "I'm Wally Tupper. I'm just here to talk about the Garden Club Gala," I said hurriedly. "Digby offered to help."

Raymond lowered his smooth, soft chin and looked at me through heavy dark lashes with the eyes of a Botticelli angel. "I've met your husband," he said. "I work at First County Bank. I'm Raymond Way."

We shook hands and he turned to Digby. "Good work on the gala gig, Digs. That"ll benefit both of us. Maybe it'll help me get that promotion. I'll be thirty soon, you know."

He turned and winked at me. "Life begins at thirty, you know."

Then he turned back to Digby. "Gotta go," he said. "I hope you'll get over this, because I'm not going to change."

He left, and we heard the front door slam. I would have liked to have slammed it on Raymond's neatly clipped head. Thirty, indeed.

I looked at Digby and felt sorry for him. "Would you rather I left?" I said. I wanted to say, "Would you like me to go knock the stuffing out of the asshole?" But that's the kind of comment even I usually keep to myself.

"No, I just have to decide if I can live with it. I don't know if I can take the frustration anymore." He swallowed hard and indicated an undecorated Christmas tree in the corner of the room. It was a large tree, at least twelve feet tall.

"Every year, I decorate the tree alone. Every year, I invite our friends in for eggnog and Christmas cheer and I clean the house and prepare the food and decorate...but Raymond will show up thirty minutes before the party starts. Then he'll charm the pants off everybody with his wit and his stories. Everyone will laugh and tell me how lucky I am to have him and how lucky we are, in this day and time, to have such a great relationship."

Digby looked forlornly toward the bedroom. "Then Raymond'll go to bed and I'll clean the house. Lucky. Ha."

He showed me out of the house looking as if his dog had died, and I drove back across the bridge feeling lower than Leona Helmsley on judgment day. And resentful.

"I don't even know these people," I said to Pitt over drinks later that night. I leaned against him on our oversized sofa, the one that had sheltered me earlier that day.

"Pluck, pluck, pluck," he said, picking at my shoulder with two fingers. Henry and Isadora, our two Jack Russell terriers, looked up with interest from where they were curled up on the sofa next to me.

"Go pluck yourself," I grumbled, but good-naturedly, because I knew what he meant. I had married Pitt because he was the one man who could look through my prickly nature and find the real person. For the first year we dated, he called me porky, and it wasn't a slur on my physical presence. It was short for porcupine, because he said whenever anybody tried to get close to me I would put out my quills.

As we got to know each other better, he would tease me with "pluck, pluck, pluck," whenever he wanted me to stop bristling and relax.

The dogs lowered their heads and resumed their nap, and I told him about my dream. "If I'm going to have dreams like that, I don't even want to get involved with LaLa's problems, much less those of some strangers," I said, knowing I was dangerously close to a pout. I could hear the whine in my voice. I hate whining. But tonight it felt...necessary.

Pitt rubbed my head, scratching me behind the ears as he would have done the dogs if they had been on his lap. It felt good. I craned my neck up towards him. The dogs crawled up and put their heads on my shoulder, as if to comfort me.

"I don't think," he said, "that you have any choice. Need a hug?"

"Certainly not," I said, sitting up. In the mid eighties, Pitt had discovered Leo Buscaglia and had gone around hugging everybody until I told him that if he didn't cut that crap out, he would end up being the butt of Thornton DeVale's jokes at the Palm Beach Country Club bar. He had rarely mentioned it again, except in teasing.

"I know what I need. C'mon kids," I said to the dogs. "Let's go get some ice cream."

They flew off the sofa and were waiting in quivering excitement in front of the refrigerator when I got to the kitchen. Henry, Isadora and I were in agreement on this: The most comforting solution to any problem is a pint of Ben & Jerry's. The dogs got vanilla.

For me, this was a chocolate crisis of a double dip magnitude.

Chapter Five

MONDAY MORNING, A FAMILIAR SCENE waited for me in the kitchen. The dogs were stalking Petal with single-minded intensity as she fixed breakfast for Pitt, who was reading *The Palm Beach Post* financial section at the kitchen table.

To Henry and Isadora, our housekeeper Petal is the goddess of food, and they pay her homage by staying within three inches of her heels whenever she is in the kitchen. Experience had taught them this is a good place to catch the fallout, and she always has their undivided attention.

On her part, Petal regards the dogs as a curse to be borne without grace. They make her life a living hell, and she sees no reason to pretend otherwise. At least, that's what she would have us believe. Secretly, when Pitt and I are not around, I know she slips them bits of steak and cheese. Which, of course, further encourages their relentless pursuit of her.

"Get out from under my feet," she fussed, as she walked Pitt's plate of bacon and eggs to the table. The dogs jumped around her as she walked—furry, fifteen-pound, spring-loaded creatures launching themselves at Petal's five-foot self. She's no match for them, since they generate a lot of thrust and she only weighs ninety-eight pounds sopping wet.

She looked at me beseechingly. "Can you get these damn dogs off me?" she begged. "They're going to ruin my stockings and I have to go to the market." I live in shorts and casual clothes; Petal lives to dress up. She works for an hour getting the Big Hair every morning and fusses with her long, arched fingernails every night.

Petal is twenty-nine but sometimes acts like she's fifteen. She's Erma's niece and Erma imported her from Alabama when she was eighteen to work for us. I offered to pay her way through college, and she graduated from Palm Beach Atlantic with a degree in home economics—her choice, not ours.

She's energetically searching for a husband. Every few months there's a new boyfriend. Lately she's been spending Saturday nights with one that seems to have real promise. God knows I don't begrudge her any fun she can find. Life at our house must be deadly dull for her.

I reached for the dog treats, which got Henry's attention. "Here, dogs," I said, and they scampered over to me, toenails clicking on the tile floor, little brown and white blurs with floppy ears. I leaned against the counter top and lobbed liver bits, which the dogs caught in mid-air.

In gratitude, Petal opened the refrigerator and pulled out a can of Diet Coke, the miracle drink that's my caffeine of choice in the mornings. In more than twenty years, I haven't started a day with anything else. And nobody who's seen me in my pre-DC moments ever wants to find themselves trapped in that situation a second time. It's not a pretty sight.

Pitt put the sports section of *The Palm Beach Post* beside him on the table and looked up. "You must have made a real impression on Rezna Saturday."

"Why?"

He reached over to a stack of newspapers, pulled out the society section of *The Tattler*, and waggled it in the air. "Check it out."

I looked around for a pair of reading glasses. I keep them scattered about the house because I can never remember to have them with me. There was a pair on the counter, and I retrieved them and put them on. Then I sat down to read where Pitt had the paper folded.

The Beach Session
by Rezna Van Daly
Society Editor, The Palm Beach Tattler

Well, wash my undies and call me Royal. It's beginning to look as if the Palm Beach Garden Club is going to pull off the gala—and in style—at Casa Besamario, the grandest estate in a town known for its estates.

It was at Casa Besamario some sixty years ago that the first charity gala was held—given, in fact, by the great-great-great-grandmother of today's Chairman, Peep Fenton.

The Palm Beach Garden Club Gala has always been one of the most exquisitely decorated balls of the season and this should be no exception. Montreaux Florists will bathe the ballroom and loggia in holiday greenery, and Digby Montreaux has sneaked me the information that the traditional Casa Besamario fifty-foot Christmas tree will not only be a focal point of the decor, but will reflect more than ten thousand lights into the Olympic-size pool on the ocean-front patio.

I wallow in recrimination after doubting in print last week that the Garden Club could be revived from its near-death experience. This year's gala promises to be the party of the season.

I'm sworn to secrecy about a special guest at the gala, but you'll be crowned a fool if you stay away from this party, my dear commoners.

P.S. Look-Ahead party-goers will also mark their calendars for New Year's Eve at The Breakers. Our flagship hotel will mark its Centennial New Year's Eve by honoring The Breakers Babies, those fortunate war infants born at the hotel during its short tenure as a hospital. Historian Reginald Wert is compiling a list, so if you are a BB, come forward and join the most prestigious processional since the Prince of Wales led the debutante march in 1942.

"I'll have to call Peep," I said.

"Do that," Pitt said. He looked thoughtful, wiped butter off his fingertips with his napkin and picked up the World's Best Boss coffee mug his secretary had given him last year. "You think I could talk this royalty into investing in Wesson?" Pittsburgh Wesson Bank was Pitt's dream, the financial institution he had planned to open since he was a little boy. Most little boys want to be firemen. My husband wanted to own his own bank.

I grabbed a piece of dry rye toast off the table—a gesture towards my perpetual diet—and walked back up to my bedroom. Peep would be ecstatic over the news in Rezna's column. Palm Beach loves nothing better than to snuggle with royalty. After all, the mayor, Paul Ilyinsky, is related to the Romanoffs, the Russian royal family that were first cousins to the Queen Elizabeth's forebears.

I called Peep and told her I would come to her house as soon as I finished a few errands. I also told her to be sure to read Rezna's column.

After further fortifying myself with a cheese omelet, I headed out the door, my first stop to pick up some books I had ordered from the Doubleday store on Worth Avenue.

Reading isn't one of the most popular pastimes in Palm Beach, and I think I'm one of the few Palm Beach residents who frequents the tiny book store. I seldom find it busy. Most townies will call the store and order books to be picked up by their drivers.

I like to stand in the back of the crowded little nook—the whole store is about as big as the average Palm Beach mansion bathroom—and surround myself with books, breathe deeply and try to imagine myself in Boston or New York.

Sometimes it works for a minute and the spell overtakes me, washing away that how-did-I-get-here feeling I've always had in Palm Beach.

Only when I went to college did I realize that most people live their lives in one world, not two. Brought up in West Palm Beach as a member of Erma's family, but schooled among those who lived across Lake Worth in Palm Beach, I had grown up with one foot on the west side of the lake, one foot on the east. On the west side, people lived in average homes and had average lives. On the east side, they lived in mansions amid all that money could buy. To be caught between them was like having each foot on a different cloud and your head in the stratosphere: you never feel as if you are standing on solid ground and you're in a perpetual state of altitude-induced dizziness.

I was always more comfortable on the west side. My dream had been to marry a college professor, like Erma did, and live a modest but interesting life in some little college town. Instead, I married Pitt, a man whose dream was to open his own bank in Palm Beach, a town that worshipped money.

I walked into the book store with a wave toward Joan Page, the store manager. "Hi, Joan."

"Hi, Wally. Looking for anything in particular? I do have the books you ordered."

"Thanks. I'm going to look around."

She went back to her paperwork. It was a routine we both knew. I would linger for a while, soaking in what little book store atmosphere the nook had to offer. Joan and I were friends, a friendship built up over years of mutual affection for books.

I didn't hear the telephone in the store ring. I didn't pay any attention to the conversation until Joan's tone of voice pulled me from my reverie.

"Well, I have the book now," she was saying, her words squeezed between clenched teeth. "You can send your driver to pick it up." There was a silence. I turned and went back to my browsing until I heard Joan say, "I don't have to take this from you." That wasn't a phrase you heard retailers use with their customers in Palm Beach. Then an even greater surprise: the sound of the phone receiver being slammed back into the cradle.

I walked up to the front desk. "Joan? Are you okay?"

"That woman." She shuffled papers without seeing them. "What a bitch! She and that married man she—" She stopped herself short. "Well, they order gifts for people, but instead of waiting for me to call them when the books have come in, they just make a scene because I don't have them. His wife is so nice. I just hate—" She stopped again. And grimaced. "I'm sorry. His wife is your friend, isn't she?"

My stomach was feeling a little knotty. "Who?"

"That Ewen guy," she said. She looked a little embarrassed. "I'm really sorry. I shouldn't talk about my customers."

I leaned forward. "LaLa Ewen is my friend, not Booth."

She showed her relief with a sigh. "She is the nicest lady. I hate what he does to her. He struts up and down the avenue with his women. You know, we all know when a man is buying a gift for a woman other than his wife."

I nodded, because Pitt had told me never to tell one retailer on Worth Avenue anything I didn't want all of them to know. They are a close society, part of the Palm Beach downstairs that knows all about what the upstairs is doing, and share it frequently within their own code of silence.

"How do you know?" I asked. I glanced up as two customers entered the store. Tourists. No one minded them, really, but they stood out from the town shoppers like a Hostess Cupcake in a patisserie.

Joan read them the same way, and didn't bother to lower her voice. "They have separate charge accounts. We keep them on file, you know—God forbid they should have to carry their plastic—and when they tell us to use such and such account, we know the bill isn't going to their home."

I made a mental note never to try to put anything over on Pitt, who already had warned me that the financial rabbit holes of the wealthy are deeply dug and often come out in another farmer's field. It was part of the game they played, sometimes with money they didn't have.

I laid the book I was holding on the stack in front of her, put my elbows on the counter and leaned forward. "Ring these up for me, would you, Joan?" I lowered my voice. "And while you're ringing, if you could just accidentally mention the name of the woman who you were just talking to, I'd pretend like I never heard it from you. Please."

She nodded, started ringing up the books, and said casually, "say, you wouldn't mind dropping off this book at Mrs. Povitch's on El Brillo Way, would you? She just called and is anxious to have the book I ordered."

Somehow it wasn't a surprise that Booth and Taffy Merriman Povitch were an item. She was beautiful, in that well-tended, carved look of Palm Beach matrons over the age of thirty. And she put on airs, which in Palm Beach is sort of like saying a pilot flew a plane. But she did it so poorly, that all but the least schooled in Klass With A Capital K saw through it.

Booth, apparently, had not.

My mind raced. "Joan, how long has this been going on?"

She looked up, her eyes searching the ceiling for answers. "I'd say about six months. There have been others."

I was shocked, and that's something I thought I had long ago outgrown in Palm Beach. I was amazed that LaLa did not know about this.

"Can you get me any more information?" I asked, edging away as the tourists approached, their paperback copies of the latest best sellers in their hands.

"Sure. Check back with me in a few days. I'm sure I can have something for you." She applied a smile to her face as she turned to the tourists. "And will there be anything else for you today?"

She winked a good-bye at me as I left the store.

I needed some time to gather my wildly racing thoughts, so I plunked my posterior down on a wooden bench just outside the book store and assumed a position not unlike The Thinker, but with my head in both hands. And with not nearly the depth of thought. I imagined The Thinker pondering what to do about world hunger. I was just scoping out Worth Avenue, wondering what my next step might be.

I contemplated my day so far and decided I might as well plug on along its inevitable path. There wasn't any way I could tell LaLa the rumor about Booth and Taffy without having some feeling in my own heart that it was the truth. Telling her the truth would be cruel enough.

From my car, I called Taffy and told her I was bringing her a book. I drove around the Everglades Club golf course and down South County to El Brillo Way, where I turned east and drove to Taffy's oceanfront villa. I pulled into a gravel driveway. Before I could shut off my engine, the double doors to the stucco mansion swung open and a butler hurried out to open my car door.

The butler showed me out to a lanai overlooking the ocean and seated me at a glass-topped, wrought iron table. As he retreated, Taffy came swinging out of the house. She was tall and scarecrow-thin. She was wearing a stylish straw hat and big round sunglasses. I had to admit she looked smashing in an ankle-length linen sheath that would have served as a showcase for all my bulges. She had a triple strand of Tiffany pearls wrapped around her scrawny little neck.

Taffy Merriman Povitch and I have known each other for years, but we rarely socialize. Taffy has always been more interested in men than women.

"Wally. Delivering for the book store are we, now, darling?" She sat down next to me. "Drink?"

"Sure," I said. I was definitely getting the hang of this drinking thing. "Make it a double."

Taffy gave me an odd look, then waved at the butler, who ran over to the outdoor wet bar and picked up a tray of bottles and glasses. He brought the tray over to the table.

She waved him away, then started mixing things from the bottles. She poured the mixture into champagne glasses, then handed me one.

I tasted it. "Um. This is good."

"Bellini," she said. "Peach schnapps and champagne."

"Actually," I said, jumping right in, "I've come to sell tickets to the Garden Club Gala."

Taffy's brows rose over tightened eyelids. "Well, that's direct. How many tickets do you want me to buy, darling?"

"A table," I said. "Five thousand." Peep was asking $500 a ticket. Ticket prices to galas have really gone up. Inflation hits everywhere, I guess.

She looked surprised. "Pauly will kill me," she said. Pauly Povitch was Taffy's current husband. Number four, I think. The heir to a publishing fortune, he was notoriously cheap.

I smiled wickedly. "So?"

She waggled a finger in my direction. "You're trying to get me in trouble, darling."

What the hell, I thought. "Oh, you don't need me for that...darling." I took a swig of the drink and looked pointedly at my Timex. "Oh, dear. I'm running late for my lunch with LaLa Ewen." I hit hard on the name, and let the end of the sentence roll only in my mind: *The wife of the man you're committing adultery with.*

She caught my drift. With a measuring look, she stood, turned and walked toward the double doors leading into the house. "You're so right, darling. A generous donation is definitely called for. I'll be right back."

She returned with a checkbook and a Mont Blanc pen—one of the gold ones. She wasn't smiling as she wrote the check. She gritted her teeth as she ripped it out of the book. She held it up, just out of my reach.

"Tell me, darling, how is our dear LaLa?"

I leaned forward and snatched the check out of her hand. "Well, she's just fine, Taffy. She and Booth will be coming to the gala—but of course they're married, so they would, wouldn't they?"

She reached up to wrap a finger around in her pearls. "One really mustn't lose one's sense of perspective about these things, Wally dear."

I folded the check and poked it down into my canvas bag. "One mustn't forget that one's, er, 'things' resulted in one's last divorce, Taffy dear."

She shrugged. "Easy come, easy go, dear. One can always find another husband. Why, there are lots of men I haven't gotten around to marrying—yet."

I chugged the rest of the Bellini and stood up. "One must remember to keep one's mitts off other people's property, dear. One doesn't want to become the talk of the town, does one?"

She stood. "So sorry you have to leave, dear. Thanks ever so for including me in your charity gala. Pauly and I wouldn't miss it." She walked to the house and held open the door.

"The butler will show you out," she said.

As I walked through the door, she slammed it behind me. The glass shook so hard the butler glanced back with a grimace. "Walk this way, ma'am," he said, prancing through the foyer with the kind of tight-assed gait you usually only see headed away from you in a pedigreed dog show.

I walked my regular old way, got in my car and drove back out to South County Road. I started to go to LaLa's, my intention being to tell her the whole story, but I changed my mind.

My thinking was, I had warned Taffy off Booth. Hell, I had black-mailed the bitch out of five thousand dollars. And she no doubt would tell Booth that I knew about his affair. Booth, not wanting to lose LaLa, whose money he lived on, would stop fooling around. *Ta-da,* I thought. *I've solved the problem.*

So instead I drove straight to Peep's house. She answered the door and pulled me inside. We walked outside through the oceanfront loggia, an open-air passage to the patio, swimming pool and beach. We sat on the patio overlooking the Olympic size pool.

"You're not gonna believe this," I said, thinking she could back me up on my strategy of silence.

"You're not gonna believe this," she said. Peep was not big on listening when she had something to say. "I called Rezna when I read her column. She has promised me—promised me—the Princess of Wales will be at my gala. She said the reason she can be so sure is the Prince of Wales is scheduled to lead the procession at the Breakers Centennial Ball on New Year's Eve, the grand climax of the hotel's 1996 anniversary festivities. The princess would like to steal a little of his thunder by attending our gala the week before."

She pointed a Chanel Hibiscus Pink fingernail at me. "Go forth and sell tickets. We have one month to put on the most important party in my life."

I went forth.

There was nothing more important than the success of this gala to Peep right now, and that would include LaLa's spousal infidelity. There was no point in opening my mouth. As a matter of fact, I thought as I headed home, it was time for me to practice a little of what I preached.

From now on, I decided, I was going to keep my mouth closed Kennedy-tight and my nose out of other people's business.

Chapter Six

DECEMBER 21

At eight o'clock on the night of the Garden Club Gala, the string orchestra was whining "I Want to Hold Your Hand." I hoped they'd pep it up later in the evening. Not that it was going to matter. Peep had sent out a thousand invitations and there hadn't been one regret. It looked like all of Palm Beach was crowding into the ballroom at Casa Besamario, the mansion built in the 1920s by Addison Mizner for Peep's grandmother, who wanted to impress and entertain Palm Beach society. She had done both.

Now Peep was doing the same. Ecstatic over having snagged a real princess, she had given the gala the theme of Cinderella's ball, and inside there were enough Prince Charmings and Cinderellas in glass slippers to make Walt Disney spin in his grave.

Dressed in a gown of burlap—Petal had designed it for me when I insisted on going as an early-evening Cinderella—I had driven myself and LaLa over earlier that evening to provide moral support for Peep, but she didn't seem to need it. She was on cloud nine, warmly greeting the very guests she had worried a month ago would snub her.

Right now, she was accepting a martini from Artie Marsh, one of the bartenders she had hired for the evening.

One of the early arrivals was Verity DeVale, draped in a strapless Versace number that must have set Thornton back a good twenty grand. He didn't seem to care. He had his arm around her waist proprietarily. He, of course, was Prince Charming. She, apparently, fancied herself Cinderella after the wedding.

I couldn't get around them.

"Wally," Thornton said. "I believe you've met my wife, Verity."

I nodded and snagged a glass of champagne from a passing tray. "A few weeks ago, at her gallery," I said. "Nice to see you, Verity. So happy you both could make it to the gala." I tried to infuse my voice with lots of sarcasm, and it wasn't wasted.

"Why, thank you so much, Wally," she said, not really trying to sweeten her voice, either. "I hope to come to many Garden Club Galas in the future."

Thornton, sensing an unprofitable turn to the conversation, interrupted. "Verity," he said to me, squeezing her so tightly around her tiny little waist that she winced, "would love to join the Garden Club and do some volunteer work for the gala board next year," he said. He squeezed again and she nodded. "I told her," he continued, "to do that this year but she didn't listen."

He turned to her. "You will listen to me now, though, won't you, dear?"

She put on a smile for me. "I certainly will. Oh, look, there's Peep Fenton. Thornton, let's go congratulate her for doing such a smashing job on this ball."

They slithered away. From the direction of the front door, I saw Pitt walking through the crowd and waved at him until I got his attention.

"Sonofagun," I said when he arrived at my side. "Money can buy forgiveness. Some of these are the same people who were saying last month that Peep killed Eaton."

We worked our way toward the bar. "This isn't forgiveness," he said. "This a shark pit anticipating a feeding frenzy—make one false step, they're saying, and you're chum."

"Verity and Thornton will have binoculars," I said. "She's seething that Peep bagged a princess as the bait for this gala."

We got our drinks, then Pitt looked around. "I've got to do some business," he said. "I think I'll go make nice with Rezna."

I kissed him on the cheek. "You little hustler, you."

I cruised out to pool side, where Peep's squad of electricians had spent a week creating a Birth of Jesus fairyland on the pool-side patio.

There a planetarium canopy had been set with thousands of tiny lights twinkling like diamonds in a December night sky. Hanging on an invisible wire was a crystal star from which beams radiated like a disco ball over the loggia, reflecting off the pool to drape the very air in bouncing fragments of light.

The star—meant to be the Star of Bethlehem, of course—traversed a track around the pool, its travels dictated by a mechanized trolley system hidden behind the canopy.

Looking up toward the star—blazing with the full force of the 220 current the electricians had installed by the pool to give Peep the effect she wanted—were a life-size contingent of Wise Men. They followed the star around the pool in on a track built into the grass Peep had installed on the patio for the evening.

At the corner of the pool was a manger scene, set up so as the Wise Men approached the manger, Mary would hold up the Baby Jesus in her arms for the Wise Men to see. The Baby Jesus was outfitted with a 220-volt halo, which glowed brighter and brighter as the Wise Men approached. As they passed by and began their travels around the pool again, Mary would lower the baby to the straw and its halo would soften to a faint glow.

The effect was magical, sort of like what it must be like to be at the North Pole when the northern lights are doing their show—especially if the northern lights are made of real diamonds.

Inside, the babble of human chatter mingled with the modulated voice of the male vocalist crooning a dance meter version of Bob Dylan's "I Don't Believe You." For the first hour or so, the guests would be too busy seeing and being seen inside to bother with going outside, so for all its spectacular decoration, this pool-side area was deserted at the moment. Later in the party, the revelers would drift out to the patio to cool off in the ocean breeze.

Something brushed the back of my neck and made the hairs there stand on end. I turned. Booth Ewen was standing behind me, so close I almost lost my balance and fell into the pool.

"Cheers, Wally dear. Having a good time?" He ran the palm of his hand over raven hair already slicked down to his head, then raised a champagne glass over my head.

I couldn't back up, because I was standing beside the Wise Men's path and they were on their way back around, so I stepped carefully sideways until I was out of his reach. "Sure, Booth. You?"

He leaned down over me, so close I could feel the warmth of his breath. It smelled stale, like an old closet. "Wonderful," he said. "The princess has arrived, you know? She's beyond my wildest expectations. So beautiful." He winked broadly. "She likes me, too, you know?"

My stomach turned. "I...,"

"Listen." He put a hand on my shoulder and pulled my ear close to his mouth. "I know you haven't told LaLa about Taffy, and I wan'ya to know how much I 'preciate that."

I nodded, trying to get my ear back. The liquor had rendered him virtually without any natural balance and he was using my shoulder to hold himself up. "Well, I...,"

He shook my shoulder. He was rough about it, and I knew it was on purpose. "I'd 'preciate it if you'd keep it our little secret, okay. What LaLa doesn't know won't hurt her, now, will it? It's over, y'know?"

I jerked my shoulder away and stepped back. "Sure, Booth, whatever you say." The creep was drunk, and the last thing I wanted was a scene at Peep's party.

"I havta go now," he said. "I promised Princess Di a dance." He turned and wobbled back inside, pushing aside a few admirers to plant himself at the elbow of the princess. If she was distressed at being in the presence of such a common commoner, her royal reserve didn't let it show—at least as far as I could see.

I sat on a wrought iron chair and stared into the pool. Now I wondered if I had done my friend any favor by not telling her about her husband's infidelity. Would she have left him if I had? And if she had, would that have made me responsible for breaking up a marriage?

I thought maybe I'd tell her the next day. If it were me, I thought, I'd rather face up to the truth about a cheating husband than see him making a fool of himself.

Digby came from the other side of the tree, sat beside me and leaned an elbow on the table.

"LaLa's husband is leaving lip marks on the royal skin. Everybody's talking about it." Digby had met Peep and LaLa at our gala planning sessions and had formed a fast friendship with both of them during the last few weeks. He and LaLa talked endlessly about their horoscopes, and he and Peep giggled like girls gossiping about Palm Beach present and past.

"Oh, my," I said. "That's definitely not protocol."

"Protocol my petunias," Digby spat. "He's behaving boorishly."

We heard a worried little sound. LaLa was standing behind Digby, fingers plucking at the bow she held in her hand. I cast a glance at Digby to see if he thought she had heard us.

LaLa stood stock still for one second, then straightened her back and squared her shoulders. She fluffed at that bow for what seemed like an eternity, then put her hands down to her side and slowly turned toward the door. A wide smile was frozen on her face.

"You know," she said, her lips barely moving. "He said he didn't want to come with me to this gala. Then when he heard the princess was going to be here, he couldn't tell enough people how he would be dancing with royalty tonight. He really gives social climbing a bad name. I guess I'd better go in there."

Digby reached over and took the bow from her hand. "I say make him come to you; what do you think, Wally?"

I stood up and took LaLa by the hand. "I agree. C'mon, LaLa, let's hit the ladies room."

She pulled her hand out of my grasp. "I'd rather go alone, if that's okay with you, Wally."

She gave a stiff little nod in our direction and headed off toward the powder room that was between the loggia and the ballroom. Even her clothes seemed depressed; they fluttered behind her at half staff.

I gave Digby a little wave and followed her through the loggia but instead of peeling off to the right toward the ladies room behind LaLa, I kept going around the tree and into the ballroom.

I snagged another glass of champagne from a passing tray and scanned the room, looking for a place to sit and think for a minute. I spotted Vanessa sitting alone on a loveseat against the wall and went over to her.

"Hi, Vanessa," I said. We'd seen each other at planning sessions several times since the day we met, but we had never talked about that first afternoon, when I had found her so bitterly drowning her sorrows in a glass of scotch.

She smiled wanly. "Hello, Wally."

"May I sit with you?" I didn't wait for an answer, just planted myself next to her on the bench.

She'd gotten some of her sense of humor back. "Please don't be shy. Join me."

I laughed. "You look great." She did. She was wearing a tan satin skirt that matched the color of her skin. The bodice was a wrap of pure white satin. She looked like a cup of cafe au lait with whipped cream on top.

"Thanks," she said. There was a moment of silence while we both watched what was going on around us. Maybe we both were remembering, awkwardly, how we had met.

"It's a little overdone, isn't it?" I said finally.

She looked at me closely. "You know what I was just thinking?"

"That rich white folks take a lot for granted?"

She laughed. "I guess that's true, too. But what I was thinking was how much people like for you to think they have money. We'd do almost anything to get it and show people we have it, wouldn't we?"

I shrugged. "I guess. It's hard for me to say, since I didn't do anything to get mine. Would you? Do anything, I mean?"

She held up her hands, palms up. "Guilty. Well. Maybe not anything. But I'd do a lot. I grew up knowing money was what made the difference. I saved and I invested and I always intended to end up letting my investments work for me."

"Good for you. I guess a bank account and a little luck will get you almost anywhere."

She finished the rest of her drink and leaned back. "I'm not the kind of person to depend on luck, Wally. I learned a long time ago I had to make the most of what I have. I've done just that. I learned a smart black woman could find ways through the glass ceiling, and I did that. I learned I could get what I wanted without subjugating my principles or bowing to the Man."

She stood up. "Even more important, I learned what to say, when to say it and who to say it to in order to impress all the right people. No, it wasn't luck that got me here, I got myself here. But...," She looked around. "I didn't learn soon enough to beware of the sharks. I will not be taken advantage of. Now, before my date gets back with my drink, I'm going to the ladies room." She started to walk away.

"I'll come with you," I said, realizing I liked the woman. She was direct and no-nonsense—things I imagined to be my own best features. *Of course,* I thought, *she doesn't sound like the kind of person whose path you want to block.*

We wound our way through the crowd; she let me lead and I headed toward the ladies room toward which I had seen LaLa moving. I had been here many times before, so I knew what to expect, but Vanessa's eyes widened a little as we walked into the powder room, because it looked more like it belonged in Bloomingdale's than in a private residence.

A mirrored far wall, some twenty or so feet away, gave the room the feeling it went on forever. On each of the other walls, there was a door: The one from the ballroom, which we had just entered, the one leading into the private potty area, and the one leading out to the loggia and the pool.

At that door stood Darla Dugan, the pudgy, piggy-nosed fetch-it person for Verity DeVale. She held the door open an inch and peered through the crack. As we walked in, she looked back at us, put a finger to her lips, and looked back through the opening.

I could hear voices on the other side of the door. I walked up to Darla and looked over her head. I could see LaLa. She was talking at a feverish pitch, and her words began to come into focus. She was angry, and speaking loudly.

"You've got some nerve, Booth. You've made so many bad investments I'm going to have to tap into the principal just to get you out of debt. I can't believe you took a loan on our home without telling me."

Booth walked into my view. He looked drunker than he had been earlier, if that was possible. "I'll take a loan on anything I want. You'd better find another sucker to marry because I don't want to put up with you any more. I don't want to support that passle of psychics you talk to every day."

The icy tone of LaLa's voice frightened me. "I've put up with a few habits of yours, Booth. If I look to the other world for solace, it's because you have made this one hell on Earth for me."

He grabbed her by the shoulder. I got ready to run out there if I needed to, but he just kept yelling; he was probably too drunk to do her any harm, anyway. "All you do," he said, "is go from one mumbo jumbo voodoo-maker to another, spending my money."

"It's my money, Booth."

"Well, you're not getting another cent and you can hire all the lawyers you want, but I'll have it so tied up in investment funds and trusts, you'll be long dead before they can unravel it."

Darla looked at me, lips clamped tightly together. Behind us, Vanessa had a stricken look. Outside, LaLa and Booth continued their argument.

"Booth, my father gave us the money to build that house."

"And I'm going to have it torn down and build a new one. That damn house was built thirty years ago and it has cost me a fortune to maintain. I want you out by New Year's."

"Not in this lifetime," LaLa said.

With the speed of a striking snake, Booth slapped her across the face so hard she reeled. I pushed by Darla, threw open the door and ran outside. I threw myself around LaLa. Vanessa, one step behind me, flung herself between Booth and me.

"Touch her again and die," Vanessa said in a low voice.

"You," he said. "I'm not afraid of you. I told you that before. Get out of my way."

He looked past me at LaLa.

"It's going to give me special pleasure to pave over that little area where you commune with your stupid spirits. Well, you are going to need all your friends plus all the dead people you can summons to help you now."

He gave a mocking bow. "Now," he said, "if you bitches will excuse me, I've promised the princess another dance." He stalked off toward the bandstand.

The three of us looked at each other. LaLa turned and ran into the crowd in the opposite direction from Booth.

"Wow." I said. I needed to immediately tell my friend the whole truth about her jerk of a husband. I was very sorry I hadn't done it before. "I've got to find her," I told Vanessa.

"Okay," she said. "I'm going to find a drink."

A few minutes later, I spotted Pitt, waiting in the bar line. I walked over and nudged him. "Hi."

"Hi, gorgeous. What's happening?"

"LaLa and Booth just had a killer argument out on the patio. I'm surprised they didn't draw a crowd. Peep would have been fit to be tied. I'm looking for LaLa. Seen her?"

"Nope. Want a drink?"

"You bet. I'm thinking of becoming one of those Palm Beach matrons who gets so happy at parties she can't remember what she did."

He handed me my drink.

"Well, I might drink more, too, if I have to listen again to Booth's boring harangue on Swiss bank accounts and why their banking system is so much better than ours. See you later."

I circled the room and still couldn't find LaLa. I did see Booth's paramour, Taffy, who gave me a cold but cordial tip of her head. Finally, I decided I still needed to pee, so I headed back to the powder room.

As I swung open the door, I heard her before I saw her.

LaLa was crying.

I hate crying.

"LaLa, what is it?" I knew very well, of course. I sat down beside her on the chaise lounge and put a hand on her shaking back.

"I just couldn't let him do that to me, Wally. I just couldn't." LaLa lifted her chin. "I swore I wouldn't let him make me cry."

I patted her shoulder. "There, there, LaLa. It will be all right. You'll see." I hate to comfort people. I'm terrible at it and I never know what to say.

"No, Wally, I don't think it will." LaLa looked up with a tear-streaked face. Her hair hung in limp ringlets around her face.

"Sure it will. You and Booth will work things out." It was a lie and we both knew it, but people said that sort of thing. Now was not the time to be telling the truth.

"I don't think so." Like a cat, LaLa kneaded her fingers into the skin of her thighs.

I was beginning to get angry at Booth, and decided it was time someone told him off. I decided it might as well be me.

I stood up. "Where is he, LaLa?"

"Out there." She nodded to the east and I walked out the door to the patio with enough anger welling up in me to tell him all the things I had ever thought about him.

I hung a left back to where I had seen him before, but before I could get there, I had to stop for an extended conversation with a Russian cousin of the mayor of Palm Beach. The cousin, it seems, was trying to drum up support for returning the Russian royal family to its rightful place as rulers of Russia. As I was pretty sure this was not likely to happen—and thought if it did, Mayor Paul Ilynsky, the mayor of Palm Beach, could probably do a better job of running the country than some of the leaders they've had lately—I agreed with her. For what it was worth. Mollified to have some support, she nodded her approval and went back inside.

When I got to the Christmas tree, I heard voices from the other side. One of them sounded like Booth. "Oh," a voice said. "What are you doing here?"

There was a moment of silence, then everything seemed to happen at once. Someone said, "Hey!" Then, "Back off."

Then I heard a splash. Booth's voice came from the pool. "Are you crazy? This is no time for kid stuff. Now I'll have to go home and change. How will I explain this to the princess? I promised her the last dance of the evening."

As I peeked around the tree, I could see Booth swimming toward the edge of the pool. He was laughing, heading for the steps out of the pool. He couldn't see me yet for the tree branches.

I saw something fly into the pool. It looked for all the world as if the Baby Jesus had done made a triple gainer into the water, but I blinked to clear what had to have been a hallucination.

For just a second, Booth kept coming. Then he saw me. He held up his hand. "Wally, help me out."

Then the full force of the current hit his body. He stiffened; his eyes got wide. His outstretched hand bent into a claw and he flipped over backwards.

After that his body relaxed, and he floated in a silent ballet, entangled in the heavy cord attaching the Baby Jesus to the outlet. Jesus rested peacefully on the bottom of the pool. His halo no longer glowed. Mary didn't seem to notice that he was gone, and in the way of animatronics everywhere, she grasped at thin air to hold up empty arms to the Wise Men, who were by now back around to the manger.

I smelled Chanel perfume over the scent of electrical wires. I turned my head to see Peep coming up behind me. A few steps behind her, Digby walked up with his arm around LaLa. Raymond was a few steps behind them.

"Pity," said Peep, wrapping her arm around LaLa's waist.

"It's not," I said, draping my arm across her shoulders.

"Girls," said LaLa. "Would you look at that? Booth has just ruined Peep's Jesus."

What could we say? He was her husband.

Chapter Seven

THE AUTOMATIC POOL CLEANER MUNCHED its way along the bottom of the pool like a flat-nosed Pac-Man. As its head passed Booth, its plastic tentacle entrapped one of his legs and as we stared in silent shock, his body began to chug around the pool like some sort of grotesque mechanical pool toy.

"Let's get him out of there," I said. "Maybe he's not dead."

"Dead?" Peep was the first to come to her senses, realizing, apparently, that while she cared very little that Booth was floating in her swimming pool, she cared very much that he might have chosen her gala at which to die.

"No. Oh, no," she moaned. "Not another one." She started shaking so violently her cigarette flew out of her hand and into the pool, narrowly missing landing on Booth. "This can't be happening."

She crossed her arms tightly to control her shaking and began to pace alongside the pool. "What will I do? What will I do?"

LaLa, eyes still on Booth, reached out a hand toward her. "Peep...,"

Peep jumped back, bumping into Digby, who had come up behind her. She pointed a finger at LaLa. "Your husband is dead right here in my swimming pool in the middle of my gala. How could he?"

I moved around behind Peep, elbowing Digby aside to grab her by the shoulders. "Cut it out, Peep."

Peep shook herself free from my grasp and waved her arms toward the house full of guests, who luckily could not see our little crowd or the swimming pool for the tree. Inside, the orchestra cranked up into a disco boogie rendition of "Staying Alive." The partiers were full-fledged into their good time.

"Don't tell me no one," she said, arms flailing wildly around her head. "If you think for one minute they aren't going to notice this, you better think again."

She stalked over to the edge of the pool and flung a forearm up and down in the general direction of Booth's body. "There's a body in my pool and I think people are going to notice that. Oh, yes, they are going to notice that. And when they do, my name will be mud in this town. Not mud. Poop. Excuse me. Worse. What's worse? I can't think. Can't think. Whatever is the worst thing, that's what my name will be."

Vanessa had moved closer to Peep. "Surely they won't blame you?" she said, hesitantly looking over the side of the pool.

Peep held her hands up in a stop motion. "Blame me? Blame me? Oh, honey, you just don't know anything about blame, do you?" She started pacing, then looked up at us.

"If three dead bodies in the same house doesn't kill a person socially, I don't know what does. I didn't do it. I didn't do it. I didn't do any of them. Now this. Now this."

Vanessa backed up against me. "Three?" she asked.

"Her first husband died here last year," I whispered—loudly, because the music from inside was deafening, even out here—"and her mother a long time ago. Don't ask."

Vanessa nodded mutely, no doubt wondering what she had gotten herself into.

Right before our very eyes, Peep's knees went out from under her and she sank to the concrete, holding her hand to her eyes. "Make it go away," she wailed.

Digby perked up. "That's it," he said, turning to me. "We'll make it go away. We'll get rid of him. Let's get him out of the pool." He looked around. "Raymond. Help me."

Raymond opened his mouth, perhaps to protest, but finally shrugged and stepped up behind Digby, a surprisingly calm look on his face. They started toward the swimming pool.

"Hold it," I said. "What about the electric current? That pool would fry an elephant right now. Well, a rat anyway."

Digby ran over to where the Baby Jesus cord still was connected to the current. Carefully touching only the rubber insulation, he pulled the plug out of the sockets.

I looked down at the pool. A little green frog the size of a quarter was hopping, happily unaware, toward the pool. He gave a three-foot hop and landed in the water, then continued doing the frog-stroke across the pool. "Looks like it's okay."

I squatted down and grabbed Peep under the armpits. She still sat on the patio, her legs tucked up under her, her head in her hands. "Help me," I said to Vanessa. She stepped over and we dragged Peep to her feet like a rag doll.

Meanwhile, Digby and Raymond were pulling on the Baby Jesus cord, reeling in both Booth and the Baby Jesus, hand over hand, like some giant dead fish.

Back over to the side of the pool, Digby and Raymond were dragging Booth's body out of the pool. They hauled him out and unceremoniously dumped him out on the pool deck. Water ran out from him as if he were being mashed from above by some unseen hand.

I'm no nurse, but I had to know for myself, so I squatted down beside him and put my fingertips on his neck, feeling for that artery people use to find their own pulse. No matter where I put my fingers, there was no pulse. Booth's lips were blue and his face had a gray color.

I stood up. "I guess he's dead," I said.

"No shit," Digby said. "I've seen driftwood with more life in it."

"Well," I said, "I just wanted to be sure."

He grimaced sympathetically. "I know. But we'd better get a move on."

"Is there a key to that powder room?" I asked Peep.

"Sure," she sniffled. "Why?"

"Where is it?"

"Inside the linen closet."

In the bathroom, I opened the linen closet door and saw the key hanging on a hook. I looked into the potty chamber to make sure nobody was in there. Then, from the inside, I locked the door leading to the ballroom. "Let's get him in here."

"Get over there," Digby directed. Raymond moved over to Booth's left foot, where Digby had pointed. To me, Digby said, "You take the other foot."

I did, and we lifted Booth and carried him to the ladies room, depositing our dripping cargo on Peep's 200-year-old Persian carpet. She didn't utter a sound.

We backed out. Digby closed the door and I locked it.

I admit it should have occurred to me at that moment that we were committing a crime. It didn't. Peep was hysterical, LaLa was speechless, Digby was barking orders. What we were doing just didn't register on my moral Richter scale. All I thought about was helping my friend, Peep. I guess I thought I was helping LaLa as well.

Finally, I said, "Now what?"

"We leave him there until the gala is over," Digby said. "If anyone asks, we haven't seen him."

"I could tell everybody he went home sick," LaLa said, speaking for the first time. "Then, later, we'll put him back where we found him. They might think he passed out and fell in the pool."

"Oh, no you don't," Peep said. "He's not going back in my pool. I want him out of my house."

"How about," Vanessa said, "we drag him out to the ocean and put him in there? They'll think he died out there?"

I shook my head. "Won't work. He's probably got chlorine water in his lungs. If they do an autopsy, they'll know he didn't drown in the ocean; that's salt water."

Peep spoke up. Slowly, as if trying out a scientific theory on colleagues. "What if," she said thoughtfully, "you take him home and put him in his own pool? People will think he went for a late night swim and died."

I looked at Digby. He looked at me. Peep looked at us all. "If you do this for me," she said, "I'll never forget it."

I picked up a drink off the table and handed it to Peep. "It's already after eleven. You get back to the party," I said. "Put an out of order sign on that bathroom and lock the door."

She nodded. "The orchestra leaves at midnight." She looked around. "Cinderella, you know...."

I bent down to Booth's body and dug into his pants pocket. I pulled a valet ticket out. I walked around to LaLa, who had her eyes shut and was reciting her mantra, and handed her the ticket. "When this dries," I said, "you take Booth's car home and make sure there are no servants awake." I poked at her and she stood up, nodded her understanding and moved toward the ballroom door.

I picked up the Baby Jesus, unplugged the cord from his little halo, and put him in Mary's welcoming arms. She didn't flinch to see that her baby had no headlights.

I looked at the others. My stomach rolled. "Let's go party, people."

An unenthusiastic bunch of nods answered me and zombielike we walked, one by one, back into the ballroom. Peep pulled the doors closed behind us. We separated, each of us retreating to a corner of the ballroom. Whenever I caught sight of one of the others, they looked as if they were, like me, almost beginning to be able to act as if the scene by the pool had never happened.

An hour later, the princess having said her goodbyes and the last guest departed, Digby sidled up to me and gave me a nod. I had kissed Pitt goodnight a few minutes before, sending him on home under the pretext of wanting to stay and conduct, you should excuse the expression, a party post-mortem with Peep. LaLa had left by the front door with Booth's valet ticket. Vanessa had to be taken home by her date; I promised I would call her.

I waved goodnight to Peep, who was supervising the caterers and cleaners. Digby, Raymond and I left by the kitchen entrance, where Digby's florist van waited. We piled into it as if we were leaving, then drove quietly around to the east side of the house. Digby pulled up beside the gate to the wall around the pool, and like so many night skulkers, we sneaked into the pool area.

I unlocked the powder room door and pulled it open, my eyes shut tight, thinking when I opened them maybe Booth wouldn't be there, like one of those bad television programs where the body disappears and the heroine can't convince the police somebody had been murdered.

But there he was, just as dead as when we had left him.

We dragged him out of the powder room and piled him on a dolly Digby had brought from the van. I thought about that movie where the two guys pretend their dead boss is alive by propping him up during a party. It doesn't really work that way, I'm here to tell you. Booth's corpse was loose and soft. The humanity—such as it was—that had been housed in this body was gone. It was now a soggy repository of fluids responding to gravity rather than a pumping heart.

I started to have a twinge of conscience. "Digby, do you think we should just report this?"

Digby rolled the body into the van and slammed the doors shut. "Wally darling," he said, "I've buried better in a shoe box in my back yard. What we have to do is protect our loved ones. Whatever it takes."

"Whatever it takes," I repeated. I didn't really like the sound of that.

Digby and Raymond climbed in and pulled away. I walked slowly around to my car—I had parked it before the valet service had arrived and they were gone now. I got in and sat in the driver's seat for just a second, wondering what the heck I thought I was doing, then started the engine.

I drove over to LaLa's, pulling in behind Digby's van as he was opening the doors. "Hold on," I said, and went to the door. I walked in and looked around for LaLa. She came out from the back of the house. "It's okay," she said. "Only the cook is home and she sleeps with earplugs."

I went back out to the van. "It's okay," I said. They pulled the doors open, then rolled the dolly down the ramp. They followed me around to the east side of LaLa's house, around to the patio where she and I had sat the morning she told me she thought Booth was cheating on her.

I wished we could go back to that day. I'd tell her to throw him out, but quick.

Raymond held the dolly while Digby pushed Booth over into the pool. He sank like a rock, rolling face down, hands and feet splaying out. The pool pump was not on and the body just lay there, not a hair moving.

I turned around. "Let's get the hell out of here."

We walked back around to the front of the house. Digby and Raymond got into the van. I kissed LaLa on the cheek.

"Will you be okay?" I asked.

She nodded and pushed me towards my car.

"You have no idea," she said. "Now go home."

I did.

Pitt must have been asleep, because when I reached the kitchen, the downstairs was dark and I didn't hear the television upstairs. Petal was spending the night with her boyfriend. But Henry and Isadora came tearing down the stairs in ecstatic frenzy.

They stood expectantly in front of the refrigerator. Trust your dogs to know what you're going to do next, even when you don't.

I opened the freezer, where Petal kept my supply of ice cream—well known to have healing qualities, less damaging than alcohol, not illegal like drugs and not habit-forming like cigarettes. Some people match their wine to their food. I match my food to my mood. But I was stumped tonight. Now just what flavor does one select after finding and moving a dead body?

Passing by the Heavenly Hash, I went for irony, and shared a bowl of Cherry Garcia with the dogs before going upstairs.

Surprisingly, I fell asleep the minute I hit the pillow. It seemed only minutes later that I heard the telephone trill. It was seven o'clock Sunday morning.

I was pretty sure I knew what it was about, so I rolled out from under the covers, hanging my feet over the edge and blinking myself into the morning. I was ready when Pitt shouted up from the kitchen that LaLa was on the line.

"Hello?" I said, into the bedside phone.

"Um, Wally?" She knew Pitt might still be on the extension.

"Yes, LaLa?"

"Can you come over?"

I paused. "Sure." I paused again. "Why?"

She cleared her throat. "It seems Booth has drowned. The cook found him in the pool when she got up. She's screaming bloody murder right now and I think I'd better call Tony. Could you come over?"

"Sure. I'll be right there." I hung up.

Figuring I might be there a while, I took a quick shower. If I go for more than about an hour after I get up in the morning without taking a shower and washing my hair, I feel like something the dogs have dug up. Pitt says until I shower I'm the Grouch Queen of the universe; he won't even talk to me, usually, until then. He says that way he knows I won't grouch us into an argument we didn't need. "Two Diet Cokes and a shower and I get a brand new wife every morning," he says. "Why mess with the old one?"

I caught myself singing "I'm Gonna Wash That Man Right Outta My Hair" while I shampooed, and wondered how Tony would react to that philosophy on Booth's death. I didn't think he would be amused.

I also did some serious thinking about whether to tell Pitt what was going on. Like most married couples, we confided things to each other about our friends, just as we confided things to our friends about our spouses. Normally, I pumped him full of my opinions on all my friends' husbands; he was aware Booth wasn't one of my favorites and I knew he held no particular affection for him, either. They had gone golfing for dollars—business golf is a prime-time sport in Palm Beach—but it never got beyond that, I didn't think.

I slid into some jeans and loafers, threw on a pullover, and headed downstairs.

Pitt looked surprised that I was dressed, but didn't say anything. I don't think he had listened over the extension—we usually are above that—but he must have figured my uncharacteristic appearance at the breakfast table on a Sunday morning had something to do with LaLa's call. He looked back at the Sunday *New York Times* business page, flipping the pages smartly in front of him. That means there's something on his mind that he wants to talk about.

I ignored him, went to the refrigerator and dug out a Diet Coke. I downed about half of it in one swallow, then said, "I have to go over to LaLa's—"

"Okay," he interrupted. "But I have to speak to you about something first."

I motioned at him to talk while I drained the can.

"I want you to do something for me," he said, putting the paper down and leaning forward, elbows on the kitchen table. "It's important."

By that time I had my head back in the refrigerator, rummaging around for my second can of Diet Coke. What he said startled me so, I jumped, hitting my head on the freezer door.

My husband and I have developed a code over the years. If something needs doing and we just want it done, without any emotion tied to it, we'll say something neutral, like "Estee Lauder is throwing herself a bicentennial birthday party and we've got to take a gift." That means, one of us can volunteer and if neither does, we'll have Petal do it.

Or, if it's a kind of special thing, the one who wants it done might say, "I need for you to go with me to the Red Cross Ball," and that means you're the preferred person to do this but if for some reason you feel like you can't do it, we'll negotiate.

But when it's got to be done and one of us is telling the other to do it, the phrase "It's important" comes out.

So I popped my top and said, "Go ahead."

"I talked to some people last night," he said, "about Pittsburgh Wesson Bank. Some important people—potential investors. They all said the same thing: I have the credentials. What I need is the head-above-the-crowd social status—the one that lets people know I have the right kind of contacts."

I swallowed and gestured for him to keep going.

"So," he said. "I was talking to Rezna, and she said I have one of the best opportunities to get myself known coming up in less than two weeks: The Breakers New Year's Eve Ball."

I was confused. "What about it?" I asked, pulling a bag of Petal's homemade-but-frozen-in-case-of-emergency biscuits out of the freezer.

"Breakers Babies," he said, not totally patiently. "Breakers Babies. Rezna said if I escorted you as a Breakers Baby in the procession at that New Year's Eve party, everybody who's anybody in Palm Beach would know where I stood socially."

"But I'm not," I protested, flopping thick pats of butter on top of two biscuits.

"You might be," he shot back, "and that's what I want you to do: Find out."

I punched the numbers into the microwave and watched the biscuits go around in circles; the butter on top began to ooze. Magic. "Look," I said. "I really have to get over to LaLa's. Can we talk about this later?"

My patience-of-Job husband, who indulges my many moods, slammed his coffee cup onto the table and said, meaningfully, "This is important to me, Wally."

The microwave beeped. I wrapped the soft, hot, greasy biscuits in paper towels, threw them and another can of Diet Coke into a Publix plastic bag, and walked over to the kitchen table.

"I can't change where I was born," I said. "And there's nothing to be gained by lying about it. But I'll do what I can to find out if it's true. Is that good enough?"

He reached up, put his hand on the back of my neck and pulled me down into a kiss. "Yes, it is," he said. "Just do it by next week."

I shook my head in amazement that anyone would care so much about so little a thing as where I was born. And, yes, with just the tiniest touch of annoyance that he would ask me to dig into a part of my past I had made perfectly clear I preferred to leave buried.

"Watch what you wish for," I said. "Booth Ewen wished last night to have his last dance with Princess Di. It seems that after the gala, he drowned in his own swimming pool. So he did, literally, dance his last dance with Princess Di. I'm going to LaLa's to keep her company until Tony gets there. I may be a while."

I admit to a certain vengeful satisfaction in seeing the astonishment on his face before I shut the door to the garage behind me.

Chapter Eight

SUNDAY, DECEMBER 22

As I backed the car out of the driveway, I contemplated the fact that I had committed a number of social crimes in my years in Palm Beach, but covering up what could be murder might be just one step over any line I had already crossed.

What could I could do about it, though? I didn't think I had any choice. I was not in this alone, and I couldn't bring myself to indulge my niggling need for some personal integrity at the expense of people who had just tried to do a good deed.

I had, however, a decidedly sinking feeling that the police might not see it that way.

LaLa was waiting for me at the front door. Before I had even walked from the car and up the steps to where she stood, I could hear her cook's keening cries from inside.

"I waited out here because I didn't want her to wonder why I'm not crying," LaLa whispered. I sort of wondered myself, given that I had not yet told my friend the things she needed to know to view her husband's death as something of a lesser tragedy.

"Is anybody else home?" I asked as we went inside.

"No," she said. "The household staff had the night off because we weren't going to be home. Marta wasn't feeling well, so she stayed here while the rest went to their own homes."

LaLa trailing behind in my footsteps, I moved toward the sound and found Marta, the cook, looking out the kitchen window toward the pool deck, sobbing at a multi-decible level. I moved between her and the view to the pool.

"Marta?" She started wailing even louder, gesturing and flopping her arms towards the patio. I knew I should look—after all, I wasn't supposed to know what was in there—but I didn't want to.

"Mr. Ewen drowned!" she finally got out. "In the pool!"

I nodded, then put my arm around her shoulder. "I think," I said, "it would be better if you went to your room. Then when the police come, they'll come find you if they need you."

I shot a glance at LaLa. "Got any brandy?"

She wrinkled her brow. "Brandy?"

"It works on television," I said.

LaLa turned around and hurried out of the kitchen towards the wet bar, her ruffled blouse and skirt combo doing little dances around her as she moved. She returned with a bottle of Corvoisier, which I took and handed to Marta.

"Take this with you," I said. "It will help calm your nerves."

Marta perked up considerably with a sixty-dollar bottle of brandy in her hands, and her step bounced a little as she headed around the kitchen counter and out the side door toward the servants quarters over the detached, six-car garage.

When she was gone, I turned back to LaLa, who looked as if she could use a little of that brandy herself. She was sort of quivering all over, not exactly shaking, as Peep had been doing last night, but not calm, either.

"Do you want a drink, LaLa?" I asked.

"Heavens no," she said, pulling me by the hand away from the direction of the pool and toward the living room in the front of the house. "The police show up and the merry widow has liquor on her breath at six fifteen in the morning. Wouldn't that be lovely?"

I credited her for thinking, which was more than I was doing. I have to admit to being a little surprised that my friend who usually had trouble staying with a conversation on this earthly plane was so sharp in this situation.

"People will surprise you," Erma would say. I realized I needed to call Erma and tell her about Booth. She had been in Alabama visiting

relatives since Thanksgiving, and wasn't due back until the night before Christmas, three days away. I missed her—Erma is usually my
sounding board—but I had planned to keep my mouth shut about
Booth and had not told anyone what I'd found out, even Pitt.

I munched on my greasy biscuit, feeling sorry now I had not confided in Pitt or Erma because I knew Tony was going to ask me what
I knew. If I had told someone else what I had found out, I wouldn't
have to decide whether to tell Tony; it would be out already. But I was
the only one who knew LaLa had asked me to follow Booth, and I
wasn't going to hand Tony an incriminating motive on my friend.

LaLa was standing by the front window and said in a low voice,
"they're here." She walked to the door and opened it.

It took a few minutes for them to get out of their car—it seemed
like an eternity. I used the time to stuff down the rest of my second
biscuit and chug my Diet Coke. Finally, Tony Taranto walked into
LaLa's living room.

"Wally," he said. "What are you doing here?"

I licked a crumb off my lips. "LaLa called me and asked me to come
over after...after...."

He nodded and gave LaLa a big hug, then me. I tried not to get greasy
fingerprints on his pristine white knit Polo shirt. He was flanked by a
detective who was so young he looked like he had just gotten out for
sixth grade recess and a brown-uniformed Palm Beach policewoman.

"Let's go," Tony said to LaLa. LaLa turned and streaked out of the
room, Tony in her tracks. The others were close behind. I hurried to
keep up with them, don't ask me why. I knew perfectly well where
they were going and what they would find.

Tony told LaLa and me to stay put at the French doors leading
onto the patio, then walked to the side of the pool. The policewoman
stepped over to LaLa's side. The detective stood beside Tony. They
were murmuring to each other. I took a step closer.

"Who's the floater?" said the detective.

Tony winced at the question. "Booth Ewen. He is...was...an inde-
pendent financial advisor."

"Who isn't, in this town?" the detective said. "Why'd you come in
person, chief?"

Tony looked around, saw me standing nearby. He grabbed me by
the elbow and guided me with him toward the house. The detective
followed. "Wally, meet Detective Mike Cassidy, just off the bus from
Orlando. Wally, tell Mike what Palm Beach residents expect from
their city employees."

"Service," I said without hesitating. "Service now."

"And what do they do if they don't get it?" he said.

"Complain to your boss," I said, again without having to think about the answer.

A corner of his mouth twitched up. "And what do they get if they still aren't happy?"

"Your job," I said, also trying not to smile, remembering we were standing ten feet away from a floating body.

"Oh," said Mike Cassidy.

Tony patted him on the back. "Now you understand working for the city of Palm Beach," he said. "And don't forget it. These people may be rich, but some of them will rub the shine off a penny trying to protect it, and they want their money's worth. And watch what you say around the family."

The detective shot me a look, as if wondering why the chief would be speaking so candidly about "Palm Beach people" with one of us within earshot.

Tony smiled. "I went to high school with LaLa—Mrs. Ewen—and Wally, here, and I wanted to check this out myself."

He pointed at me. "You stay here. I can't have you walking all around here until we find out what happened."

Tony stepped again to the edge of the pool, looking down at Booth, whose face was a little bloated, as if he'd had too much to drink. "Get me a medical examiner and a photographer," Tony said to the detective. "Call the DA."

Mike Cassidy scurried off to a corner where he sat down at a table, pulled out a cell phone, opened it up and started dialing. He looked excited. I guessed the opportunity-to-serve-the-chief situation didn't come along often.

As if echoing my thoughts, Tony walked over to me and said, "We don't get many questionable deaths here," he said. "Much less murder or mayhem. These things usually happen on the other side of the bridge."

"Questionable?" I said. "Murder?"

He gave me a sharp look. "Sorry," he said. "Didn't mean to startle you. When somebody doesn't die in the hospital, you know, with a doctor around, I have to consider it questionable."

"He drowned in his own swimming pool, Tony," I said. "How questionable is that?"

"You'd be surprised," he said.

He sure would.

LaLa shook herself away from the policewoman and came over to my side, sort of bumping me along until we were out of Tony's hearing range.

"Wally," she sniffled. "They brought a policewoman. That means they are going to take me into the police station. They can't do that, can they?"

I shook my head, but answered truthfully. "They can if they want to, LaLa, but they won't. They have no reason." I hoped I knew what I was talking about.

"I can't go to jail," LaLa mumbled pitifully between trembling lips. "They'll put me in a dark room and lock me up—oh, Wally, don't let them!"

I sat her down in a corner of the patio, waved off the policewoman when she moved toward LaLa, and walked over to Tony, who was making copious notes in a neat, cramped printing in a tiny little notebook.

He looked down at me.

"Is there any reason," I said, "that LaLa should have a lawyer here?"

He glanced over at her. "Do you think she needs one?"

I shrugged. "Hey, I'm not the police."

He looked over at the detective, still dialing numbers on his cell phone, and the officer, watching him dial. Then he looked back at me.

"It can't hurt," he said softly.

I pulled my telephone out of my purse and dialed a familiar number, that of Erma's oldest son Benson, known to family as Bunky. His wife answered.

"Frances?" I said.

"Yes?"

"Wally. Need to talk to Bunky."

"Sure, hon. Hold on."

I smiled up at Tony, who had returned to his note taking. If anyone understood that it was better to offer the polite and generous gesture, it was Tony, who had been brought up in an Old Money family—so old that the money had evaporated long before he was born. Still, his mother had brought him up with the gentle values of the well-bred. Class meant treating everyone with the same good manners, no matter what the situation. Social pleasantries must be honored. Old Money would probably apologize for staying so long in the coffin and holding up the funeral guests. I had always loved that about Tony. He was equally polite to everyone.

"Something wrong?" Bunky asked.

"Yep. I'm at LaLa Ewen's house and Chief Taranto is here...,"

"Say hail to the chief."

I turned to Tony. "Bunky sends his regards." Tony rolled his eyes.

"Listen," I said. "It seems Booth Ewen has drowned in his own swimming pool but we just wonder if you think LaLa needs for you to be over here with her."

"Damn right."

"Uh, huh," I said.

"Tell her not to say a word until I get there."

"Okay."

"Not one freaking word, do you understand me, Wally?"

"Sure do. Thank you, Bro."

"You're welcome, Sis. I'll be there as soon as I can."

I pushed the End button on the telephone and put it back in my bag. "Bunky's on his way over," I said. "Thank you, Tony."

I walked over to LaLa. "Listen," I said. "Bunky's coming over to be with you. He says don't utter one word until he gets here."

She smiled with trembling lips and nodded her head in quick, jerky little nods.

I walked back over to Tony. "You don't seriously think this is anything but an accident, do you?" I looked up for the lightning bolt that might strike me any minute now, but the sky was Florida blue, not a cloud to be seen.

He ran his hand over his eyes, massaging his forehead. "Look," he said softly. "I know Booth Ewen was a bastard. I know what goes on in this town. I have wondered why LaLa put up with him. I also know he was going through her money like it was water, and money is a pretty large motivator to kill somebody."

He looked down at Booth's body, shrugged his shoulders. "Do I think this is homicide? I can't say right now. Maybe this was just an accident. Maybe Booth just fell down boom in his tuxedo in his own swimming pool and drowned. But the question I have to ask is, was there something for which LaLa—or anybody—hated Booth enough to kill him?"

Well, duh. Lots of people. Booth was an unfaithful husband who was involved with other men's wives and, according to Pitt, a number of shady business deals. I went home that night unsure whether I wanted to know the answer to Tony's question. I went to sleep that night certain I didn't want to be involved in finding out the answer.

Monday morning, I was still obsessing over the details of the very thing I didn't want to think about, when, at about nine o'clock, I stuffed the morning *Tattler* into my bag and headed out the door. I backed the car out of the driveway like a madwoman. I screeched west on Barton, hung a quick right on Cocoanut Row and shot onto the Flagler Memorial Bridge into West Palm Beach. Right in the middle of

Monday morning rush hour traffic, I might add, which didn't help my nerves.

I was headed for Phil Foster Park, a little blop of land in Lake Worth between Palm Beach Shores and the mainland. The park was located just beneath the Blue Heron Bridge, which was the next one north of the Flagler Memorial Bridge into Palm Beach, but you couldn't get there on A1A, the beach road. The barrier island on which Palm Beach is situated comes to an end at the Lake Worth Inlet on the north end of Palm Beach. A lot of Townies would be just as happy to dig an inlet just south of the Southern Boulevard Bridge on the south end, thereby cutting off all land connection to the mainland.

I turned north on U.S. One, not admiring the view. In the 1890s, Henry Flagler created West Palm Beach as a place to house the workmen and servants who would cater to the resorts he was building for the wealthy on the island. Predictably, the decline in America's cities that hit in the seventies hit West Palm, decimating much of the business district along the waterfront. To its credit, the city had done much to pull itself up by the bootstraps in recent years. The older residential neighborhoods such as El Cid, where I had lived as a child with Erma's family, and Northwoods, where I had visited Digby, were being renovated and brought back to their historic charm. Meanwhile, like everybody else, I tried not to look at the empty and rundown buildings on my left as I drove north.

Instead, I occupied my mind by thinking about Digby's phone call at eight that morning, which luckily came just as Pitt was leaving for work. I had decided with Pitt's growing obsession about his social place in Palm Beach and how it was going to affect his plans to start his own bank, it would be best if he didn't know that his wife had committed what I assumed would be a felony. Obstruction of justice at the least; maybe accessory to murder. I had convinced myself overnight that maybe if you didn't know who did it, it wasn't a crime. But I still suspected there was some law somewhere against moving a body when you knew the person had not come to a natural end.

"Must come," Digby had said on the phone. "No one must know."

In the interest of secrecy, of which there was little, if any, in Palm Beach proper, Digby and Peep had cooked up a scheme for the Garden Club gang to travel in separate cars to a place where no one we knew would be.

As a meeting place, they had selected the dock of the Palm Beach *Princess*, the tourist boat that takes people south on Lake Worth to view the homes on the shores of Singer Island and the north end of Palm Beach. Palm Beach residents would rather be staked out naked on Worth Avenue in front of the Everglades Club than be seen on a tourist boat. Safe from prying eyes it was, indeed.

I was the last to arrive. I parked and walked up on the wooden deck where the others stood. I went inside and bought a ticket, then we all milled around on the dock looking guilty as hell, waiting to board the boat. Nobody said much. Vanessa stayed to herself. LaLa hung on Digby. Peep stood, chin lifted high, looking out over the water.

A deep gray cloud hung over the west side of the lake. Scared away by the oppressive overcast sky, only a few tourists, foreigners mostly, clustered in a knot at the end of the gangplank, their cameras hanging from their necks. Their children played, running in circles, oblivious to what country they were in.

Finally we boarded, seating ourselves sulkily at a white metal table at the opposite end of the boat from the tourists.

Peep, who had a boat twice the size of this one docked at the Palm Beach Marina, curled a lip at the dirty white plastic chairs. Digby wiped off the chair for her and we settled in, silent as if by agreement until the boat got underway. Digby made his way to the little snack bar on the boat and brought back coffee in Styrofoam cups.

I slapped my copy of *The Tattler* onto the gritty metal table top. Vanessa picked it up and read out loud.

The Beach Session
By Rezna Van Daly, Society Editor
The Palm Beach Tattler, Monday, Dec. 23, 1996

Rezna sez: Where are our manners?

There's been much discussion at all the best parties about the general lack of manners today. Much tsk-tsking has gone on over Dom Perignon that it's getting more and more difficult to collect a crowd of committed partiers who know all the rules and agree—albeit silently—to play by them.

No one in the Old Guard has to be reminded of the sorry state of affairs that has existed around here since wives started suing husbands and scions of our most popular families were accused of unspeakable crimes.

We hoped, my dears, that last year's excruciatingly rude episode at the Palm Beach Garden Club Gala was the end of all the messy affairs, many of which were interfering with the more serious fundraising events of the season.

It seems, however, that the discourteous behavior continues.

Once again, the night of the Palm Beach Garden Club Gala has marked an event that one reluctantly must refer to as rude.

Although certainly since it just occurred Saturday, and the gentlemen of the Palm Beach police have as yet no official opinion, the fact that Booth Ewen, a town financier, was found in an unfortunate state in his own swimming pool must be viewed with the same skepticism with which we viewed their official pronouncement regarding the accidental nature of last year's event.

It pains this writer to be compelled to bring it to the gentle reader's attention, but, my dears, the man was found dead in his own pool in a tuxedo in last year's style.

While criticizing the departed may seem cruel, all who aspire to reach the heights in Palm Beach must be cautioned that no one who is Anyone in Our Town would be caught dead in last year's cut.

"I'm going to kill Rezna," Peep said.

I shot her a look. After all that's happened, you'd think she'd get over the use of that particular phrase.

"You can't blame Rezna for reporting Booth's death," I said.

"She didn't have to tie it to the gala," Peep said. "She doesn't know."

"Let's get down to business," Vanessa said. She didn't see Peep glare at her. Peep still had not warmed to Vanessa the way I had. No small wonder. Peep was guilty of the "NOK" thinking of some Palm Beach residents. "Not Our Kind," was the kind of thinking that for years had kept Jews out of the most exclusive clubs—as for people of color, even the beautiful cafe au lait color of Vanessa's skin, forget it.

Vanessa continued. "I hate to sound selfish, but I can't afford to be involved in a scandal. I'm a trial balloon for my company, and they've got a white guy waiting in the wings to take my place as CEO if I don't perform."

"Ditto," said Digby. "Well, not about the white guy, but my florist business lives and dies on the good will of my Palm Beach customers. If I lose that, I might as well hang up my wire cutters."

We all moped for a minute while a voice over the loudspeaker droned loudly as the boat passed Singer Island, a small but exclusive enclave of rich folks. The captain-slash-guide read his historical notes with booming enthusiasm into the microphone; his speech took over my thoughts.

"The island is named after Paris Singer, son of the sewing machine magnate," he read. Paris, I knew, was the one who helped Addison Mizner set up the ritzy Everglades Club in 1918. Paris had courted the famous dancer Isadora Duncan in Palm Beach, only to lose her to the more hospitable and forgiving social life of Europe.

Like Isadora, my friends were now feeling the pressure that can result when you need the approval of Palm Beach Society. Isadora had chucked Palm Beach completely, something I had considered many times, and would have done if not for Pitt.

The guide took a break. I took advantage of the silence.

"Look," I said. "I saw the Baby Jesus fly into that pool, and I'm pretty sure he didn't jump. So that means somebody threw him. I suggest that we find out who, and that we do it quickly. That way, there won't be time for any of us to be affected." *And that way,* I thought, *chances are good Pitt won't find out I'm involved.*

Digby held up a Styrofoam cup. "We find who threw the Hail Mary pass. Are we agreed? Let's toast."

"To the end of it," Peep said.

"To the future," Vanessa said.

"To Booth's soul, in whatever dimension it now resides," LaLa said.

"To justice," Digby said.

I looked around. "Isn't anybody going to say, 'to the truth?'"

Chapter Nine

TUESDAY, DECEMBER 24

Tuesday morning, I walked under the gothic arched entrance of Bethesda-by-the-Sea Church on South County Road just as the bells in the tower were clonging nine forty-five.

The building is the second Bethesda-by-the-Sea Church in Palm Beach. The first, the 1894 cypress-shingled original, still stands at the north end of the island. This "new" 1927 church reeks with history and dignity. If you've got to have a funeral, this is the place to have it, but my stomach was rolling with the antics of drunken butterflies as I walked into the bon voyage party for Booth Ewen's farewell cruise into the great beyond.

The service was to begin at ten o'clock, and LaLa had purposely kept the viewing time short. She was flouting the tradition of paying respects prior to the funeral. I could understand LaLa's wishes not to open the church to gawkers until fifteen minutes before the funeral. What I could not understand was her decision to open the casket.

Sure enough, as I walked into a church already full of early birds who had sneaked in despite her instructions to the contrary, there lay Booth, in state, at the front and center of the sanctuary. What a challenge to the mortician's magic wand, I thought.

Now, most people don't like funerals. I mean, someone's dead and that's not usually good. But I'm letting you in on one of my deepest, darkest secrets when I tell you the tears I shed at funerals most often are tears of laughter.

Erma says I'm too afraid to show my soft side. LaLa says I'm afraid of the undead. Peep says I don't want to ruin my makeup. They're all wrong. I just hate to be taken in by the hypocrisy of weeping for someone who wouldn't have walked across the street to speak to me.

I know I'm the exception. I had to quit bringing Petal to funerals. She would break out in sobs even if the closest she had come to the late lamented was brushing their sleeve in the aisle at Green's Drug Store. I look around and see people sniffling who I know would—you should excuse the expression—cut the corpse dead when he or she was breathing.

Add to that the eulogy given by someone who worked hard to think of fifteen minutes worth of nice things to say about the dear departed, and I get downright giddy. I compose my own eulogy during funerals and always find myself about fourteen minutes short of good works. Inevitably, I leave vowing to be a demonstrably better person so my funeral won't embarrass anyone in its brevity.

Usually I struggle not to make snide cracks to people who say things like, "He looks so peaceful." Usually Pitt gets furious, and almost won't sit with me. But today he was right behind me as we walked into the church in which we were married. LaLa and Booth had married here, too. Married here, buried here. A certain symmetry.

I stopped, though, in the narthex, the little anteroom at the front entrance to the church. Inside the church, in the nave, a small crowd gathered around the entrance to an alcove off to the side of the main pew area. A few more people lingered around the casket, shaking hands and greeting each other as if it were a cocktail party.

Some of the most illustrious of Palm Beach citizens were here, and I thought Booth, looking down—or up—from wherever, must be frustrated at not being able to schmooze.

Pitt wasn't, though, and he started working the room while I hung back and scanned faces and the backs of heads. Peep and Mitch stood by the front row, talking with someone I didn't recognize. Darla Dugan stood alone, a few paces away from the coffin, staring at it. Thornton and Verity DeVale were progressing slowly up the aisle, stopping at every row so each could chat somebody up. Vanessa was at the entrance to the alcove and behind her I could just make out LaLa's blonde hair among those who would comfort her. Near the front, in a pew by herself, Taffy touched a lace handkerchief to a tear duct.

Digby spotted me and made a beeline for the door into the nave, where I stood. He wormed his way through the crowd as if I were in need of medical attention and, when he stood in front of me, breathlessly announced, "I must speak with you, Wally."

His hands fluttered and his eyes were cutting back and forth. I took his arm and pulled him back into the narthex.

"What on earth is wrong with you?" I asked in a stage whisper.

"I'm just so upset," he said. He bit his lip and rapidly blinked his eyes. "You just have to help me."

I nodded, grabbed his hands with mine to hold them still. "Of course."

It has to be the funeral, I thought. *He's had some sort of guilt attack about what we did the other night and he wants to spill the beans.* He was looking down at our hands, which were tightly gripped together.

"Are you feeling bad about Booth and what we did?" I asked in a conspiratorial whisper.

He jerked his head up. "What? Booth? Goodness, no!" His hand flew up to the side of his face, Jack Benny style, but he wasn't doing an impersonation. He was just surprised.

He wrinkled his nose as if he smelled something foul. "Not Booth. Not that. It's Raymond. I'm worried about Raymond."

I stepped back. "Raymond? What about Raymond?" I was really confused.

Digby leaned in and put his mouth near my ear. "He's being blackmailed," he whispered, breathy with emotion. "We got in an argument Saturday night when we got home and I confronted him with our bank statement." He stopped talking, completely out of oxygen. He was gasping for air.

"Exhale," I said. He did.

"Again," I said. He did.

"He always takes care of the bills," he said, more slowly. "I take care of the house and he takes care of the bills. But the statement was on top of the dresser and I opened it and looked at it and...," He was inhaling like an asthmatic Pekinese.

"Exhale," I said. He did.

"He's taken out a lot of money," he said, with a big emphasis on the last word. "Big withdrawals from our joint account. At least a hundred thousand dollars."

"Wow," I said, while he took a deep breath and exhaled again, without my direction. "Did he tell you he was being blackmailed?"

"No. He wouldn't tell me anything. He said it was none of my business. None of my business," he repeated sadly.

He looked crestfallen. "I told him I could lose my shop if I don't have the money to buy inventory." His arm swept the room, and I figured he was indicating the dozens of flower arrangements standing and piled on the floor behind the coffin.

"And the mortgage," he said. "There was barely enough in the account to pay the mortgage on the business, much less the house. And the inventory...,"

"Digby," I said, patting his arm. "I'm so sorry. What can I do?"

He looked at me as if I had just asked what color is the sky. "Why, follow him," he said. "LaLa told me you were following Booth to find out if he was having an affair."

"So?"

He swept his arm out again, this time toward the coffin. "And you certainly don't have that job anymore."

My stomach sank. "So?"

He grabbed my hands. "So, please follow Raymond now, and find out who's blackmailing him."

My mouth was dry, as if I had a mouthful of sand. I just didn't like the way things were going lately. "Why do you think anybody would blackmail Raymond?" I asked. "What has he done that somebody can blackmail him?"

He looked at me as if I had just grown a third eye. "His family," he said. "I have to tell you who his family is."

"Who?"

"Ever hear of the Reverend Loyd Bateman?"

I grimaced. Leader of the Christian Right. "Sure."

He nodded in Raymond's direction. "His father."

I gasped. "You're shitting me."

"Shhh...No. I'm not. Raymond changed his name when he moved away from home. They don't know where he lives or his...lifestyle. The information would be big time news."

It sure would. CNN would bring in liberal talking heads by the dozens to discuss a gay son among the ranks of the organization that had boycotted Disney World because they extended health insurance to life partners of gay employees.

"Holy crap," I said. "But who...?"

"I don't know," he said, "but I'm begging you to find out." He looked around the room. "I've got to go now. We'll talk." He hurried back up toward the front of the church, his demeanor now calm, as if he had just stopped to say hello.

I walked slowly toward the front of the church, my head reeling. Had someone put something in the Palm Beach drinking water? In the past few days I had stepped into a what looked like a murder and a blackmailing. And my husband was crabbing at me to stick my nose into my own family history. With four generations of Pennsylvania family behind him, Pitt could never understand that my philosophy about being an orphan was that I wouldn't be disappointed over not finding that for which I never looked. I shook my head and shoulders to get it all off my back. What next?

As if to answer my question, someone touched me on the shoulder. I swung around to find Verity DeVale standing behind me.

"Wally, how nice to see you again, but how sad we must meet under such unfortunate circumstances."

I thought of responding, "I'm thoroughly enjoying the occasion, but I hate seeing you here," but thought better of starting something. Pitt gets pissy when I do that sort of thing.

"Verity," I gushed, hoping my breakfast would hold. "How delightful of you to come. I know how close you and Booth were."

She gave me an odd look. "I wanted," she said through clenched teeth, "to make sure you and Pitt would be at Thornton's Dining for Depression benefit Thursday. Thornton will just be devastated if Pitt can't come. He says," she stopped and looked meaningfully at Pitt standing in a group near the front of the church, "he's invited backers for Pitt's venture."

My butterflies whooped. They knew I was caught. "I'm sure Pitt appreciates it," I said. "I'll check with him, of course, but I assume we'll be there."

She smiled, victory hers. "Eight for cocktails," she said. She turned on one heel and slithered away into the crowd toward the front of the room.

The crush at the front of the room swelled as people greeted each other with smiles and hugs. There was a lot of hustle and bustle as people tried to get to each other through the crowd. I wondered if somebody might ask if they could move the coffin to make room for dancing.

Pitt had paid his respects at the coffin and was heading in to speak to the grieving widow. The church organist came in and sat down, but it was a flutist who started piping a new age melody of the type that used to make Booth grit his teeth and spit out a snide comment about LaLa's choice of music.

Nice touch, LaLa, I thought, sidling up to the coffin to pay my respects to the not so dearly departed.

I looked first at his face, made up all cream and pink, the way they do. His cheeks had a healthy color to them and his face was nicely drained of the fluid that had collected in it during his unfortunate demise.

His Armani suit draped just so over the shoulders—*must be tucked in the back,* I thought—and he had a white carnation in his lapel. How natty.

His hands were curled gently on his abdomen, thumbside up. I noticed two things. One, he was not wearing his wedding ring. And two, nestled in the curve of his right hand was a turd.

Large, black, dried and cracked.

I started laughing.

Not a giggle. Not a chuckle. It was one of those loud belly laughs that jumped up from my stomach and out of my mouth before I even knew it was coming. And then, like those people on the funniest bloopers shows, I couldn't stop.

People formerly staring at LaLa now turned to stare at me. I was clinging to the casket, weak in the knees. Pitt was the first to arrive, no doubt ready to give me a stern talking to about decorum. But instead, he stepped back from the casket with a look on his face I can only describe as stricken.

Despite the fact that I frequently accuse Pitt of having an anal-retentive personality, despite the fact that I do occasionally call him a shithead when he is behaving badly, I know from experience that when an actual turd of canine origin presents itself he is so put off, he'll rush from the room and fix a martini forthwith.

So while Pitt was backing up, stepping on Darla Dugan as he did so and pushing his way backwards into a crowd that included Digby, Raymond and Artie Marsh, everyone else was pushing toward the casket to see what was causing such a reaction.

Thornton DeVale leaned past me to look into the coffin with Peep and Mitch right behind him. The clatter of tongues grew as word was passed back in the crowd. Peep stepped up to me and poked me in the ribs with her finger.

"What the hell is going on?" she asked. I pointed, unable to speak, at the casket. She looked in, then looked back at me. She broke and started laughing with me. Helpless, we hung onto each other in gales of laughter while saner beings stood around us. As everyone got the word, the noise abated and changed into a shocked silence broken only by Peep's helpless peals and my hearty barks of laughter. I realized LaLa had reached us and was looking into the casket.

Peep and I managed to suck it in and were holding in our laughter out of respect for LaLa as she turned her head back toward us.

"You just can't escape karma," she said. Then the three of us fell into a pew, clinging to each other in the helpless throes of uncontrollable laughter.

The priest leaned solicitously over LaLa.

"Mrs. Ewen," he said. "If you don't mind, we'll start the service now."

LaLa nodded contritely, tears of laughter still wet on her cheeks. "By all means," she said. "We better get on with it."

We all moved to our places, where for fifteen minutes my mind was on everything but what was being said at the front of the church. Someone who knew Booth—apparently not that well—droned on for a while, then there was a religious service and then, finally, the service was over.

I checked Pitt to make sure he had survived his ordeal, told him to go on home while I rode with LaLa to the cemetery in West Palm Beach where she had decided to lay Booth for his eternal rest. Peep and I got into the limousine with her.

We shut the door and looked at the faces outside.

"Lordy, Lordy," Peep said, lighting a cigarette. "I hope they remember to remove that thing from his coffin before they bury him."

"I don't know," I said. "It might be nice for him to have some company."

We had barely stopped laughing again when we arrived at the cemetery, where Booth was duly buried in a scenic plot with a view of a marble fountain and a formal garden. The ceremony was mercifully short, and it was back in the limo after the burial that we really sobered up.

"LaLa," I said. "This is not really so funny. Somebody threw the Baby Jesus into the pool with Booth, and now it looks like whoever it was isn't too happy with you. I'm getting a little worried."

"In my wildest dreams," she said, "I can't imagine who could be behind all of this."

"Do you think," I asked, "we should tell Tony the truth?"

"NO!" my friends shouted. The limo driver cut his eyes at us, catching the excitement even if he couldn't hear the words.

"They will think I did it," LaLa said. "They might even try to put me in jail. Bunky said without any evidence to the contrary, they would be looking at me first and that I should be very careful what I say. Somehow I think admitting that I allowed my husband's body to be moved to our pool, then letting him stay there overnight, might look a little suspicious."

"It wasn't overnight exactly," I protested. "It was really just a couple of hours."

"People already say I killed my own husband," Peep exhaled with a stream of smoke. "I don't think the gossip is going to get any better if they find out Booth died in my pool. No. No. No. Wally," she begged. "I'll be ruined in this town if we can't keep this our secret."

I sighed. I hate secrets. I had spent a lifetime building a marriage with no secrets and trying to live an open, honest life in a town rife with gossip, innuendo and social subterfuge.

"Okay," I said. "But LaLa, I do have to tell you something and before I do, remember I didn't tell you before because you're my friend and I love you."

Lala narrowed her eyes at me. "Yes?"

"I actually did find out that Booth was having an affair."

Peep blew out a blast of smoke. "Really?"

LaLa tilted her head like the RCA dog. "Do tell. I suppose you know with whom?"

"Taffy," I mumbled.

"Taffy Povitch?" Peep leaned back and threw out her hands. "LaLa, how could he?"

LaLa's hair, blown by the limo's heavy-duty air conditioner, flew up around her face as if to express its own amazement. "He's definitely coming back as a cockroach," she said. "I'm going to speak to Velma. I need to find out about Booth's life on the Other Side. If he's sending me messages on toilet paper, I want to know about it."

"Girls," Peep said. "Before we get home, I have something serious I need to talk to you about."

"Wait a minute, Peep," I said. "LaLa, you don't seem very surprised to hear about Taffy. Did you know?"

LaLa watched the scenery go by as the limo traveled along North County Road. "The universe has many secrets," she said. "Sometimes it shares them with us, sometimes it doesn't. I have always had to realize with Booth that he was living out in this life his bad karma from a previous one. Even," she said, "back when I thought I loved him, I knew he was capable of evil."

She brushed at her cheek. "I tried not to know these things, Wally. I tried to live in a better place. I counted on my spirit guide to lead me around the truth when it would be hurtful to me."

I looked at Peep, whose face was blank.

"Huh?" I said.

"She doesn't want to say," Peep—master of verbal evasion—said.

I shrugged. "As long as you forgive me for not telling you."

LaLa patted my knee. "For more than forty years you've been painfully honest to us about our shortcomings. I guess I can forgive you for keeping Booth's shortcomings to yourself."

I bit my lip. I'm aware I'm too quick to tell people what's wrong with them. My direct current seemed to have short circuited in the events of the last few days, however.

"Ah hem," Peep said. "I believe I said I need to say something."

LaLa leaned back and closed her eyes.

"Shoot," I said.

"I'm being followed," Peep said. "Someone is following me."

"What?" I said.

LaLa's eyes flew open and she leaned toward Peep. "Who?" she said.

"Well if I knew who, I'd say who, now wouldn't I?" Peep said. "I can't tell who. It's a black Mercedes S600 with tinted windows."

"Black Mercedes S600," I said. "Great. Half of everybody in Palm Beach has a black Mercedes. Pitt has a black Mercedes S600."

"So does Mitch," said Peep. "I know there are hundreds of them, but I can't help that, now can I? I certainly would like it better if it were someone with a more recognizable car, now wouldn't I?"

She had a point. "When were you followed?"

"For weeks," she said. "Not every time I leave home, but lots. I'll see it behind me when I go to volunteer at the Flagler Museum, or to work in the thrift shop or shopping."

The limo pulled in to Peep's estate.

The driver opened the door and Peep got out. Then she leaned back in and looked at me. "I want you to find out who's doing it, Wally. Get on it tomorrow, please."

She shut the door and I looked at LaLa.

"Do I have a sign on my back?" I asked. "Does it say 'For Hire' back there?"

LaLa smiled. "No, sweetie, but you can hardly refuse us, now can you?"

A couple of minutes later, the car was pulling into LaLa's driveway; she gathered her things and got out.

Then, like Peep had, she stuck her head back into the car for a parting shot. "After all," she said, "if you had told me what you found out in the first place, none of this would have happened, now would it?"

She closed the door.

Leaning back in the car, I let the stereo sound wrap around me and the events of the week swirl around in my mind as the car drove the short distance to my house. I thanked the driver and went in the house through the front door.

I changed clothes and curled up with Pitt and the dogs on the sofa in the family room. Petal brought me a brandy and tucked an afghan around my feet, fussing over me as Erma used to do when I had a bad day as a child. I'm sure Petal thought going to the funeral of my best friend's husband was enough to put me into the blue funk I was feeling.

I told Pitt the truth: "I've spent fifty years trying to extricate my-self from the sometime tawdry, sometimes elegant but always emo-tional grip of life in Palm Beach. I went to college until you dragged me back here, and I've spent the years since gritting my teeth and trying to think of something more pleasant as I've gone to party after party."

His eyebrows went up. He took a sip of martini.

"I'm sorry," I said. "I realized today I've been called blunt, but be-cause I told the truth about the wrong things. You need to know I have been close to asking you if we can move to Boston."

He drained his martini, then reached over and gave Isadora a scratch behind the ears. He took my empty glass from my hand, stood up and walked over to the bar.

I waited for him to say something.

He didn't.

"Pitt," I said.

He shook the martini shaker, then poured himself a martini and splashed a dollop of brandy into my snifter. He walked over, gave me the drink, then sat down beside me. He took another sip. I felt him sigh deeply. "Are you telling me you want to leave me?" he said. "Are we having a marriage crisis?"

The question shocked me. "No." I sat up. "No." I didn't think. Were we?

"Then what do you want?" he asked.

I leaned back against him.

"Beats the hell out of me," I said. "All I know is I don't want to be looking for murderers, blackmailers and stalkers. I want to go back to my meaningless life as a student of everything and master of nothing. I want to go to Boston, where people actually discuss ideas, instead of each other, at parties. I want to go somewhere where I feel at home."

"Well," he said. "Speaking of parties, I hate to bring this up, but New Year's Eve is only a few days away and you made me a promise. You said you would find out if you are a Breakers Baby so maybe we can march in the procession at the New Year's Eve Ball."

"Careful," I said. "Peep lost a husband last year. LaLa lost one this year. Obviously these things can be arranged."

He looked hurt. I felt a little guilty.

But only a little.

Chapter Ten

WEDNESDAY, DEC. 25

Christmas morning, Petal informed me that Erma had called while I was sleeping. I breathed a sigh of relief and picked up the phone in the kitchen.

"Welcome home," I said when she answered. "And Merry Christmas."

"How's my baby?" she asked; the same question she had asked hundreds of times since I left her house to start college more than thirty years before. I wasn't her baby—five children of her own had come after Erma married Ennis George, a young school teacher, when I was a little girl—but she had called me that from my earliest recollection, so I guessed her baby I would always be.

"Much to tell you," I said. "When do you want us over there?"

"Come on," she said. "We have the tree lit and the grandchildren are beginning to arrive."

Pitt, Petal and I got ourselves ready in unusually short time. It was Christmas, and to all three of us, going to Erma's was going home at Christmas.

Pitt piled the presents in his black Mercedes SL600, squeezed Petal in among them in the back seat, and we headed south on County Road to the Southern Memorial Bridge. The El Cid neighborhood, where Erma and Ennis live, is an old, well established neighborhood in West Palm Beach. Erma, Ennis and I had moved into the brand new, sprawling ranch house right after their wedding in 1951. The house was built on what passed for a hill in West Palm, a flat rise of land overlooking Flagler Avenue, which runs parallel to Lake Worth. From the front porch of Erma's house, you could look across Lake Worth and see the Mediterranean cupola of Mar-A-Lago, a symbol to me always of Palm Beach, of its rich history, a history made by people of great wealth and, sometimes, great weakness.

We arrived at the same time as Bunky and Frances and their three children. Christmas at Erma's grew larger every year, as her five children multiplied into couples and then families. There were, at last count, seven grandchildren. Bunky, at thirty-three the youngest of Erma's children, was the most prolific with three. The others continued to present me, at a slower rate, with the closest thing I would ever have to nieces and nephews.

Once inside, I headed straight for the kitchen, where Erma would be overseeing the cooking of enough turkeys and hams, squash, turnip greens, yams, green beans and mashed potatoes and gravy to feed a small army. There would be at least one congealed salad, possibly one green salad, dozens of angel biscuits dripping with butter.

For dessert, there would be red and green Christmas cake, pecan pie, mincemeat pie and ice cream and little fried peach pies. Erma had left Alabama more than fifty years before, but she had never given up Southern ways.

My stomach hurt just thinking about the meal to come as I walked toward the back of the house, which was now beginning to reverberate with the sound of dozens of combined voices, all chattering over one another. The roar would get louder and more raucous as presents were delivered and opened and would not stop until dinner, which would begin promptly at one o'clock with grace said by Ennis.

I swung open the door and saw Erma with a soup ladle in her hand, dripping brown juices over a turkey the size of a beach ball. The kitchen was rich with the combined smell of the turkeys and ham. Pies cooled on the window sill.

Erma handed the ladle to one of the cooks and came at me, wiping her hands on an apron I had made her in home economics class in seventh grade. Over the years that her hair had grayed from coal black to snow white and her skin had wrinkled and begun to sag around her eyes and mouth, she had worn that apron every Christmas. It didn't look much worse than the Christmas she unwrapped it. It crossed my mind that she must treat it like some sort of treasure for it to look almost new.

I hugged her and suddenly there were tears in my eyes. The full weight of what we had done Saturday night hit me like a swimming pool full of cold water. I started to blubber.

"Baby? What's wrong?" she asked. She grabbed my shoulders and guided me into Ennis' den, just off the kitchen in the back of the house, and sat me down on a plaid sofa draped with a multicolored afghan.

"Booth Ewen was killed," I sobbed. "I found him. Dead. The funeral was yesterday." I was sure my mascara was running down my cheeks; crying has never been my most attractive look. Women always look so beautiful in the movies, with tears running down their perfect peach cheeks. In real life, my eyes get all red-veined and I look like a raccoon with an eye infection.

Erma grabbed a bottle of Courvoisier off of Ennis's leather bar, poured two deep glasses, handed me one, sat down beside me and patted me on the back. "I'm sorry, baby. He was your friend?" She pulled a box of tissue from a bookcase beside the sofa and handed it to me. I saw Ennis smiling at me from dozens of photographs on the wall as he greeted visitors to the small college from where he had recently retired as president.

"Nnnn...no," I wailed, "that's just it. I didn't like him. I never liked him. I didn't care that he was dead. I'm a bad, bad person, Erma. I've done something really terrible."

She took a pull from the brandy and patted me on the knee. "What did you do?"

I shook my head. "I can't tell you. But it was bad." My tears had worn away to a sniffle now, having confessed, or at least admitted, to acting in what now seemed an unbelievably stupid way.

She looked a little shocked. "You didn't kill him, did you?"

"Heavens no," I said, amazed she would even ask such a thing. It shocked the tears right out of me.

"Okay then," she said when I got my composure back. "My baby wouldn't do a bad thing," she said flatly, "unless she had a good reason. Did you have a good reason, sugar?"

I nodded. "I thought so." I felt guilty now that I had failed to appreciate the finality and seriousness of death—even the death of someone you didn't like.

"Well," she said, "if you won't tell me what you did, all I can say is you have only two choices: to believe you did the wrong thing for the right reason and keep on trying to do the right thing, or admit you did the wrong thing for the wrong reason and try to make amends."

I felt better, and nodded my agreement. "I know."

"Is there anything you can do about it today?" she asked.

I realized there was not. "No," I said. "Nothing that I can think of."

"Then," she said standing up, brushing off her hands with finality, "get in the living room and tell those lazy sons of mine to get ready to hand out presents, because it's Christmas, and that's what we do on Christmas."

I looked up at her. "Erma," I said, "let me ask you one more thing."

She sat back down. "What is it, baby?" She spit on a tissue and dabbed at my face, I assumed to clean me up.

"Reggie Wert thinks I could be a Breakers Baby and Pitt is just panting to have me be one—"

"What's a Breakers Baby?" she interrupted, brushing my hair back off my face.

"Apparently some babies were born in the Breakers during wartime, when they turned it into a hospital, and I'm the right age."

She nodded. "Oh. Well, I don't know what to tell you. You were almost a year old when your parents hired me. I never asked where you were born and they never said. Of course, we didn't have but a couple of months of knowin' each other before they went away...."

"My question," I said, "is this. I really don't care if I am a Breakers Baby. I really don't even want to know. But Pitt wants me to find out. Can I just tell him no? Can I tell him I'd rather not find out—that it hurts too much to think about those people that I never knew?"

Erma took my hand and stood up. "Come with me," she said. We went back into the kitchen and out the back door of the house and into the large yard. She pulled me around to the south side of the house, from where you could see the Southern Boulevard Bridge and Mar-A-Lago.

"Look across the water, Baby," she said. "You have always held yourself emotionally on this side of the bridge, on our side of the bridge. There's nothing wrong with that. But your people lived over there and it's time you learned as much as you can about who they were. It was wrong of me not to do that for you, but I just thought you'd be happier if you were just one of us."

She patted my hand between her own. "And you are one of us, but you belong to them, too, and it's time you found out who they were."

"Now," she said, "get inside and let's have Christmas."

I followed her—Southern earth mother in Georgio pants and sweatshirt—into the kitchen with a feeling of dread about the search everyone wanted me to make.

Why did I think I wouldn't like what I found?

We left that night stuffed with food, heavy with gifts and buoyed with good cheer. I told Pitt in the car I would talk to Reggie first thing in the morning, and he rewarded me when we got home.

"I've saved something special for you—a Christmas present," he said. He leered, lifting eyebrows. "I'll give it to you upstairs."

Oh, no, I thought, *I'm so full of turkey I might pop.* But what I said was, "Okay, sweetie, I'll be right up. Let me take the dogs out." Isadora and Henry were standing by the door, eyes eloquently begging. Mind you, they have a doggie door leading to a very expensive dog run in the back of the house, so they can relieve themselves at their own whim. But I guess it's not the same without an audience.

When I got upstairs, Pitt was in bed, sitting up with pillows propped behind him on the satin sheets he likes so much. He was wearing the Ralph Lauren pajamas I had given him for Christmas. "Give me a minute," I said, and went into the bathroom where I showered off the sticky handprints of seven children and the grease from dinner and hoped that being clean would put me more in the mood.

Back in the bedroom, I climbed into bed and leaned against Pitt's shoulder. He was watching the umpteenth rerun of Christmas with Andy Williams and his family, where Andy and Claudine Longet were crooning Christmas songs at each other. *Fitting,* I thought. Soon after that Christmas special was made, she was accused of murdering her lover and she and Andy divorced.

Pitt turned and reached under the bed and brought out a red and gold wrapped present tied with gold cord. "Here you go," he said.

Surprised, I stared at it. He had given me several Christmas presents at Erma's; nice, useful kinds of things. This was unexpected.

"What is it?" I asked. It was heavy, about eight or nine inches high.

"Open it," he said.

I ripped open the paper to find four wrapped presents inside. Books, I could tell from the size and shape.

I unwrapped the first one. A first edition Carl Hiaasen, *Tourist Season.* One of my favorite books. The next one was a first edition Zora Neale Hurston, one of my favorite authors. The third was a first edition John D. MacDonald, one of my idols. And the last, purposely, I was sure, was a first edition Stuart McIver, *Yesterday's Palm Beach.*

I didn't miss the hint, but I wasn't about to fuss at him. I treasure first editions and these would be the pride of my collection, which centered around my love of Florida history.

I kissed him.

Then I kissed him again. Suddenly I forgot how full I was and just concentrated on a little Christmas gift of my own.

The next morning, on Thursday, Pitt was already up and gone to work when I woke. Petal was playing her new Garth Brooks CD at full volume. The dogs were barking at something in the back yard.

I knew I didn't have any excuse for not following through on my promise. After breakfast, I called Reggie to ask him if I could meet him at the Breakers. There was no answer at his home, so I assumed he would be at the hotel.

I got dressed and drove over there.

I found Reggie in his office looking as if he had lost his best friend. In his hand was the telephone, which he hung up as I walked in. His warren was a cubbyhole off the suite of marketing and sales offices of the Breakers staff. The place was a virtual landfill of papers, books, stacks of photographs and albums piled everywhere. Reggie had his own little niche at The Breakers, in more ways than one.

"What's wrong, Reggie?" I asked.

"Burglary," he said. "Right here in my office."

"Cash receipts?"

"No, no," he said, long-faced. "Cash receipts are put in the safe and deposited every night. Besides, those are in the business office, and they didn't go there. Only here, to my office."

"What happened?"

"Yesterday, apparently, while no one was here in this part of the hotel, someone broke into my office and rifled through my papers," he said.

"Did they take anything?"

"I can't tell yet. I'm still looking around." He stood and started rummaging through piles. There was stuff everywhere. It wasn't clear to me what amount of clutter was caused by the intruder and how much was just Reggie's natural pack rat mentality. He was a lover of historical trivia and minutiae, and kept bits and pieces of information about Palm Beach history everywhere.

"Did you call the police?"

"Yes, they're sending someone over."

"Oh." I sat down on a velour armchair that looked like a refugee from the recent lobby remodeling. I was hesitant now to ask what I had come to ask. Was it thoughtless to bring up your business to someone with their own problems?

"Uh, Reggie? I wondered if you had any information about my family."

He slapped a stack of papers down on the desk in frustration. Then he gave me a pitying look. "Not much, I'm afraid. I found out you don't have a birth certificate. Did you know that?"

I didn't. "Are you sure?"

"Have you ever applied for a passport?"

"No. I've never gone out of the country."

He gave me an odd look, and it was understandable. One of the big benefits of money is being mobile. Unhampered by the pesky need to arrange their own transportation—staff does that—and with a circle of friends who own houses in all the world's playgrounds and jets to take them there, the wealthy hop oceans at a whim. Thus the term jet set. I, on the other hand, don't fly. "Well," he said. "I suggest you go to the courthouse and see for yourself."

I turned when I heard a knock on the office door. Detective Mike Cassidy stood there, looking in. He was wearing a Tommy Hilfiger sweater, a Christmas gift. I could tell because it still had gentle creases where it had been folded for wrapping. He was sending off major cocky vibes and I bristled as I always do when I encounter cocky men.

"Mrs...."

"Ms. Wally Tupper," I snapped, annoyed that he didn't remember my name just two days after we had met—and, I am a friend of his boss. "Hello, detective."

"Ms. Tupper, were you here when the burglary occurred?" he asked, pompously, I thought.

"No, detective, I just now arrived."

"Then," he said, overly politely, "may I ask you to step outside while I speak with Mr...." He glanced at his little notebook. "Mr. Wert."

I patted Reggie on the knee. "I'll come back later. Thanks for your help."

"Don't give up, Wally," he said. "There's an answer to this."

I smiled weakly as I left his office. Maybe the answer was I didn't exist at all.

I walked back to the portico of the hotel, and stared out at the three bare-breasted women holding up the bottom bowl of the Renaissance style fountain in front of the hotel. I knew how they felt, having to hold that thing up. I'll bet sometimes they just wanted to shrug it off and lie, without burden, in the sun.

Cassidy had gotten on my nerves sufficiently that I also had the passing thought that the fountain was obviously designed by a man. No woman would condemn her sisters to sit eternally bare-breasted in the middle of a parking lot in the Florida sun.

The valet brought my car before I could formulate a plan to free us all.

Driving west out of Breakers Row, along the line of parking places, I spotted someone I knew. Raymond Way was standing in the parking lot talking to Digby. Digby was waving as he got into the Montreaux Florist van. Raymond was standing next to a black Mercedes SL600.

They did not notice me driving by. That was lucky, since in my little red 1962 Corvair convertible, I'm not too hard to identify if you see me. My Corvair has been with me since she was shiny new in the summer of 1962, the summer that Connie Francis sang "Where the Boys Are" with a cry in her voice that spoke to me of the promise of love that life offered—and I knew my little red convertible was going to take me to that promised land.

Now, remembering my promise to Digby, I pulled my car out onto South County Road, turned immediately back into the next little road, a private drive leading to the Breakers Condominiums, and made a U-turn. I pulled back into Breakers Row just in time to see Raymond pull out. I whizzed past as he was looking the other direction and drove to the other side of the fountain. When he came toward the fountain to make the circle, I drove around to the other side. I felt like part of a Peter Sellers movie.

I followed him to Worth Avenue, where he pulled into a parking space—wonder of wonders—got out and ducked down Via Mizner, now a little grotto of shops, but once the residence of Addison Mizner, who had built himself a home over the street he helped create.

There were—of course—no parking spaces for me. I pulled into a loading zone and crossed my fingers. My car wears the sticker that identifies me as a resident of Palm Beach, which usually keeps me from getting a ticket. Parking tickets, it is understood, are for outsiders.

I hopped out and walked around the corner where I saw Ray disappearing into Bice restaurant. I peeked in, looking through the crowd waiting for a table. I saw Raymond greet Artie Marsh, my favorite bartender at the Breakers.

The two looked chummy, seated at a small table for two. I didn't think it was a business lunch, although I could have been wrong. I knew the answer for sure when I saw Raymond reach over and cover Artie's hand with his own, and give it a squeeze.

"Uh, oh," I said to myself. I turned and left as they were giving their order. I was already late for my own lunch with Pitt, and I still had to get back to Reggie this afternoon.

Back at my car, I found a small white envelope tucked under my windshield wiper. I snatched it out from under the wiper and looked at it to be sure I was right. I was. It was a ticket. Just as I opened my car door and got in, my purse started to ring.

I fished my cell phone out of my bag.

"Yeah," I said.

"Woof. Bad mood?" Pitt asked.

"I just got a ticket," I said.

"Where are you?"

"Worth Avenue."

"Here? Why didn't you park in our lot?"

"Yeah. Well. It's a long story. I'll be right there."

"That's why I called," he said contritely. "I've got to cancel."

"What's up?"

"I forgot about the DeVales' thing tonight and I have some stuff to wrap up this afternoon. I'll be home about seven."

"Oh, damn," I said. "I forgot, too. See you then."

I realized that Reggie would be at the DeVales' that night, so I decided to postpone my trip back to the Breakers.

But I did have something I wanted to get off my chest.

I drove to the Palm Beach police station and parked in a ten-minute space. That would be all it would take.

Ticket clutched in my hand, I climbed the brightly painted tile-edged stairs, went in and asked the desk officer if Tony were available. Luckily, he was, so I went on up to his office.

"Wally," he said, rising and coming over to give me a peck on the cheek. He looked great, all tanned and hard-bodied, casually dressed in khakis and a knit shirt. I shook my head to clear it and tried to growl at him.

"Look," I said, holding out my hand, which clutched the ticket, and shaking it at him.

"What's that?"

"A ticket."

"Oh....tsk. Tsk." He held out his hand.

I handed it to him, gratified I didn't have to ask for a favor.

The ticket had suffered from being clutched in my sweaty hand for the past fifteen minutes. He unfolded it and read it. "You parked in a loading zone, Wally."

I hung my head. "It was an emergency." I would never ask Tony to fix a ticket for me. I have some moral fiber. Whether I have the strength of character to refuse if he were to offer to fix it, we'll never know, because he extended his hand, ticket held out, to me.

"Here," he said. "You can pay this downstairs."

I whined, sounding much like Henry when Isadora has stolen his favorite toy.

Tony smiled and shook his head. He reached down, pulled up my hand, and pressed the ticket in my palm. "I don't fix tickets, Wally. You ought to know that."

I guess so. "I didn't...really...expect you to fix it," I stammered huffily, wishing that were totally true. "I just wanted to tell you I was only there a second." I said. "Really."

He smiled in a maddeningly understanding way. I didn't fool him for a minute, it said. "What's the point of being police chief if you don't obey the law?" he said. "And once I cross that line for one person, where do I stop?"

What could I say? I certainly could afford the twenty dollars, and I didn't have any principle to stand on. I sighed.

He squeezed my hand. "I'll buy you a drink to make up for it."

I squeezed back. Hard. He wasn't hitting on me—would a man who had just refused to fix my parking ticket be stupid enough to hit on me? I didn't think so.

"Sorry," I said. "Gotta go. Got a parking ticket to pay."

He walked me to the door, shaking out his fingers.

"By the way," I said. "Was anything taken from the Breakers?"

Tony shook his head. "Some paperwork, as best as we can tell. We'll know more when Reggie completes his inventory—or comes down from his snit, whichever comes first. He's really hot that someone violated his inner sanctum."

I laughed. "Who would be brave enough?"

"Oh," he said, "the autopsy results on Booth Ewen will be in tomorrow. I pulled in a favor from the state lab. Tell LaLa I'll call her if there's anything unusual, but I'm sure there won't be."

I gulped. "Sure thing. Er...could you call me first, so I can be with LaLa when you talk to her?"

"Better idea. Meet me at the hospital for lunch tomorrow. We'll catch up on old times and I'll pick up the report."

I was pretty sure I wouldn't be very hungry. "See you there at noon."

Chapter Eleven

THURSDAY, DEC. 26

I was feeling as if I had just hit a speed bump while moseying down the road of my own quiet and purposely underwhelming life. On the other side of the speed bump was a detour sign that was sending me off into uncharted territory.

It was a few minutes before seven o'clock Thursday and Pitt and I rocked on the waves created by our pre-party sex on the king-sized water mattress. He likes to have sex before we go to a party because he says it makes him more relaxed. Who am I to argue?

I stretched, feeling pretty relaxed myself. "God," I said, savoring the feel of satin on my skin.

"God had nothing to do with that, thank you," Pitt said. "Give Him credit for the birdies, if you must, but when I've got you going like that, I'd like a little credit, please."

"Screw the birdies," I said, sitting up.

"If you want. But you'll have to catch 'em for me. I don't have time." Pitt sat up, slung himself over the edge of the bed, hit the floor and headed for his shower. "We have to be at dinner, remember?"

"Do I. I'd rather be strung up by my fingernails than go to the DeVales'." I glared at him. "You know how little it means to me to go to this damn Dining for Depression. I'm depressed just thinking about having to go. I'll send a check. Why do I have to go eat caviar, too?"

He returned my glare as he stopped at the bathroom door. "Wally, I don't often ask you to lower yourself to pimping for me at these parties, but the president of CitiCorps is coming to town tonight for this event. Is one night too much to ask?"

We retired for a few minutes to our respective bathrooms, and when we returned to the bedroom, silence reigned.

Pitt see-sawed a towel over his back, wrapped it around his waist, sarong style, and stepped to the Bauhaus armoire where he kept his collection of CK briefs.

The armoire, like the rest of the bedroom, reflected Pitt's taste. Despite having taken architectural and design courses at Georgia Tech, I acquiesce to Pitt's wishes when it comes to the house. Even though the house is mine, I always let him make the decisions about it.

It isn't, I reflected as I watched Pitt pick out black briefs and socks, that I don't care about how our house is decorated. It is that he cares so much. He wants so badly for everything to reflect the height of taste and status, so early on I had yielded the decorating decisions to him rather than try to make myself care any more than I did.

Satisfied at his selection, he threw his choices onto a chair. "Yes, I know how little you want to go. But you agreed. To go. For me."

Knowing there was no serious threat to my going—I always protest, but I always go—Pitt turned his attention back to his wardrobe and pushed the button that activated the mechanical closet, sending a rack of shirt selections, arranged in shades of white, yellow, blue and pink, whirling past him. He stopped it at the tux shirts, took a minute to pick out one that was no different than a half dozen others, and hung it on a rack. Then he stepped to the suit rack, repeated the action, and pulled out an Armani tux.

As he passed me on his way from the closet, he pulled the towel from his body and snapped at my butt with it. "It's after seven o'clock. What are you wearing?" He dropped the towel and walked, naked now, back over to the underwear, and sat on the chair.

"I'm wearing the Adolfo. The new one. The one you like so much." The only good thing about buying couture clothing is that they will fit it to your shape, no matter how odd that shape is.

He nodded. "You'll look beautiful, as always. You do understand this man is very important to my career?"

Of course I did; I'd certainly heard it enough. "By the way," I said, remembering. "I was at the Breakers earlier and I saw Reggie Wert."

"Did he find out if you are a Breakers Baby?"

"No. I don't have a birth certificate. I have to go to the courthouse and see if they have any records."

"New Year's Eve is only five days away."

"Three if you don't count the weekend."

"Hmm. Sarcasm. I'm just asking. Does he have anything for me?"

"We didn't talk about it. Somebody broke into the Breakers."

"Get anything?"

"Not sure yet, Tony said."

He gave me an odd look. "Maybe we should have your friend the police chief over for dinner. I think I need to make his acquaintance."

I thought about that for a minute. "Okay."

Pitt, who looked as good as any model in the CK briefs he slid onto his nude body, was as smart as he was handsome. He and I met while I was studying archaeology at Penn and he was getting his doctorate at Wharton. He finished first in his class every year.

We hit it off from the beginning. He loved my money and I loved his brains. Since money is not important to me and he takes his intelligence as a matter of course, neither of us minded that the initial attraction was more shallow than the friendship and love that later developed. When we married, it was with the understanding that he could pursue the career he wanted with my money, if I could count on him not to take the pursuit of social prestige too seriously. It had worked out.

But he wanted something more now. It had been eating at him lately; an itch he had to scratch. I understood. I had my own itch. At least he knew where to scratch his.

Thirty minutes later, we arrived at the DeVales' nouveau ocean-front estate on the south end of Palm Beach. As we inched up the drive toward the portico where valet swarmed like bees around hibiscus, I thought of Eva Stotesbury and Marjorie Meriweather Post, the two Palm Beach society queens who had started the "estate wars." In 1919, Stotesbury commissioned Addison Mizner to build El Mirasol, the first of the grand estates in Palm Beach. Post had Mar-a-Lago built in 1924 to eclipse El Mirasol and the wars were on.

The DeVales had taken up the battle cry. Their estate was not the largest in town, but in ornate and ostentatious design, it could compete with any place in town. They had torn down the 1920 estate of an early Palm Beach resident, plus a newer house on the adjoining lot, to build their fortress.

The point, I guess, is to impress those who were here before you, which is why people like Thornton and Verity DeVale never stopped trying to top people like Peep—whose grandmother came along in 1925 and built an estate bigger than Mar-a-Lago.

It makes Palm Beach parties great fun—if you're a shark looking for fresh blood. It spawns an air of hysteria, emits the tangible smell of anxiety of those who want so badly, like the DeVales, to be accepted.

Verity approached us slowly, the shark teeth disguised behind a wide smile. She was decked out in diamonds so thick it looked like some sort of white rash had broken out on her earlobes and bare-to-there chest. From across the room, Thornton saw her making her way toward me and, I suppose fearing a repeat of the funeral encounter, hurried to head her off.

She beat him to me and, apparently deciding I was worth courting, grabbed my hand and pumped it. "Wally and Pitt, how delighted we are that you could come. Pitt, here comes Thornton. I know he has some people he wants you to talk to."

Indeed, at that moment, Thornton arrived, smiling his smug little smile and draping a hammy little hand around my shoulder.

Pitt, sensing trouble in the making, spoke up. "Are you two going to be at the Breakers Centennial Ball New Year's Eve?"

Thornton nodded. "Of course," he said. "We've had many invitations. But I'm sure we'll drop by."

Pitt preened. "Wally," he said, pulling me toward him and out from Thornton's grasp, "is going to be in the procession of Breakers Babies."

I saw Verity's eyes narrow; Pitt did not notice, and kept on talking. "Breakers Babies, you know, were born right there in the hotel, during the war. Her family lived here before the war."

Thornton looked thoughtful. "I heard something about that—your family was killed in the war, Wally?"

I took a deep breath. This was a conversation I avoided. Not so much because it was uncomfortable, but because I had so little to say it was embarrassing.

"They disappeared," I said. "On a flight to the Bahamas. In the Bermuda Triangle."

"Like Amelia Earhart," Pitt said. I didn't correct his geography.

"How interesting," Thornton said. "Isn't it, Verity?"

"Lots of people were born here," she snapped. "That's really nothing to brag about, is it?"

Pitt's radar was down. He kept going. "Really," he said, "only a few babies were born at the Breakers."

"We've found seventeen of them," Reggie Wert said, coming up from behind me. He shook hands all around, then continued. "But we believe there are more."

"Why?" Thornton said.

"Why would anyone care?" Verity asked.

Reggie smiled benignly at her. "Because, my dear. It's history. The Breakers is a historic place with many stories to tell, and none more interesting than when the army took it over in 1942 to make it into a hospital for recuperating servicemen and women."

Verity smiled snottily. "You certainly don't look your age, dear."

I lifted my eyebrows at Reggie. When you're over fifty, the babblings of twenty-somethings are of no consequence.

"Babies were born at the hotel through much of 1944," Reggie hastened to add, not that it mattered to me. Age, it seemed, gave me a clearer view of the world. Lately, the scales were beginning to fall from my eyes, as the saying goes, about a lot of things. Or was it the encounter with death that had changed me? I wasn't sure. I only knew my life had changed, suddenly, subtly and without my having made any conscious move.

"What's the big deal?" Verity snarled. "It's just a hotel. You might as well be born in a—" she stopped suddenly as if a thought had sneaked up on her, unexpected. "A Holiday Inn," she finished sullenly.

Reggie gasped as if he had been slapped in the face with a glove. He drew himself up to several inches over his five feet and cast an icy glance at Verity.

"Certainly not, my dear. Why, to be born at the Breakers is a great feather in one's cap—"

"What's it done for her?" Verity broke in, gesturing at me. "Just look at her."

I leaned in her direction, about to give her what was left of my mind, when Pitt grabbed my arm and Thornton grabbed Verity's and both men pulled with all their might.

"Thornton, I'm raring to meet those investors you mentioned," Pitt said. "Where are they?"

Lifting his hand, Thornton jerked a thumb toward the bar. "Getting a drink."

Pitt gently pushed his shoulder in that direction. "Let's go, then, and get some business done." He tried to pull me with him, but I jerked my arm loose and stood my ground.

Verity stood hers.

The three men took off. Cowards.

"Wally," she said, her eyelids blinking out a Morse code to beware what came from the mouth. "Let me level with you." My lack of response threw her for a second, but she continued.

"I have worked very hard—on Thornton's behalf, of course—to make myself...useful...in this town. I have volunteered on every board worth my time. I have tried to be nice to the right people. I have donated money to the right causes." Her decibel level had gone up and someone standing nearby glanced at us, so she dropped her voice, moving a step closer to me and raising her face closer to mine.

"But what I'm doing isn't working," she said.

I stepped back a step and raised a cautionary hand in her direction. "Hold it, Verity. You really are talking to the wrong person. For one thing, you have confused me with someone who gives a—"

"I'm not," she broke in, "courting your favor. Precisely the reason I am telling you this is that while you do have a certain standing in this town because you've been here so long, I know you are indifferent to your position in society. Anyone," she said, her little slitty eyes boring into me, "can see that when they look at you."

I was opening my mouth to tell her just how much I particularly didn't care what she thought, when she continued. "But your family's longevity here doesn't impress some of us. Your husband, on the other hand, seems to be very concerned about his position in Palm Beach society."

She looked across the room where Pitt was glad-handing some fat cats. "And I suspect he wants your cooperation on that."

I shut my mouth and waited.

"So," she said. "I'm putting you on notice that I intend to chair the Garden Club Gala next year, and that between now and then I will expect your help in putting in a good word for me with the right people."

"Peep Fenton chairs the Garden Club Gala," I said.

She smiled and wrapped her arms around herself, leaning back. "Not anymore, I can assure you. I'm certain—quite certain—that by New Year's Eve Peep Fenton will be lucky to be on the guest list for the unveiling of the new cheese spread at the Palm Beach Publix."

She gave me a "so there" nod of the head, and turned to her left to greet another guest, but not before flinging one final threat. "And that goes double for her friend LaLa Ewen, who won't be nearly as beloved in this town when people find out the real truth about her."

I stood back and watched with a weird fascination, like when you see the big fish eating the little fish at an aquarium.

I heard a familiar voice behind me, booming deeply amid the mean-ingless nattering of the party guests.

"Why didn't you call me, baby doodles? I would have taken care of it." Mitchell Fenton sounded a bit rankled at his wife, Peep.

"I didn't want to disturb you, sweetie. There wasn't anything you could do. Not one teensie-weensie thing."

I turned around to see Mitch pulling at the collar of his Brooks Brothers tux.

"Hello, Mitch."

"Wally. Look, Peep. It's Wally," he boomed.

She shot him an irritated glance and stepped a half step closer to me.

Mitch followed, crowding us both.

"I hear you've been talking to our police chief, Wally," he said. "Do they have any idea who killed that sonofabitch Booth Ewen? Who is this Society Killer we are reading about, anyway?"

I shrugged, not wanting to get Tony into any more trouble.

Peep answered him. "They don't know, Mitch. LaLa thinks they suspect her, but they would, wouldn't they?"

Her husband caught her meaning. "They do seem to look at the spouse first, honeybunch, but I'm sure LaLa is as innocent as you are."

"You know," Peep said, "it wasn't right, what they said about me and Eaton. I knew—know—that everyone always loved Eaton. That made what they said about his death hard to accept then and now."

She glanced at Mitch, but I felt it would never occur to him to base his self-esteem on Peep's feelings for her late husband, or to think himself a second choice; I saw him as thinking of their marriage only in terms of her becoming available when he needed her. After all, the story around town was that Mitchell had put his first wife, Desdemona, in a high-priced hospital for rich women who couldn't cope with real-ity and then divorced her.

After years of playing the field, he married Peep because, for social reasons, he needed a wife. This callous behavior made me shudder, but it never seemed to bother Peep.

"But," Peep continued, still on her own conversation, "pretty much everybody hated Booth. Remember what a nuisance he made of him-self our senior year?"

"He was a pain in the ass," Mitch nodded. "I remember Desdemona said he hit on her at the senior picnic."

"Really?" Peep said. "I can remember, as if it were yesterday, the night—it was just a few days before the prom—he came up to me at a party at the Everglades Club and took me for a walk in the courtyard. Then he started to paw me and I thought I wouldn't get away from him. If Eaton hadn't come looking for me, I don't know what would have happened. Eaton was furious with him, and threatened to turn him over to the police. I talked him out of it, of course, but he moped about it for months. In fact, Eaton seemed to brood about it more, as time went on, not less."

"Well, Eaton was a good man." Mitch leaned down to peck her on her cheek and patted her bottom. "And I'm a lucky man."

"Thank you." Peep looked back and forth between the two of us. "Mitch?"

"Yes, honeybunch?" His hand slid around her waist.

"Someone really is watching me."

"What do you mean, baby doodles?" Her husband's voice was bored—his eyes were scanning the room.

"I mean, I see a car sitting on South County Road sometimes, like someone is watching the house. And I've seen the same car on the Avenue. I've told you."

"Whose car is it, snuggums?"

"I don't know, Mitch."

"Who is in the car when you see it?"

Peep shifted away from him slightly. "If I knew that, Mitch, I'd know who it was, now, wouldn't I?"

"Don't get your panties in a wad, tiger, just tell me what kind of car it is."

"It's a black Mercedes S600."

"Shit, Peep, half of Palm Beach drives a black Mercedes S600. I drive a black Mercedes S600. How do you even know it's the same car?"

"I just know, Mitch."

"Honey, you know the women in your family have a tendency to be a tad, well, imaginative. Not that I'm saying there's anything wrong with you, of course, but you have to admit there must be something genetic." Mitch had said it all in the most concerned of voices, but even I could read between his words: *You might be crazy, too.*

"What should I do, Mitch? Should I tell Tony?"

There was no reply for a moment. "I see somebody I gotta go talk to, sweetie. I'll be right back." He moved off into the crowd.

"Maybe," she whispered as he walked away, "Desdemona wasn't all that crazy until she married you."

She looked up at me. "I married him thinking he would be a tree to cling to in the winds, like Eaton was. But he twists and turns when the gusts come. I sometimes wonder if he doesn't want me to swing in the wind when trouble threatens." She shuddered. "You've got to help me."

"What do you mean, help you?" I asked, looking behind her to see if there was a gun pointed at her. There was not.

"It happened again this morning." She looked around the room, eyes narrowed, as if expecting to be jumped at any moment.

"What?"

She exhaled heavily in exasperation. "Followed me. I told you. Someone is following me."

My patience with humanity in general was eroding like one of those California mudslides. I knew that even if Peep imagined this threat, there were other, more real ones at hand. First, I needed to convince her this was her imagination.

"Listen up," I said. "Eleven o'clock tomorrow morning. It's Friday, and you always volunteer at Whitehall on Fridays. I'll be waiting on Polmer Park when you come by at five 'til, and see if there is someone following you. Okay?"

"Okay," she agreed, mollified. "How will you know? What if there's traffic?"

"You said it was a black Mercedes, didn't you?"

"Mmmhmm."

"I'll see if there's a black Mercedes behind you. If so, I'll follow it."

Taffy Povitch approached us looking as if she had just fed on an entire school of marlin. "Darlings. I have the most amazing news."

She was bone thin. Her little turkey neck looked like it would barely hold up her head, which was piled with hair like Audrey Hepburn in that movie. She draped a bejeweled claw over my shoulder.

"What is it, Taffy?" I asked about one quarter heartedly.

She sniffed the air and made a face indicating displeasure. "Oh, not here, darling. You must come to my house for coffee tomorrow morning at ten. I'll tell you every juicy detail, yes?"

I shook my head. "Can't come until after lunch." I was already working on the excuse I would come up with tomorrow following my lunch with Tony.

I saw a spark in the dark eyes, but no facial muscles actually moved. She turned to Peep. "Terrible. Terrible thing about Booth, my dear. And on the night of your gala. Why, when Pauly and I found out, we were simply aghast. To think we were all there together that very night. Tell me," she leaned forward over Peep, her triple strand of pearls swinging loosely around her protuberant collarbone. "Did he really drown in his own pool? Was LaLa there?"

Peep and I exchanged glances.

Taffy continued. "It's all a little, well, weird, isn't it Peep, considering."

Peep nodded her head. "It really is, Taffy. I don't know what you thought about Eaton's death, but I always counted on you to know the difference between the truth and the gossip."

Taffy closed her eyes for what seemed an eternity. I looked at Peep. What was Taffy Povitch thinking?

After a moment, Taffy's eyes opened. "At first I hated you. I thought you had killed Eaton like everybody said, and that the police had let you go." She stood up, threw her head back. "I would have done anything to get back at you for killing the man I loved."

Peep gasped quietly. I held my breath.

"But," Taffy continued, "I finally realized that you loved him, too. And that he loved you. You had no reason to kill him."

I exhaled.

Peep lit a cigarette with shaking hands, forgetting, I guess, that Mitch was in the room.

Taffy looked out over the crowd. "It's funny, you know. Even if Booth hadn't died that night, your gala brought back memories I thought I had exorcised." She took a sip of her drink.

Then she smiled, and I saw the toothy smile of the ex-cheerleader, the eighteen-year-old who had charmed everyone with that thousand-watt smile.

"I still had hope that night of our senior prom. You and Eaton were dating, sure, but he was always nice to me, and lots of couples broke up after graduation. I thought you might, too, since Eaton was going to Emory and you were going to, what was it, Sweetbriar? I had begged my parents to let me go to Emory too, but I didn't have the grades for it, and so I went to Florida. I wrote Eaton several times inviting him to Gainesville for sorority parties—I bet you never knew that, did you?—but he never would come." She paused, looking out over the water again.

"But that night I had hope, so I followed Eaton outside when he went out to get some air. We sat out on your loggia for a few minutes and I asked him to take me for a walk." She gave Peep a rueful smile. "He was too nice to turn me down."

Peep's lips pressed together, tight.

"Anyway," Taffy went on, "we walked the beach, and we talked about college, and what our lives were going to be like, and he told me it was hard to know what to do when you didn't have to do anything. His parents were older; he would inherit such a huge fortune, he would never have to work. But he wanted to do something that was worthwhile."

"The museum," Peep said softly.

"I gave him the idea," Taffy said. She leaned forward. "Peep, I always wanted you to know, that whatever happiness you and Eaton had, I was glad for. And I was glad we took that walk that night, because that's when he decided he wanted to study history and become the curator of the Flagler museum. I reminded him how much the history of Palm Beach infiltrated our lives, growing up here."

Peep nodded. "It was hard, wasn't it, being a teenager in Palm Beach."

She meant that Palm Beach children face their rebellious years with confusion: How do you rebel against parents who already break every rule society has to offer? With the exception of the social rules, there were no "don'ts" in Palm Beach. Drugs, sex, booze were everywhere. How do you rebel against that?

"It was," Taffy agreed, "and some of our teachers helped us get through it without killing ourselves in fast cars or in crazy drunken nights on the beaches by telling us the stories of the terrible things that had happened here before us. So I suggested to Eaton that he carry on the tradition...what is it? Those who do not know history are doomed to repeat it? He said that. That's one of the things I remember most about that night."

The smile faded. "The other thing I remember about that night is Noelle. We were best friends; co-captains of the cheerleading squad. We did everything together, then she was just gone."

I let my thoughts run to a girl we had all known in high school. Cheerful, peppy, smart and talented, she was loved by girls and boys alike. Then she had simply disappeared—she didn't show up for graduation, even though she was valedictorian, and no one ever heard from her again. No explanation was ever offered, and Palm Beach never had even a morsel of gossip to chew on. Her parents seemed as baffled as everyone else.

"Taffy," I said gently, "I wonder if you can think of anyone who would want to harm Booth?"

Taffy lifted her chiseled chin. "Oh, well, that's what I was getting to. I don't know, of course, but I do remember something from that night that has always stuck with me. Eaton and I ran into Booth that night on the beach. He was LaLa's date, you know, but he was out there on the beach, by himself. He stopped and flirted with me, and I could tell he had been drinking—everyone was that night. But he and Eaton barely spoke.

"And when he walked off, Eaton said to me, 'someone is going to kill that son of a bitch some day.' Of course it stuck with me, but I thought it ironic last year that Eaton was the one who died and Booth was still alive. But it turns out Eaton was right."

Peep looked shaken. "I've got to...powder my nose," she said, and tottered off into the crowd.

We stared after her for a moment, then Taffy shook her head, as if coming out of a reverie. "Come see me, my dear. Three o'clock. Maid's afternoon off. I'll leave the door unlocked—come on in," she said, and moved on, her little nose quivering like a bunny. I suppose she had gotten a whiff of a healthy credit rating. Taffy was never one to slack off in her dedicated search for the next husband.

I was staring at her bony butt as it disappeared into a sea of bony butts, when I felt hot breath on my back. I turned to find Darla Dugan looking up at me, the top of her bleached-within-an-inch-of-its life hair practically under my nose.

"Aren't they a bunch of phonies?" she said with a nervous little laugh. "Don't they just make you want to puke?"

It wasn't the kind of talk you usually heard at a Palm Beach soiree. I liked it. "Well," I said. "That's refreshing."

She gave a little snort and pursed up her mouth. Above the piggy nose, deep green eyes searched nervously through the crowd, as if fearing she would be overheard.

"If you have money," she said conspiratorially, "you can be refreshing. People call it eccentric."

She did have the money. The Dugan fortune had been building for centuries. As the sole heir of a fortune that made mine look like pocket change, Darla owned several conglomerations. Gossip had it, however, that she was a recluse and left the running of the businesses to others.

She didn't look so reclusive tonight. Other than seeming a little wary, she was standing right here in the middle of Palm Beach society, blasting them. Maybe that explained the wariness—she knew she had to watch her back.

"What brings you to Palm Beach?" I asked, making polite party conversation.

"I came to see old friends," she said.

"Oh, who?"

"Listen," she said sharply. "I don't have time to chat. I just wanted to tell you—because you are one of the nice ones—that you cannot trust anybody here. They are out to get you and your friends."

"Yes, go on." She had my attention.

She looked around and lowered her voice. "They will treat you like dirt if you let them see a weakness. They will hurt you. They will make fun of you."

"I just wanted to warn you." She squinted up at me. I considered myself warned, but I wasn't quite sure about what.

Suddenly her shoulders jumped. "I have to go," she said, scurrying off into the crowd.

I shook my head. I knew she was right about everything she said. I was just totally in the dark as to why she had said it to me.

Chapter Twelve

FRIDAY, DEC. 27

At ten forty-five Friday morning, I was sitting in my car on Polmer Park Road, sipping a Diet Coke and wondering what my life was coming to.

Peep's Jag streaked down North Lake. She was headed south to the Henry Flagler Museum, to volunteer as she had three times a week since her first husband Eaton had become curator some fifteen years ago.

I started my car and watched the road. Son of a gun if a black Mercedes didn't streak by. Speed limits are low in Palm Beach, but people travel as if there's a fire and they have the only hose, especially on the north end of town, where the traffic is mostly local residents or the help.

I pulled up to the corner of North Lake. The Mercedes windows were tinted black, so I couldn't see a face. I didn't think right then to look for a tag number, but decided to see if I could catch up with him and do just that.

It didn't happen. I made the turn onto North Lake Way, but the Mercedes had slipped on down to where the road zigs at Miraflores Drive. By the time I zigged, I had lost him. There was more traffic along that stretch of road, and there were three black Mercedes S600 with black tinted windows that I could see from where I sat.

I gave up the chase. It was almost eleven-thirty; close enough to lunch time, I thought, so I kept driving south until I came to the police station and found a legal parking space.

Figuring Tony would be leaving soon to meet me at the hospital anyway, so I might as well interrupt him, I went on up to his office.

I interrupted more than I bargained for.

Tony's secretary—a six-foot bombshell—undulated toward his open office door.

"Rose," I heard him say as soon as she hit the doorway. "It's time we ended this little game."

I didn't know of what game he spoke, but I could see a pout on her face. She was a beautiful woman, in the way that employees who work near the rich are beautiful; more carefully dressed, more carefully tended, more aware of their looks than their wealthy employers.

"You have to stop flirting with me," he said. "We have a job to do here, Rose, and I expect you to do your job, and that's all. Do we have an understanding?"

She tossed her mane of shining hair and turned on her heel. "Yes, sir," she said on the way out, closing his door just hard enough to make her point but not hard enough to provoke another rebuke. "We certainly do."

She reached into a desk drawer, pulled out a Louis Vuitton bag that had probably cost her a week's salary, gave me a haughty glance, and strode out of the office and toward the stairs.

Why she flirted with Tony when she probably had her heart set on becoming head of the household in one of the town estates was a mystery to me. I opened the office door and peeped in.

"Hiya," I said.

He looked up at me. "Weren't we meeting at the hospital?"

"So arrest me."

He smiled, just a sardonic twitch on one side of his mouth. "Just as well. I have the medical examiner's report right here." He leaned back in his office chair and waved at me to sit down. I did.

He studied the papers in front of him. "I can't decide," he said as he read, "whether this is good news or not. I don't want to arrest LaLa for Booth's murder. I'd rather find out that the son of a bitch got drunk and fell in the water and drowned himself to death."

"But...?" My spine was ice cold with fear, the word *murder* shrieked in my brain.

"But the report says otherwise," he said, scratching his head. "Something's rotten in Denmark."

"What's the problem?" I asked, innocent as all get out.

"When I saw Booth's body in the pool, I assumed he'd drowned in his own swimming pool," he said. "The only question I thought I had to answer was how'd he get in the pool? Now, there're other questions, lots of them."

I cleared my throat of the giant tree frogs who had taken up residence. "Questions?"

"It appears Booth did not drown," he said.

"What?" I said. "Whatever do you mean?" Lieutenant Columbo couldn't have done it better.

"His autopsy reports indicate his manner of death was consistent with electric shock." Tony put down the report, pulled a file out of his desk drawer, and flipped through what appeared to be photos of LaLa's swimming pool.

"But look," he said. I stood up and walked over to his desk. They were of LaLa's pool. "No electric source near the water."

"Taranto?" We both jumped, and looked up from the photos to see the vice mayor of Palm Beach, the second in command to the mayor of Palm Beach, standing in the doorway. Paul Ilyinsky, the mayor of Palm Beach, is a classy, polite and intelligent leader. Mullen Dumar, his underling, is all that the mayor is not, and seems to fancy himself playing the role of Edward G. Robinson in a gangster movie. He is given to issuing orders and ultimatums, I have heard. I try to avoid him when we're at the same parties.

The man walked into Tony's office. I smelled oil as his greasy head passed my nose. He was wearing a blue blazer, open-collared shirt with an ascot, white slacks and loafers without socks.

"Mullen," Tony said. "How good to see you. Would you like to sit down?"

"Rose, bring us some iced tea," Tony called toward the general area from which his secretary had just disappeared.

"She's gone," I said. "I'll get it." I only said that as an excuse to get out of the office. I knew I was in the way.

"I'll have coffee," the vice mayor coughed, then settled his rotund body into the guest chair and waited for Tony to be seated.

I left the office, then skulked around behind Tony's door, standing so I had a view inside through the crack in the door, but they couldn't see me.

"Chief," he wheezed, pulling a rumpled handkerchief out of his pocket. "I need that you know something."

Tony nodded gravely. "Know what, Mullen?"

"I need that you know that the Prince of Wales is coming to Palm Beach."

Tony smiled. It was not news. The town had been making plans for months to welcome the prince to the Breakers Centennial Ball. Tony sighed. "If it's about the arrangements, I've already spoken to the county about helping us with the detail while the prince is here."

Mullen shook his head, his jowls continuing to move after his head stopped. "No, we have a new problem, and you're the only one who can help us."

Tony wrinkled his brow. "What's the problem?"

Mullen leaned forward, the pressure on his bulging midriff causing his breathing to be even more tortured than normal. "The prince," he said, the sound coming more through his sinuses than his throat. "The prince won't come unless the killer's arrested."

Tony cocked his head. "Killer? What killer?"

Mullen Dumar ran the handkerchief across his face. "Booth Ewen's. The Society Killer. That's what they're calling him in Britain. Those papers you have in your hand went out to the press yesterday through some leak at the hospital, and some British reporter got aholda Booth Ewen's murder and made it sound like there's some sort of lunatic killing people at society parties here. Society killer strikes! Charles at risk!" He drew headlines in the air with his hands.

"Mullen, this is absurd. I don't know who killed Booth, but I know for dammed sure they are no threat to the Prince of Wales, for Christssake."

Mullen Dumar pursed his lips. "You may know that, Tony. Let's say even I know that. But that doesn't matter, now does it?"

Tony cocked an eyebrow. "It doesn't?"

Mullen lifted himself laboriously from the chair. "Nope." He walked around the chair and braced his hands on the back.

"It doesn't matter, because we don't matter, you and me. The prince matters. And those people who are giving parties for him when he comes, they matter. And the mayor, he matters. And all of these people have to believe the prince is going to be safe."

Tony leaned back in his chair, apparently still not quite sure what he was supposed to say.

"As I mentioned, the county...."

"County, shmounty." Mullen leaned over the chair, his breathing audible. "Do I have to spell it out for you, Tony? I thought you was smarter."

Tony smiled grimly. "I thought I was, too, Mullen. What do you want me to do?"

Mullen Dumar wadded his handkerchief into a ball and stuffed it into his pocket, then turned and walked to the door.

"Arrest somebody," he said softly as he got to the doorway.

Tony stood up. "But...."

Mullen's voice was deep and feral, coming from somewhere within his throat. "Arrest somebody," he ordered. "And do it soon." He pulled open the door and walked out.

He didn't see me.

When he was out of sight, I went back into the office.

"Son of a bitch," Tony said. "Can we skip lunch? I gotta think."

"Come to dinner tonight," I said. "We need to talk."

"Okay."

"See you at seven."

I left for Whitehall to tell Peep someone was following her. I drove south to Cocoanut Walk and then east to Whitehall, built to be within walking distance of Flagler's first hotel, the Royal Poinciana, which closed during the Depression.

I parked out front with the tourists and walked up the imposing sidewalk to the front of the white-columned mansion. Flagler built the home in 1902 for his third wife, Mary Lily. He divorced wife number two after having her committed to an asylum in 1895 and spent a few years playing the field. He finally convinced Mary Lily to marry him by bestowing on her one thousand shares of Standard Oil stock and building her Whitehall. The home still represented to me the very essence of Palm Beach. If the Breakers is the pulse of Palm Beach, Whitehall is its heart.

My Nikes squeaked on the marble floors as I made a beeline for Peep, talking to some tourists near the columns at the far end of the Marble Hall, what some might call the "living room" of the mansion. Or maybe it's a 140-by-40-foot foyer.

Anyway, I caught up with her, snarled at the tourists to chase them away, and when they were out of earshot, said, "I saw him."

"I didn't see you," she said, hands on Chanel-covered hips, stomping one sensible, low-heeled Ferragamo. "I thought you'd forgotten."

"I didn't."

"So, who was it?"

I grabbed her by an elbow and steered her a few feet away and into the Elizabethan Breakfast Room, so called because the table only seats six instead of twelve, like the Francis I Dining Room. Ornate homes make me itch.

"I don't know," I admitted.

Her bottom lip popped out and her eyes narrowed. "Just what was the point of having you follow me if we still don't know who it is?"

I leaned against a door jamb and threw my arms up in supplication. "I'm sorry. The windows were tinted and I couldn't see."

"Did you get the tag number?"

I tightened my lips. "I missed it."

She looked away.

"Peep, I'm sorry. I'll get him next time."

"If there is a next time," she said, sullen.

"Don't be overdramatic."

She reached up and grabbed me by the shoulder with one hand. "LaLa says there's danger. She saw Death in the cards and it happened. Now she says we are all in danger."

I didn't know what to say—I'm not one to put too much stock in LaLa's communications with the spirits. But I also know lots of things happen that we can't explain. My reasoning: If we believe in God, whom we cannot prove exists, who is to say other things we cannot prove exist are not also true?

But I was pretty sure there was nobody after Peep; I couldn't think of a reason anyone would be.

"I have to go see Taffy," I said. "Wanna go?"

Her eyes flew open in surprise. "Why on Earth would you go see Taffy?"

"She asked me to, last night."

"Mmmph."

"What?"

"Nothing." She waved me off, distracted, and wandered out into the hall. I followed her back to the front door, where another tour group awaited.

She turned her back on them and whispered to me, "I'm going to St. Augustine to talk to Desdemona. I want to find out if Mitch followed her like he's following me."

"I don't think your own husband would follow you," I said, trying to maintain the tone of someone who is reasoning with her friend and not put the hell out with her for being such a ninny. "And what the hell good do you think it's going to do you to talk to his ex-wife? I think you've lost your mind."

She stiffened as if I had slapped her, turned on her heel and walked a few feet. Then she turned, raised a pointed finger and aimed it at me.

"You are no better than he is, not taking me seriously. You just leave me alone and don't worry about it—but when I end up in some funny farm somewhere—or worse—you remember what I said."

She stalked back to her tour group.

Confused, dejected and not a little angry at almost everybody I knew, I went back to my car.

A few minutes later, I pulled up in front of Taffy's house, tires crunching in her gravel drive. Her black Mercedes S600 was in the driveway. I noticed that her front door was ajar—quite the welcome, I thought.

I pushed the door open and stuck my head inside.

"Taffy?"

No answer.

No doubt by the pool swigging something cool and exotic, I thought, and stepped lightly toward the back of the house. The air in the dark foyer was cool and dry—typical super-cooled Florida interior temperature. Harry Connick Jr. was crooning a love song to somebody via the wall speakers of the inbuilt home entertainment center.

Taffy's house was one of those estates where you walk a labyrinth of rooms to get from the front to the back, and I didn't notice anything amiss until I neared the Florida room, a casual, enclosed room with windows and sliding glass doors that can be opened or closed, depending on the outside temperature.

Florida rooms are handy down here—thus the name—because Floridians love to sit outside but must deal with rain, bugs and the occasional cool night. Taffy's Florida room opened out onto her pool patio.

Anyway, as I approached the Florida room I felt humidity blanket my skin and the temperature went up—a sure sign a door or window was open somewhere.

Sure enough, one of the sliding glass doors in the wall of glass doors that spanned the back of the house was open—and with temperatures and the humidity in the 80s, that was like throwing money out the window of a moving car.

So I was curious.

I went through the door, closing it behind me. The pool area was quiet. There was a tray of drinks on the table—Bellinis again, I saw—and next to it a stack of scrapbooks and photographs. Taffy was sitting in her chaise lounge, which was pointed away from me and toward the pool.

"Taffy," I said. "It's Wally."

She didn't turn around.

Still in a fog of naiveté, I walked around her chair, still talking. "Well, when you said...."

I stopped when I got to where I was facing her.

She wasn't listening.

She wasn't even breathing.

She was dressed in a Lilly sheath, Chanel sandals and her triple strand of pearls.

The dress was twisted a little, around her knees, as if she had shifted her weight and gotten it caught underneath her.

One of her shoes had come off, and lay near her foot, on the chaise.

The pearls were hanging around her neck, loosely draped beneath a deep red strangle mark on her neck, which was bent sideways; her head lolled near her shoulder.

Her mouth was open.

Her eyes were open.

She was dead.

A door slammed.

I jumped. It had not occurred to me Taffy and I were not alone. I crept back to the Florida room door and peered inside. Was there someone here with me?

I hated to be silly. Maybe it was her maid, coming back home. Maybe the wind had blown a door shut. Maybe Taffy had invited someone else over. I felt a little foolish about the goose bumps charging at full speed up from the base of my spine to the back of my neck.

On the other hand, people were turning up dead of unnatural causes, and some prudence was in order.

All the television shows where women walk through dark rooms while the killer lurks behind the door raced through my mind. I pictured myself being overpowered by someone with a gun, a knife and a grenade, holding me at bay and doing seriously painful things to my body.

Slowly, I slipped into the Florida room. Keeping my back up against the wall, I crept front-side out around the room, as if keeping my flank covered would protect me from the devil himself.

Feeling thoroughly foolish, I rounded the corner of the doorway back into the living room, shoulder blades hugging the door jam like a cat scratching its back on a scratching post.

I heard a car engine, then tires crunching on gravel.

Lurching forward, I made it to the front door in three steps—noticing that it was closed, when I knew I had left it open—and flung it open in time to see what I had assumed was Taffy's Mercedes spraying gravel every which way as it pulled full speed out onto El Brillo Way.

My heart was going just as fast as the car, and while I was tempted to see if my car could catch up to it, I knew it was hopeless. For one thing, my car is not the most powerful engine in town, and can't really hold candlepower to a Mercedes.

For another thing, the Mercedes was already, no doubt, on South County and I had no idea which way it was going.

And for the last thing, I knew my urge to get in the car and drive off was more a serious desire to just get myself the hell out of whatever was happening here.

I went back out to the swimming pool, called Tony on my cell phone and sat down to wait for him in a wrought iron chair at a table near the unfortunate Taffy, who did not look her loveliest.

Having twice seen death up close in less than a week, I am qualified to tell you it does not look in real life like it looks on television. On television and in the movies, when people die, they look pretty much like they did when they were alive. Oh, their eyes may stay open until someone gently reaches over and closes them. Or their heads may loll backwards onto a bed or a chair. They may even have bullet holes in them and fall off a horse.

But real death doesn't look like that. Real death is a head hung at an angle that functioning muscles will not allow. Real death is glazed eyes half open, half closed. No actor can portray the utter lack of humanity that comes only when the soul departs the earthly shell, leaving it with as much life as shed snakeskin.

So I was trying not to look at Taffy, out of respect for what I know would have been the wishes of a woman whose life was pretty much dedicated to looking good, when my cell phone rang.

"Wally?" LaLa said.

"Yeah."

"My spirit guide is telling me you are in danger."

"Where are you?"

"In my car. You need to find Peep. She told me when she leaves Hermes she's going to St. Augustine to find Desdemona. Don't let her do that—it will be dangerous for her."

"Speaking of danger—"

She interrupted. "We are all in mortal danger."

"Well, some more than others."

"What do you mean?"

"Taffy's dead. I'm sitting by her pool looking at her...." I meant to say "body," but couldn't get it out. "At her," I finished lamely.

There was a long silence, with only the sound of LaLa's Mercedes in the background.

"What are you doing there?"

"Taffy invited me—last night."

"Why would you go—knowing what you know? Knowing she slept with my husband? You are bringing some very bad karma on yourself."

"I'm sorry, LaLa. It's not like I was coming to be her friend or something. I just came, that's all."

There was another silence. Then nothing. My best friend had hung up on me. I watched a Florida lizard zip across the patio and felt lower than his little green tummy.

"Fine mess you've gotten us in."

I jumped for the third time that day.

"Hells bells, Tony. You scared the stuffing out of me."

He grinned wryly and motioned toward Taffy. "I scared you?" he said, with an emphasis on the I.

I shrugged, grumpy and frightened. "Can I go home?"

"No. Sit." He turned around and walked back out to the front, and when I saw him next he was followed by two Palm Beach cops carrying bags of equipment.

A hour later, I was sitting in the front seat of Tony's car, headed to my house. He had refused to let me drive home, citing his invitation to dinner as the excuse. We both knew I wasn't in any shape to get behind the wheel of a multi-ton hunk of steel, and I called Petal on my cell phone to tell her not to panic when the police car rolled into the driveway.

"You know," he said, making conversation, "After two tours of duty in cramped tents in Nam and twenty years in low-budget FBI cars, I swore I'd never again take a job where I'd spend more time in a car than it took to get me from place to place. But here I am, continually driving around three and three-quarter square miles."

"Why did you come back?" I asked. "Wasn't this a step backward for you?"

"I needed something to do," he said. "After my wife died, my son moved halfway around the world to run an American conglomerate in Japan, and suddenly I was alone."

In his rearview mirror, I watched the cars stack up behind us on South County Road. They'd pass any other car at a breakneck speed. Ironic that Tony could save lives just by driving around in a patrol car.

Tony took a left on Barton, then a right into our driveway. He came around and opened my car door for me. Petal rushed out of our front door in a state of anxiety I thought was more like what I should be showing. But I felt numb. The world seemed to be revolving around me, but I couldn't quite catch up.

Pitt wasn't home yet, Petal said. She hustled me out to the small but lushly landscaped patio area around our pool—not realizing the sinister place pool patios were beginning to assume in my life—and sat me down in a sunny spot. Tony followed.

"You just sit right here," Petal said. "I'll get drinks."

She brought a pitcher of martinis. Desperate times called for desperate measures, or something.

"Tony, what's going on?" I said, when Petal had gone back inside.

He shook his head. "I wish I knew, Wally. None of this makes any sense to me."

"Are you going to arrest LaLa?"

There was a long, long silence.

"Here's the deal. I can't arrest LaLa. I don't have any evidence against her, even though she would normally be the most obvious suspect. But I have to solve this crime, and I have to arrest somebody, or I may not have a job when contract time rolls around. Do you understand?"

I nodded.

"So I am looking pretty hard at what kind of evidence I do have," he said. "I'll give you a rundown."

He snagged a sterling silver toothpick from the little sterling cup next to the bowl of olives, and placed it on the glass top of the table, idly rotating it.

"One, it appears Booth did not die accidentally, as I told you."

He picked up another toothpick and put it at a diagonal to the one on the table. "Two, Booth did not die of drowning in his own swimming pool."

He picked up a third toothpick and lay it so it was pointing straight down, at a diagonal to the second. "Three, if Booth did not die at home, then somebody—and LaLa is the obvious suspect—is lying."

I pressed my lips together and kept my eyes on the table.

"I won't arrest her just because they are pressuring me," he said. "But I will if I think she did it," he said.

"And four, I have witnesses that overheard LaLa and Booth arguing at Peep's house at the Garden Club Gala. And I will have to report that to the DA." He put an olive at the bottom end of the third toothpick.

On the table, dotted with the olive, was a sterling silver question mark.

Chapter Thirteen

SATURDAY, DEC. 28

The Beach Session
by Rezna Van Daly
Society Editor, The Palm Beach Tattler

Christie had her Indians. Hammett had his falcon. And it seems, my dears, that Palm Beach has its own little mystery right here in town.

Did Booth Ewen drown in his own pool the night of the Garden Club Gala? Or did he die of some other cause?

Once again, the Palm Beach Garden Club Holiday Gala has been the scene of what one reluctantly must refer to as a murder.

We are shocked to discover that Booth Ewen's death was caused not by his drowning in his own swimming pool, as previously reported, but by electric current passing through his body. How such a high voltage exposure occurred is still a mystery that puts a new light—once again—on last year's unfortunate events.

To add insult to injury, it seems that Taffy Merriman Povitch, long time Town socialite, has been spotted wearing her pearls in an—shall we say—inappropriate venue.

Taffy's death illustrates that some people just don't know the worth of Tiffany pearls, or they would certainly not use them as a weapon.

Where are our values?

You don't ignore a summons from Rezna Van Daly, so when she called Saturday morning and wanted to see me in her office, I agreed to meet her for breakfast.

I pulled into a diagonal parking space on Royal Poinciana Way across from Testa's, the town's oldest restaurant.

It was a gorgeous Palm Beach morning, the air cool but dry, the sun coming up blazing. I lucked into a table in the awning-covered outdoor seating area; on a Saturday morning at this time of the year there's usually a waiting line.

While I waited, I sipped on a raspberry iced tea, a house specialty, and watched people stroll by. Though I worked at not letting it happen, my mind kept rolling back to what I had seen the day before.

Rezna arrived amidst a flurry of attendants—a driver who rushed around to open the door of her Mercedes, a secretary who followed her from the sidewalk to the front rail of the restaurant, taking intense notes on a steno pad as Rezna talked nonstop, and another lackey whose job was not clear but who hopped to attention outside the door of the car.

She spotted me at the table by the front rail, waved off her entourage, nodded at the two young women greeting guests at the *maitre d'* stand, and marched to the table.

One of the young women hurried behind her with menus, which she placed in front of us as soon as Rezna was seated.

"Coffee," Rezna barked. Then apparently realizing she wasn't giving orders to her own crew, she changed her facial expression to a beatific beam. "Please," she cooed, fluttering a hand ever so beseechingly, putting on her best society editor manners.

When they brought her coffee, I ordered the blueberry pancakes and she ordered an English muffin. Then I sat back and waited to find out what she wanted.

"What's going on?" she demanded.

I shook my head wearily. "Wish I knew."

She reached over and grabbed my wrist with an age-spotted but soft, perfectly manicured hand, making me aware of my own stubby nails and cracked cuticles.

"I got a call," she said. Her hair was pulled back in a turban and worry lines converged in the middle of her forehead.

"And?" I said, thinking she was being pretty dramatic about something.

She cut her eyes back and forth and then locked them on mine. "It was a threat," she said in a stage whisper. "Somebody—I couldn't tell if it was a man or a woman—told me if I wrote another word about Breakers Babies it would be the last word I wrote."

I sat up. "What the...?"

"That's not all," she said. "Call Reggie. You have to hear his story."

As the waitress brought our breakfast a Mercedes pulled up in front of the restaurant and Rezna glanced over as her driver hopped out and ran around to the passenger door.

"Got to run, dear," she said, blotting her lips with her napkin. She made her way to the Mercedes and got in without another glance.

Puzzled, I finished my pancakes with whipped cream, had another raspberry tea, and tried to sort things out. Since I had a lot of thinking to do, I polished off her untouched muffin with strawberry jam.

Booth had been bragging about something the night he died. I couldn't remember what—so much had happened since then, that it hadn't crossed my mind again until now. Why? Because Taffy had been bursting to share something with me—gossip, I had assumed— the night before she was killed.

What was it they wanted to tell me?

I pulled my phone out of my purse and called the Breakers, asked for Reggie and waited. In a minute, he came to the phone. I told him Rezna wanted me to talk to him and that I'd be right over.

When I got there, he was sitting in his office—still not completely back together since the robbery—wringing his hands.

He looked like he was going to cry.

"My history," he said, tugging at the lapel of his crimson coat.

I sat down across from his desk. "I don't understand, Reggie."

"All they stole were my historical files," he said.

Now I understood. The history of the Breakers was as dear to Reggie as their own family history is to some people. He had lived much of it, doted on all of it, loved to share it.

I was at a loss as to how to commiserate with this. "Is there anything I can do?" I asked.

"Yes," he said. "There is. In the basement of the Palm Beach County Courthouse, there are all kind of original records such as newspapers from before the turn of the century and the books they used to use for recording births, deaths and marriages before they started using computers."

I waited. I wasn't sure what this had to do with me.

"I can't go down there," he said. "I have asthma. That kind of dust and mold could kill me. But you can."

"Me?"

"Yes," he said. "Remember, you need a birth certificate? While you are there, you can search through those records for information about goings on at the Breakers. It's there—I just know it. If you can get me copies, I can get started rebuilding my files. I've only got three days."

"Why three days?" I asked.

"New Year's Eve," he said. "The Breakers Centennial Ball is New Year's Eve and we are going to have the procession of Breakers Babies. My list was in that box. I have to have a list, or the whole thing will be chaos."

"Is it really that important?" I asked gently.

He sat up and ran his hand across his shiny, bald dome.

"It's the most important thing there is," he said. "It's history. It's truth."

How do you argue with that? I didn't. I promised him I would go to the courthouse on Monday, and walked slowly through the crowded hotel lobby back out to the *porte cochere*.

I handed the valet my ticket and was waiting for him to bring my car around when my phone rang. I pulled it out of my bag and answered. It was LaLa.

"You've got to get here to Peep's right now," she said.

"I'm...."

"I said now," she snapped. "She's getting in her Jaguar and saying she's going to St. Augustine."

"I'll be right there," I said as the valet pulled up with my car. I slapped a five into his hand, hopped in and started the engine. I almost ran down a little old lady on my way around the circle, gunned it when I passed her, and swung my car in a perilously speedy turn onto South County Road.

It took me five minutes to get to Peep's, and another five to talk her out of her Jaguar keys and into the deal that I would drive her and LaLa to St. Augustine.

We took a detour. Thus it was that at four o'clock that afternoon, I pulled Peep's Jag into a gravel parking lot so small the car took up all the available space. If anyone wanted to back out of their space, they would have to wait until we moved on. Luckily, no one was leaving the little parking lot at the hotel in Cassadaga, a tiny town established to be a home for spiritualists.

We climbed out of the car at the corner of the hotel, which had a covered porch that ran along the entire short block length of the hotel. White railing ran between simple white columns along the porch.

We walked up the steps at the corner of the building and into a small cafe-type sitting area leading into a gift shop and the hotel lobby. The hotel lobby consisted of a few more tables and a check-in desk about five feet long. There was a door between the check-in desk and the gift shop so that one person could handle both duties.

Peep dropped to a seat at a table with an ashtray, and LaLa headed to the desk to check us in. She had convinced Peep that stopping in this little town was the logical first step to a visit with her husband's loopy ex-wife.

I sat down next to Peep and looked around. Three bored-looking, middle-aged women sat at a table in the corner, drinking coffee and smoking cigarettes. Alone in the room, they appeared to be doing nothing but hanging around.

I pegged them as being some of the spiritualist residents of the hotel. I call them psychics. LaLa always corrects me and says they call themselves mediums. Whatever. I'd came to the little town with LaLa once before and heard the story of the nineteenth century spiritualists who decided to establish their own little town where they could set up their own church. Out of the fifty or so homes in the little crossroads town, about half are owned by practicing mediums. Like stockbrokers to Wall Street or lawyers to Washington, D.C., I guess mediums are drawn to Cassadaga as a place where their particular skills are understood and appreciated.

LaLa was walking toward our table from the lobby when one of the women caught sight of her. "Does she know you're here?" the woman asked.

LaLa nodded. "She always does."

The woman nodded and looked away. LaLa sat down at our table.

Peep's eyes were wide. "How does she know?"

"It's a community of mediums, Peep. They just know."

I couldn't help a small scoff. "You called and made an appointment, didn't you, LaLa?"

She nodded sheepishly.

"How the hell else do you think they know?" I asked Peep. "You think the psychics just know who's going to show up every day?"

"Medium," LaLa corrected.

"Furthermore," I said, feeling a bit grumpy after the long drive, "I once met a psychic who was divorced. Now wouldn't you think they would know better?"

"Ahem," LaLa said, and looked up, behind me.

I felt something brush my shoulder and looked up into the ample bosoms of a woman in a bright red, button-front shirt that was challenged to cover all it was charged with covering.

LaLa laughed. "See? I told you. This is Velma Myrtlewood."

The woman looked at us with some disapproval, especially me, I thought, but didn't say anything.

"I'd like my friends to come along, okay, Velma?"

The woman nodded and stepped back. "Sure. Come along."

I followed Velma, LaLa and Peep up a narrow wooden staircase into a hotel hallway lined with simple doors. I could easily reach out and touch both walls of the hallway, so the postage stamp room that she led us into wasn't a big surprise. It had two rectangular frame windows; one housed a window air conditioning unit, the other was open, its frame raised to open a screenless, two-foot hole that had a view of the top of the roof of the outside porch.

LaLa went to a worn wooden chair at a cheap round table covered with a lace shawl. I backed into a plastic lawn chair on the other side of the table and Peep primly settled herself into a faded armchair between us.

Velma closed the door behind us. "Tea?"

I shook my head, as did Peep, but LaLa nodded. When Velma left the room—to go into a kitchen, I assumed—LaLa leaned over and whispered to me.

"Please don't tell anybody about this, okay? What would people think?"

"For God's sake, LaLa, Nancy Reagan used to consult a psychic before she would make out Ronnie's activities for the day. People are used to this stuff."

Peep nodded her head. "It's downright fashionable, LaLa."

LaLa trapped a piece of flyaway hair and tried to anchor it behind one ear. It escaped. "Nancy Reagan got astrological charts done, not readings," she said. "Anyway, I think the fashion has passed," she said. "So many of those people coming through Palm Beach were charlatans, now I think people think...well, it's a bit suspect."

This coming from a woman who keeps dead friends in her back yard and has a spirit guide located somewhere in the beyond. I was suspecting something myself. "You mean you don't want people to know right now, right after Booth's death, don't you?"

LaLa took a sip of the tea Velma had just set in front of her. "If you must know, yes. I don't need people thinking I'm strange, now, do I?"

I almost laughed, but Velma shot me a look, so I settled back and waited to see what was going to happen.

Velma settled herself into the chair opposite Peep. She pulled out some cards. "Tell me your birthdays."

"Don't know," I said.

"Don't know?"

"I was orphaned at about age one," I said. "So I don't know, exactly."

"Hmm," she said, then looked at Peep.

"Do I have to?" Peep said.

"Yes," LaLa said.

Peep poked a lip out. "June six."

"Time and year, please," Velma said.

"Midnight," Peep said. "Nineteen forty-four."

Velma picked up the tarot cards.

Slowly, she lay them down in a pattern, looking at each one as she did.

As she lay the cards on the table, LaLa looked at me. "Did I tell you Velma told me Booth was going to die?"

I sat up straight. "Did she tell you who was going to kill him?"

Velma reached up and tugged at a Mamie Eisenhower bang in deep auburn, looking at me. "And what would you want me to do about it if I knew?"

"Tell the police, of course," I said.

She shrugged and gave me a patronizing look. Then she patted a card. "I'm a little worried about what I'm seeing here. For all of you. Do you want to hear it?"

LaLa nodded emphatically. Peep shrugged. I just stared at her, experiencing a menopausal moment of annoyance at being ignored.

"I'll start with you," she said to me. She pointed at a card. "There's something you value that you are in danger of losing. Or someone."

I sat up. "Where do you see that? Is someone going to die?"

Velma patted another card. "Someone already has. No, I see this as you separating yourself from something you don't know that you value."

LaLa looked at me. "Is that true, Wally?"

I shifted uncomfortably. "Not forever," I said, half under my breath.

"What?" Peep said, leaning on the table.

Velma silently replaced the cards Peep had pushed out of place and watched me with sharp eyes. "One more thing," she said. "You will find something you didn't know you lost."

I sighed. "Before all this happened—Booth—I was thinking of moving to Boston."

"Does Pitt have a new job?" Peep asked.

"Obviously not, Peep," LaLa said. "Think about it."

Peep did, for a second. "You are thinking about leaving Pitt?" she said in amazement. "You love Pitt."

I nodded. I agreed. I did love Pitt. But I didn't love Palm Beach and lately I had felt out of sorts and out of place. Inexplicably, since I had—except for college—never lived anywhere else. But it was as if I had suddenly awakened from a dream that had been meaningful while I slept. But I couldn't remember the dream, no matter how much I reached for it. It was bugging me.

"I'm not thinking about leaving the marriage," I said. "Just the town. Pitt comes to Boston. We could commute. People do it."

Peep put on a pout. "Well, you can't. I need you."

LaLa nodded. "I need you, too, Wally."

I didn't know what to say, so I stood up and walked into the kitchenette where Velma had made the tea. I pulled one of six or seven unmatched drinking glasses from a shelf over the counter and ran tap water into it. By the time I went back into the living room, I had worked myself into a little fit of resentment. I wasn't sure against what.

"Stop trying to make me feel bad," I said. "You know I've never felt part of Palm Beach."

Peep shook her head. "No, I didn't."

LaLa nodded in agreement. "Neither did I."

I shrugged. "Well, maybe neither did I...frankly, this has just come on me. Maybe it's the realization that I'm two-thirds of the way through my life. Maybe it's...I don't know what brought this on."

I took a deep breath. "Go on, Velma. Get onto somebody else, would you?"

Velma glanced up at Peep. "Someone is following you."

Peep gasped. "Yes."

Velma nodded. "That person does not wish you well."

"Who is it?" I asked, sorry I hadn't taken Peep more seriously.

"I can't tell," Velma said. "But there's a shadow—someone shadowing her. It's odd—almost as if they are shadowing each other."

Peep grabbed my hand and squeezed. "Tell me more."

"I can't," Velma said. She looked at LaLa. "But you are going to lose something, too. A possession. Something you own or possess."

LaLa's blue eyes sparkled with, what? Unshed tears? "I lost a husband," she said.

"Something else," Velma said, tapping another card. "Someone from your past coming back into your life. Plus, I see a danger in motion and a loss of freedom."

Peep stared balefully at her unlit cigarette and picked up a cookie instead. "Maybe you're going to prison."

"Peep," I said. "Cut that out."

"Sorry," she said. "Just kidding, LaLa."

"That's not funny," LaLa said.

"Well," Peep said, "you never should have married Booth and if you did go to prison for killing him, it would be worth it. He was a rat when you married him and he was a rat until the day he died. He and Eaton never got along and Eaton used to say Booth had no right to walk the streets. And I saw him cut Eaton dead at parties; not even speak to him. You know the reason we never socialized as couples is because Booth and Eaton didn't speak."

I held up a hand but Peep was getting worked up and didn't stop.

"LaLa," Peep said. "Why did you marry that man anyway? We told you Booth wasn't good for you, you didn't listen. Where was your precious spirit guide then, eh?"

I touched LaLa's shoulder, which was uncharacteristically clenched tightly toward her neck. She brushed my hand away and glared at Peep.

"My spirit guide has gotten me through things you'll never know about or understand, Peep. But who do you think you are, telling anybody who to marry? Why, you just married a man who had his own wife put in a rest home. Do you think that's a good move?"

Peep opened her mouth but LaLa kept talking.

"Let me tell you this, Peep, if you think you are so smart. Booth told me Mitch told him he made Desdemona go into the hospital because she wouldn't have a face lift and she had gained weight and he didn't want to take her to parties anymore. So he made her go away. How's that for picking a husband, hon? I guess you'd better put that cookie down or you'll be in some hospital before long, too."

Peep looked at LaLa and at the cookie in her hand.

Slowly, she lowered it to the plate.

Chapter Fourteen

SUNDAY, DECEMBER 29

After an hour-long drive through silence as dense as a lowland fog, we arrived at Flagler Resort, a pricey hideaway for wealthy women unable to cope with reality. We found the "resort," which looked more like the campus of a small and very expensive girls college, amid moss-draped live oaks in the countryside between historic St. Augustine and the St. Johns River.

I parked and we walked into the Spanish-style administration building, the largest building in our view. Surrounding it were what looked like dozens of tiny fairy cottages. Resident cottages, I supposed. Small, but lush.

We walked into a spic-and-span circular reception room, with a tile-topped desk forming a smaller circle in the center of the room. White-uniformed staff turned to look at us from their little fortress.

In the lobby area, several women sat at a wooden table playing cards. Near them, several other women sat knitting or reading. Residents, I assumed. They were all nicely dressed, coifed, nails manicured. They were well tended.

Peep put her hands tentatively on the tile.

"I'm looking for Desdemona...Fenton," she said.

A receptionist walked over, took a slow measure of the number and size of jewels on Peep's fingers—an impressive array, if I do say so—and smiled broadly.

"And whom may I say is asking?"

"Mrs.—"

"Her sister-in-law," I interrupted. "Bringing presents from the family."

Peep shrugged. "That's right. Presents."

The receptionist pursed her lips and frowned. The others in the center of the circle went back to their business. A few of the residents were staring.

"Mrs. Fenton..."

"Yes?" Peep said.

Luckily, the nurse thought Peep was encouraging her, not answering, so she continued. "is no longer in residence here...exactly," she said.

Peep blinked at her.

I moved closer. "No longer in residence?" I repeated. "What do you mean?"

The nurse cleared her throat. "I just assumed she had told her family...I mean, she told us she contacted Mr. Fenton but...."

"We need for you to be a little more helpful here, Miss...Nugent," I said, reading the ID badge she wore.

"Yes, well. Mrs. Fenton is traveling extensively in Europe. She keeps her room here, but she has not been here for some time. She sends postcards from her travels, but I am not," she said firmly, "allowed to give you any more information. I shouldn't have told you that. It was Mrs. Fenton's request that her family not know that she is traveling."

"What?" Peep's mouth was working up to asking more questions, but I knew from the expression on the receptionist's face we weren't going to get any more answers. I grabbed Peep's arm and tugged. As we left, I put my card on the tile, asking to be notified if they heard from her.

Just outside the massive mission doors, a frail, white-haired woman approached me. "Don't let them know I talked to you," she said. Her voice was aged, soft and frightened.

"Who are you?" I asked.

"I can't tell you," the woman said, looking around nervously. "But find Darla Dugan and you'll find Desdemona Fenton."

"What?"

"Desdemona left with Darla," she said. "We were all friends. We ate dinner together. And when Darla said she was going home, she asked Desdemona if she wanted to come with her. She went."

"But Darla..." I started.

"New Smyrna," the woman said as she turned and walked, hunched and slow, back into the building. "End of the spit, last house at the very southern tip end of the island."

We got back into the car in silence.

"Food," I said. "We need food and we need it now. It will give us time to think."

I turned the car toward St. Augustine, where a charming historic district has been built around the town's legacy of being one of the first Spanish settlements in the New World.

Thirty minutes later, we had placed our orders from a roughhewn wooden booth in the middle of a small, period-theme restaurant smack in the center of St. Augustine's Old Town.

Peep looked at me and shook her head. We were all trying to make some sense out of what we had heard.

"How the hell can she just be gone?" Peep said.

LaLa leaned over the scarred wood table toward Peep. "It's not so difficult, Peep. She was in there voluntarily. She always has been able to check out any time she wanted."

"But Mitch will be furious."

"Why?"

Peep opened her mouth to answer but held her reply when a waiter dressed as a monk deposited a cheeseburger on a pewter plate in front of me, removing the two empty vodka glasses in front of Peep and replacing them with a full one. "Aren't you going to order, dearie?" he said to Peep.

"When I damn well want to, sweetie," she snapped. The monk nodded and backed away, and Peep lit a cigarette.

"Mitch...hates it when he doesn't know about things." She flicked an ash and took a deep drag. "He's pretty adamant about knowing everything that goes on."

I chewed thoughtfully on my burger and swallowed. "She's not his wife anymore."

Peep nodded. "I know, but...I've heard him on the phone with the rest home and...well, I know how he is with me, so I guess he was the same way with her."

I didn't know. "You mean he keeps up with your whereabouts?"

"It's more like he acts like I can't make any decision for myself. Like, if I say I'm going to work at the Flagler Museum, he'll say, 'Is that the best use of your time, Peep?' as if to question whether I should do that or something else."

"Just about the museum?" I asked. The monk arrived with a steaming pewter bowl of corn chowder for LaLa. "You're going to eat something," I said to Peep. "House salad for her," I told the waiter, pointing at Peep. "And lots of bread." The monk nodded.

"Oh, no," Peep said, ignoring the exchange between me and the waiter. "If I say I'm going to have veal for dinner, Mitch'll say something like, 'If that's what you think you want,' like I'm not making the best decision, but he'll just let me go ahead and make a mistake."

LaLa blew on her spoonful of chowder. "Do you mean he questions everything you do?"

"Yes, that's exactly what I mean. Say, I'm going to the Garden Club, he'll say, 'Do you really think the Garden Club has enough prestige for you, Peep?' Or, if I'm going shopping, and I say I'm going to Sak's, he'll say, 'Why don't you shop at Lily's? She has better clothes?' Do you see?"

I put my chin on my hands. "So, he's not going to like it that Desdemona left without telling him? They haven't been married for years, you know."

"You don't do things without telling Mitch. He doesn't like it. And he paid her bills, so even though he didn't have any communication with her, he'll be mad that she left and didn't tell him."

I thought about that. "I don't think he's going to like the Flagler Resort's explanation that they didn't notify him because she told them to keep her bungalow—that she would be back."

Peep shook her head emphatically. "He especially won't like that. It means he's been paying for a bungalow she wasn't living in."

The monk deposited a salad and a basket heaped with rolls in front of her.

I picked up a roll, broke it in two, and handed her half. "Eat up," I said.

"You know," Peep said slowly. "I've been afraid if I stayed with Mitch for twenty-five years I might turn into what he says I am."

"What does he say you are?" I asked.

Peep tried to stop her hand from shaking as she brought a forkful of lettuce to her mouth. "Crazy," she said. "But I'm crazy like a fox. We're going to New Smyrna."

We drove south on I-95 and crossed the bridge to New Smyrna Beach, an upscale little beach community. Once on the barrier island, I turned south. I suggested we stop for directions but LaLa shook her head.

"I'm getting a vibe," she said. "It's right up here. On the ocean."

A few miles later she practically shouted, "Here!" and I stopped at the entry gates to a walled ocean estate. Woven into the wrought iron gates was a giant letter D.

"Dugan," I said. "Now what?"

"Hang on," LaLa said, and hopped out of the Jaguar. She ran up to the gates and pushed on them. They moved. She pushed on one gate until it was open wide enough for me to get a car through. After that, she climbed back in and we drove through the open gate and down a sand-covered path toward a mansion amid the dunes.

The Mediterranean stucco building was surrounded by overgrown weeds.

"She's not taking care of her place very well, is she?" LaLa said.

"Well, she's been in Palm Beach," I said.

Peep bristled. "One has servants," she huffed.

I shrugged. Darla Dugan obviously did not have servants, or if she did, they were very bad at their jobs. I pulled up under a stucco portico wide enough to accommodate three cars. We all got out, and I pushed on the double front doors. One of them swung open.

"Ain't nobody here," a voice rang out from inside. A man's voice.

"Holy crap," I said. Not too brightly, I stepped through the door to see a foyer leading to an expensively furnished living room. Something was odd, though, and I couldn't figure it out for a second. Then I realized. No lights. Despite the somewhat overcast day outside and a darkly furnished interior filled with heavy furniture and draped windows, there were no lights on.

"Go away!" the voice called, from somewhere off to the rear.

Huddled together like three teenagers in a slasher movie, we walked through the house. Head poking out from behind dark drapes, cringed a short, emaciated man with a full beard and bad teeth.

"Who the hell are you?" I asked, moving towards him.

Suddenly the head disappeared. The curtains moved, and he was gone. I walked over and pulled on the curtains, revealing an open French door. The man was scuttling down some stairs leading to the beach from the greenest, scuzziest swimming pool I have ever seen. He disappeared around a corner of the house.

"A homeless man, I guess," I said as I walked back into the room. "We'd better tell Darla when we get back that she needs to check on her house." I looked around and vowed to thank Petal for keeping my house in order. The house reeked with a sour, acrid smell. It didn't look any better. Papers lay on the floor; pictures hung at odd angles on the walls; dishes encrusted with food grew mold on tables.

The question on all of our minds: What was an heiress with her fortune doing abandoning such a grand oceanfront estate? And where had Desdemona gone when she left Darla Dugan's? I remembered Desdemona as waif-thin, a wispy, clingy sort of person with Coke-bottle glasses. I couldn't imagine where a person like that would run to.

We climbed back into the car and drove south with little productive conversation. We crossed Lake Worth on the Flagler Memorial Bridge and were driving east on Royal Poinciana Way when I looked in the rearview mirror.

"You're not going to believe this," I said. "But there's a black Mercedes S600 with tinted windows following us."

It was pretty close behind the Jag, just a half a car length. I tapped my brakes. The Mercedes didn't slow down. He was literally on my bumper.

"Oh, my God," Peep breathed.

"Danger in motion," LaLa shrieked, just as the Mercedes pulled around on my right side, pulling so close to the Jag I could see the dirt on the tinted windshield.

Frightened, I slammed on my brakes to let the Mercedes get past me, then floored it. I accidentally pulled on the steering wheel, sending us all into a full tilt.

"Wally no!" Peep screamed, and I jerked the steering wheel back the other way. The Mercedes slowed down and pulled even closer to my right side, and there was nowhere to go.

I was trying to decide what to do when I saw the Girl Scout troop crossing the road in front of me. Six or seven little girls dead ahead.

I slammed on the brakes and jerked the wheel to the left and pointed it into the median. *Grass will be soft,* I thought in a rational nanosecond.

The Mercedes was on my right.

The little girls were screaming, scattering all across the road.

And there was a palm tree in the median.

I stomped on the brakes.

We hit the tree. There was a loud bam.

The airbag deployed.

And I saw stars.

When you see somebody get bumped on the head in the movies, they always wake up and go on about their business as if nothing had happened. Call me a wuss, but when I woke up sitting in the front seat of Peep's Jag with a bump that felt like a baseball on the side of my head, I was not about to go anywhere.

It hurt like hell and the first thing I did was put my hand up and poke at it, which made it hurt even more.

"Ow," I whined, to nobody in particular because I hadn't even fully opened my eyes yet. I didn't have any desire to move again, so I just sat still for a few minutes, listening to the sound of the nearby traffic, men shouting, doors slamming.

Time passed—I have no idea how much—and I heard voices around me. Hands pressed at my neck and held my wrist. I was either safely alive or already dead, because they didn't seem too concerned about moving me anywhere, so I stayed put.

"Wally?" came Pitt's voice from somewhere beside me.

"Where did you come from?" I mumbled, resisting the temptation to turn my head and look at him. "What are you doing here? Where are LaLa and Peep?"

"They're fine. Tony heard the call on the radio and called me at the bank," he said. "I figured I'd better see if you lived."

"Did I?" I said.

He laughed. "Apparently you all did, no thanks to your driving. What were you thinking?"

"I...Ow...." I started to get up, then changed my mind when a stab of pain shot through my head. I leaned back.

"Wally?"

"Tony?"

"Wally, the ambulance is here and the paramedics are taking you all to Henry Flagler Hospital to be checked."

"I'm okay."

"Sure you are. But let's just humor them, shall we?"

"No," I growled. "Let's just humor me."

I opened my eyes to see Pitt and Tony leaning into the car with worried faces. Behind them and around the car, well-built men in blue T-shirts with white letters reading FIRE RESCUE were busy doing God knows what.

"Wally, you've got to go...."

"Shut up," I said to Pitt, the husband I swore to love and honor. "You," I said to Tony. "Get in here."

Pitt backed up with a hurt look on his face and Tony stepped closer, wary. I suppose he had reason. I might not have appeared to be totally rational.

"They're trying to kill us," I said. "They tried to run us off the road."

"Who?" he said.

I knew he was going to ask that and I knew it was going to make me mad. "How the hell do I know?" I snarled. "You're the cop. You figure it out."

A paramedic came up behind Tony just then and whispered something to him. Tony backed up. The paramedic leaned in.

"We're going to move you, now."

I looked down at my feet and willed them to do something. They just sat there. "Move, dammit," I said to my right foot.

The paramedic had my left hand, or rather I had his right hand. I must have been squeezing.

"Nothing wrong with her grip," he said over his shoulder. Then, to me. "Look at me."

I turned my head to the left. "Ow," I said. "It hurts."

"What hurts?" he said.

"My head."

"Could you let go of my hand?"

I did.

"Can you get out of the car?"

"Sure."

"You're not moving."

"Oh."

"Never mind," he said, and leaned in. He put a collar around my neck and buckled the strap. Then he put his left arm under my knees and his right arm behind my back.

I would have been happy to just let him carry me, but I swear I heard him groan with the effort.

"Hey," I said. "Just let me do it, then."

"No, you're getting a little ride," he said. Another pair of hands grabbed my legs and together they lifted me onto a board. I felt straps tighten around my thighs.

"Don't let them kill me," I said.

"What'd she say?" one of the men asked.

"Dunno," the other said. "Let's move."

I opened my eyes as I was being lifted into the ambulance. Peep was on a gurney in the back already. LaLa sat in a little seat, next to a solid young man who was grabbing the end of the gurney on which I was riding.

"Peep, are you okay?" I asked.

"Just fine, darling. They won't let me smoke, though."

There was a pause.

"Danger in motion," LaLa said, as the ambulance started moving. "That's what Velma said."

"Damn right," I said. "And as soon as my head quits hurting, we're going to find out who the hell it is."

Chapter Fifteen

MONDAY, DECEMBER 30

I had a headache the size of Donald Trump's ego when I woke up Monday morning, and I was beginning to get a little annoyed that someone seemed to wish harm on my person.

Despite the fact that I was alone and safe in my own bed, Vice-mayor Melvin Dumar's fear that the press was going to latch on to the Society Killer-on-the-rampage story seemed more realistic today than it had earlier in the week.

Even more important, I realized how much I had taken for granted the safety and security I felt in my little niche in Palm Beach. Suddenly I found myself wanting to make a bargain with God that if She could arrange for me to go back to that time before death and fear had touched me so closely, I wouldn't complain any more about dullness as a quality of life in Palm Beach.

Of course, life doesn't allow you to go back, only forward or full stop, so I turned my head to see the time. As I did, I discovered my head wasn't the only thing on my body that hurt. My neck ached, and, as I tried them one by one, it seemed every muscle in my body was checking in with its own complaint about having been moved beyond its normal range during the accident.

It was ten o'clock, very late for me to sleep. I had to attribute it to the pills Pitt poked down my throat the night before.

Toe by toe, muscle by muscle, I inched my way out of bed and gingerly got on my feet.

I made my way slowly and carefully to the bathroom and stood for a few minutes, staring at the bottle of muscle relaxants on the vanity, wondering if I should just take a handful and go back to bed.

Since my pill-taking usually is limited to vitamins, hormones and the occasional antibiotic, I decided to take a pass on the downers and just feel the pain for a while. Of course, that was what I had said about hot flashes, too, when they first began, and I sure changed my mind about that in a hurry.

I crept toward the stairs, making it only as far as the top of the landing before the click of toenails on tile alerted me to the fact that the dogs were aware I was on my way.

I sat down on the top stair as they bounded toward me, Henry getting to me first and planting wet, licky little kisses all over my face. Isadora was right behind him, pushing her way in to hide her head shyly on my shoulder, her more demure way of demonstrating unconditional dog love.

Petal walked out of the kitchen and looked up at me. "The phone's been ringing all morning," she said. "I unplugged the one in your room so it wouldn't wake you."

She held up a Diet Coke, popped the top, and brought it to me at the the top of the stairs. It was the kind of generous gesture that endears people to you. "Thanks," I said. "Give me a few minutes and I'll catch up with you."

She nodded, went back down the stairs and disappeared into the kitchen. The dogs experienced a moment of uncertainty as to who they would go with, but to their credit, they opted to stay with me rather than see if Petal was headed toward food.

When I got to the kitchen, I saw that Pitt had gone on to work, as I had suspected. Petal put a plate with two of her hot, flaky biscuits in front of me, along with a stick of butter.

Then she put a stack of message notes in front of me. I rifled through them. Tony, LaLa, Rezna, Digby.

I couldn't quite break through the fog in my head well enough to dial, so I asked Petal for a Diet Coke to go. Then I creaked back upstairs for a long, hot shower.

Afterwards, I slipped on a knit pants set because it was easy to pull over my still-sore body, put on as little makeup as I could get away with and not frighten small children, and gave my hair a disgusted look and a quick fluff with the blow drier.

I went back downstairs when I heard the phone ringing again. I walked into the kitchen and Petal covered the phone. "Artie Marsh," she said.

Curious, I took the phone. "Artie?" I said to the bartender at the Breakers, who had never called me at home before.

"Ms. Tupper. Sorry to disturb you. But I thought you might be interested in something."

"What's that?"

"You remember a few weeks ago we were talking about who was trying to do in who in Palm Beach society?"

"Sure I do."

"Well, there's some serious dirt being spread around over here right now, and I thought, since you are Mrs. Fenton's friend, you might want to check it out."

"What's going on?"

"Well, I think you'd better get over here and find out for yourself, but it's Mrs. DeVale talking about Mrs. Fenton, if that gives you a clue."

It did, and I hung up with a promise to hurry right over. My annoyance factor at what was going on lately was rising like winter prices on Worth Avenue, and I welcomed the chance to chew somebody out. Especially Verity DeVale.

Also, I have to admit, I was seeing Artie in a whole new light after spying on him and Raymond Way, Digby's so-called partner. And I knew that since Ray knew the truth about where Booth had died, there was a chance that Artie knew, too. I wondered where it would lead.

I told Petal where I was going, ignored her protests, and backed my car out of the driveway. I hadn't gone very far east on Barton before I saw the black Mercedes pull out behind me.

Thoroughly ticked off, I decided I had been somebody's victim for the last time. The Mercedes tailed me to the corner of South County Road, where I signaled to turn left, as I would to go north to the Breakers. I turned, but as soon as I did, I floored the gas pedal, willing my car to jump farther, faster than ever before. She did, and a block later I rounded a quick left into Pendleton Avenue, pulling into the first driveway and concealing myself behind a ficus hedge. I saw the black Mercedes go past on South County, and pulled out a couple of cars behind it.

Staying several cars behind so that my car wouldn't be noticeable, I saw the Mercedes turn into the Breakers. I drove into a little road leading into the Breakers Golf Course and sat there a few minutes until a Mercedes pulled out, turning north. I couldn't be sure it was the same one, but I figured my chances were good, so I pulled out behind him, again staying a safe distance behind.

We drove and drove, crossing the Flagler Memorial Bridge and weaving in and out of downtown West Palm Beach traffic, for about ten minutes. I was just about to throw in the towel, figuring if I didn't I'd end up on I-95 south to Miami, when the Mercedes pulled into the parking lot of the Palm Beach County Courthouse, built after the county blushed at embarrassment at the horror of having its old courthouse flashed worldwide on the news during the William Kennedy Smith rape trial.

Imagine my surprise when Ray Way got out of the car.

Imagine his surprise when I pulled into the parking place next to him.

"Why, Wally Tupper," he said, smooth as silk. "What a pleasure."

"I guess so, Raymond," I snapped. "Since you were following me."

He raised his eyebrows in what I was sure was mock surprise. He was lean and elegant, like Frank Sinatra in the Rat Pack years. And he had the same wary look behind his eyes. "Following you?" he said. He gestured at my car. "Looks like you followed me."

"What's going on?" I asked, tired of someone with his youth and good looks being so sure they could bamboozle me just because I have crow's feet and a body that shows the effects of fifty years of unchallenged gravity. "What's going on," I repeated, sounding more sullen and resentful than I meant to, "is that Digby thinks you were being blackmailed by Booth Ewen. And I have seen you with Artie. And putting the two together, I think I need to tell the police chief he better have a little talk with you."

He scanned the parking lot, as if seeing whether anyone was watching us, and a little thought scampered through my mind that if this was a killer, I'd be pretty stupid to confront him alone, in the middle of a deserted parking lot.

But here we stood.

"Booth Ewen wasn't blackmailing me," he said finally, not quite looking me in the eye. "Digby has it all wrong, as usual."

I waited.

"So," he said, jiggling the coins in his pants pockets, the way men do when they are nervous. "That's that. And it's really none of your business."

He started to go around me, toward the courthouse.

I grabbed him by the worsted wool sleeve and pulled him to a stop. He brushed off his sleeve disdainfully, and looked at me.

"Yes?" he said coolly.

I pointed my index finger at him. I didn't waggle it at him, because I was a lot madder at him than that. I poked it right into his chest, hard, a couple of times.

"Digby is one of the nicest people I've ever known," I said. "If you don't tell him about Artie, I will. I'm giving you twenty-four hours."

He shrugged. "Dig's doing the flowers for one of the ballrooms at the Breakers Centennial Gala tomorrow night, and Artie's tending bar."

I nodded. "How will you get in?" If you're not invited to one of these things, you don't get into the ballroom. That's one of the most visible signs of that A-list, B-list thing that Peep's always so worried about.

He chewed on his lip for a moment, then stuck his hands in his pockets and hung his head. "I'm invited."

I raised an eyebrow.

"Digby worked it out with Reggie Wert to get an invitation." He threw up his hands in mock excitement, "so we could all get into this 'once-in-a-lifetime' event."

Shiver me timbers, I thought. Invitations to a big-time do like the Breakers Centennial Gala would be scarcer than rhinestones at the Red Cross Ball.

"See that you make sure Digby comes out of this unharmed, heart and soul," I said through my teeth, my eyes squinched into little slits from which I shot my fiercest glare.

He bowed at the waist and gave a flourish with his arm. "Why certainly, Your Majesty. Whatever you command. Now, if you'll excuse my absence from the Royal Presence, I've got business to do in the courthouse." With that, he strode off toward the door.

I definitely did not like this little smart-ass.

As I leaned against my car, trying to decide which way to go, Tony pulled into the parking lot, spotted me and aimed his car for where I stood.

"Get in," he said, leaning over to open the passenger side door.

I did.

"Spill," he said.

"I don't know what you mean," I said.

"Yes, you do."

"I got a call from Artie Marsh, the bartender at the Breakers, this morning, telling me I should go over there. But when I pulled out, I was followed. That's all I know."

He started the car engine. "We're going to the Breakers and we're talking to Artie," he said. "There's something you're not telling me, so maybe he will."

I gulped. "Nonsense," I said, somewhat weakly, I have to admit.

As we drove east on the Flagler Bridge, I took a deep breath. "Tony, I think it's all connected."

"What do you mean?"

"From Booth's murder to Taffy's murder and even to somebody trying to turn me into a bookmark today. I just can't help but feel like it's all part of one big thing."

"What kind of thing?"

"If I knew, I'd tell you." Well, most of it, anyway.

"Start from the beginning and tell me everything you know," he said.

I started almost from the beginning. "There was the turd in Booth's coffin, which was clearly some sort of message. Then at the DeVales' party, Taffy invited me over the next day because she had something important to tell me. Look what happened to her."

"Then somebody tries to run you off the road," he said.

"And, oh, there's something else strange."

"What?"

I told him about Desdemona and the homeless guy in Darla's house. "You might want to tell her to contact the police and have them check her house out," I said. "There's no telling what might have been stolen. If that guy could get in, others could."

He nodded. "I will. But what does that have to do with anything here?"

I was stumped. "Nothing, I guess, but it's been an exciting week."

We pulled into the Breakers. Tony parked in the fire lane and gave the valet a glare as he ran toward the car. The valet backed off and we walked under the *porte cochere* and into the lobby.

At the door to Reggie Wert's office, we ran smack into Verity DeVale.

"Oh," she said. "Speak of the devil."

It's just an expression, I told myself. "Verity—you've been busy this morning, I hear."

She smiled at Tony. Behind her, Reggie stood, arms crossed in a waiting position. Reggie is a veteran of the social wars.

"Chief Taranto," she said. "Some of us are wondering why you are not arresting the women who are killing their husbands. I have a petition right here signed by more than one hundred Palm Beach residents for you to arrest Peep Fenton and LaLa Ewen for the murders of their husbands."

I opened my mouth to give her a piece of my mind, but Tony's hand gripping my arm stopped me. I saw why when Melvin Dumar stepped from behind the door.

Verity had a cat-who-swallowed-the-canary smile.

"I warned you, Taranto," Dumar said.

"Tomorrow is New Year's Eve," Verity piped up. "The Prince of Wales will be here tomorrow night. But if you don't do your job, he won't come."

"Malarky," I finally contributed to the conversation. I could barely speak, and what I really wanted to do was grab Verity's perfect blonde hair and pull it out by the roots. Maybe first I'd scratch out those big blue eyes. "The Prince of Wales is coming to The Breakers Centennial Party and I doubt he's even heard that anybody died here." I hoped I was right.

"Wally," Reggie said with trepidation, "it's true. His people are expressing some concern." Reggie stood up tall and straight. "But chief, I don't want to pressure you."

Tony looked at me and rolled his eyes. "I'm sure," he said dryly.

Verity shook the papers at him. "We mean business, chief. Do something." She hooked her arm into Dumar's. "Right, Melvin?"

Dumar put his face inches away from Tony's. "If that prince don't show up at the gala tomorrow night, I'm holding you responsible."

He and Verity walked out of Reggie's office arm in arm.

Reggie gave us a shrug of apology and came over to me.

"There is something else you might want to know about," he said. "Something odd."

Odd was beginning to lose its meaning to me.

"What's that?" I asked.

"I've had calls," he said. "Three of them. I think they're from the same person— it sounds like a woman—but I can't be sure. Each time, the person pretends like they are interested in talking about the Breakers Babies, but each time, there's some sort of veiled threat that maybe the Breakers might not follow through on the Procession of Babies."

"What kind of threat?" Tony asked.

"Very subtle," Reggie said. "Like, 'Maybe there's a curse on the Breakers because it burned down twice before and you don't want to bring up any bad karma'."

"What the hell does that have to do with anything?" I said.

Reggie shook his head. "It didn't all make sense, and I can't say it was a direct threat, but it definitely sounded sinister." He looked at Tony. "I just thought it would be a good idea to let you know."

Tony puffed out an exasperated breath. "Thanks, Reggie. It was." He grabbed me by the arm. "Let's talk to Artie. I've got to get back to my office."

It was noon, and usually there would be a few early birds hitting the sauce for business or pleasure, but today Artie stood alone, wiping crystal glasses at the Tapestry Bar.

He threw two cocktail napkins up on the bar as we approached. "Ms. Tupper...Chief Inspector...what can I do for you?"

I plunked down on the same barstool I had occupied that day a month ago when my life had started to churn like a stopped-up sink freshly doused with Drano.

"You called me, Artie," I groused. "I think for a reason."

"Oh," he said breezily. "I just thought you would like to know that Verity was over here dishing dirt on your friend Mrs. Fenton...hoping I'd spread it around. She had three of the A-list biddies with her, and she was making sure they got an earful."

"What was she saying?"

"Well," he said, giving Tony a glance. "She was saying that the chief here was going to arrest Mrs. Fenton for murder, and Mrs. Ewen, too, and that it just looked bad for Mrs. Fenton to chair the Garden Club Gala when she was clearly going to be in prison next year."

"Well, that will straighten out quick enough if I don't arrest her," Tony pointed out, pulling his cell phone out of his breast pocket as it chirped. He turned away to talk, walking to the other end of the bar.

"What's going on with you and Raymond, Artie?" I said. "I've seen the two of you together, and I don't want Digby to get hurt."

Artie wiped at an invisible spot on the bar.

"Can I trust you?" he said, giving Tony—who was still talking softly on his phone at the other end of the thirty-foot bar—a glance.

"Well...," I started.

"Look," he said sharply. "I just asked that to be nice. Frankly, you know as well as I do that if Raymond decides to spill what he knows about the Garden Club Gala, you are all liable to charges of accessory to murder. So, I have your cooperation, yes?"

I shrugged. This is how the devil gets you, you know. One bite at a time. Because I have something to hide, I will forever be at the mercy of those who wanted a piece of me. "Sure," I said.

"Here's the thing," he said. "Raymond approached Booth about a...er...donation to Raymond's investment fund."

"Why would Booth do that?" I asked.

"Because," he said. "Raymond happened to...make an acquaintance...of someone who works at the firm that does Booth's taxes, and he heard the guy say he suspected Booth of underreporting his income on some investments. So last summer, Ray arranges a game of tennis with Booth at the B&T, and makes him an offer he can't refuse."

"Such as?"

"Such as that he pay Ray a little monthly income—say, ten thousand dollars—not to mention this to the feds."

"And Booth had been paying?"

"Yep."

"So," I asked. "Why are you telling me this? What do you want from me?"

"We just want one thing," he said. "Ray meant to tell you this morning, and that's why he followed you, but you surprised him at the courthouse and he chickened out."

He patted the area of his heart. "He knows all of this is going to hurt Digby and he feels bad. We just want to get out of it gracefully."

"You mean the blackmailing or the relationship?"

"Both," Artie said. "It's going to be hard enough for Ray to tell Digby the truth. But if you can help us, we think we can get out of the blackmailing thing clean enough."

"How?" I asked. My eyes cut over toward Tony; I was going to be asked to do something less than Nobel-prize worthy.

"Go through Booth's financial records," he said. "Mrs. Ewen will let you do that. We think somebody might be on our trail...we don't know who, but Raymond has gotten calls. If there's no evidence—such as check carbons written to Raymond, there's no proof. Get his checkbooks, tell Mrs. Ewen we'll pay her back every cent, and we'll all be happy."

I thought about that for a minute. I thought LaLa might go for it. What did she have to lose? "Okay." I hopped down off the barstool, hoping Tony would hurry up.

"Oh, one more thing," Artie said, "about Mrs. DeVale. She's working an angle to get Mrs. Fenton barred from the Breakers Centennial Ball tomorrow night. Went to talk to Reggie about it. She says by the time the Palm Beach *Tattler* comes out tomorrow morning, Mrs. Fenton won't be welcome at a Democratic fund-raiser with a check in her hand."

Chapter Sixteen

TONY PULLED HIS CAR INTO my driveway, turned off the engine, and turned to look at me.

"We've been here before," he said.

I wasn't sure what he meant, although my memories of some front seat smooching sessions were pretty strong. There was a lump in my throat that told me I'd better not answer him.

He leaned over to me and kissed me on the cheek.

"Take care of yourself," he said. "I'd hate to lose you, now that I've found you again."

I got out of the car and lifted one hand in a wimpy little wave.

Petal was waiting for me just inside the door. I wheedled her into taking me to LaLa's by promising her the afternoon off for a movie and dinner on me.

I wasn't sure how LaLa was going to react to my request that we paw through her financial records—who among us wants anybody to know how much we really spend at the grocery store?—but it seemed it would be to her advantage for us to do so.

Petal waited in the car, talking on the phone with the latest boyfriend, while I told the housekeeper I'd find LaLa myself.

She was in the sitting room—sitting. She had a piece of paper in her hand.

"Yoo hoo," I called from the doorway.

She looked up, put her hands behind her back, and crunched up the paper. "Wally. What are you doing here?"

She stood up and oh, so casually, tossed the paper into a wastepaper basket as she came to give me a hug. "Come on," she said, "let's go outside."

We went out her patio, overlooking the ocean on a winter Florida day so beautiful it made me want to cry. The sun was gentle, the breeze was gentle. I was not.

"Listen, LaLa," I said. "Booth had more secrets than Estee Lauder has lipstick shades. We're going to have to look under some rocks, if we want to get this thing over with."

"I don't know what you mean," she said, an unusual stubborn streak making an appearance.

"What I mean," I said, "is there are snakes about. For instance, Verity DeVale has been sniffing around Reggie Wert asking all sorts of weird questions. She asked about Noelle, can you believe that? Even more important, she's got a petition signed by one hundred people in Palm Beach to have you and Peep arrested for murdering your husbands."

LaLa was looking up and away, as if listening to a faraway voice. "Noelle?" she said.

"Yes," I said. "I haven't thought about her in years, have you? But listen, Tony is between a rock and a hard place, and I know he's not going to arrest you or anything...."

LaLa's attention snapped back to me. "Arrest?" She stood up and started pacing around the patio, a virtual symphony of linen rippling around her. "I can't possibly be arrested. They'd put me in a small, dark place. I'd die."

She was creeping me out. "Well, there is something we can do to help avoid that," I said.

"What?"

"Artie Walsh and Raymond Way were blackmailing Booth because he underreported income to the IRS. They want us to find the checkbooks before the police do. If we can do that, they'll give you back the money. So, let's go up to Booth's office and prowl around through his records, shall we?"

LaLa's mouth was pursed so tight you couldn't have put a straw between her lips. "Certainly not. Not even you can go looking through his personal things."

I was taken aback. Here is a woman who would walk in front of a speeding truck if her spirit guide told her to. I'm just suggesting we poke around in her dead husband's office files. "LaLa, it's got to be done."

She laughed, but it wasn't from humor. "No, it doesn't. Just let things lie."

"Things aren't lying," I said. "Things are hopping about like frogs on speed. Now do you want to help yourself or not?"

Walking over and putting a hand on my shoulder, LaLa glared at me with a ferocity I had never seen in her eyes. "You aren't talking about helping me, that's for sure. I don't want you digging around in my—or Booth's—past. So stay out. And get out."

I jerked upright. My best friend for more than thirty years had just ordered me out of her home. My stomach dropped about a foot and my heart was heavy. What could I do?

"You've lost your mind," I said. "We dragged your husband out of a swimming pool for you."

She looked away.

I was blinking furiously as I walked inside. She stayed on the patio. Neither of us said a word. I was not going to cry, I promised myself. But I couldn't have felt any worse if I did.

And I was curious. Here was a friend I had known since grade school. Except for when I was in college, we hadn't missed talking to each other many days out of our entire lives.

What could she be hiding?

A few minutes later, Petal dropped me off where my car still sat in the parking lot of the Palm Beach County Courthouse. As I unlocked the door, I turned back to where Petal waited.

"Want to make a fast C note?" I asked.

Her eyes lit up.

I rummaged in my purse, pulled out my wallet and fished out a one hundred dollar bill. "I don't care how you do it, but get LaLa's housekeeper out of that house within the hour and keep her gone." I looked at my watch, which read one-thirty.

Petal lit up like a six-year-old in a candy store. She loves to play games. "You got it."

I handed her another fifty dollars. "As a matter of fact," I said, "If you can get LaLa out of the house without suspecting anything, you've earned this. Mum's the word."

It wasn't as crazy as it sounds. Petal is in close cahoots with a gang of metaphysical gurus in Boca Raton and LaLa is always eager to go visit them for some spiritual maintenance. "Take her down for an aura cleaning," I suggested.

Petal also loves intrigue. "Hot damn. She'll be gone within the hour, or my name isn't Petal T. Posey."

As soon as I cranked up my car, the Honda CRX Pitt and I had given Petal for her college graduation present jumped ahead like it had been goosed by a GMC Jimmy. And she was gone.

I drove east on Third Street and turned left on Olive Avenue—or U.S. 1, as it is more commonly known—on my way to the Flagler Bridge.

I had to pass Montreaux Florists to get there, and I considered that a sign. I pulled into the postage-stamp size parking lot and lucked into a space in front of the pink stucco dollhouse that is Digby's place of business. The area around the six-foot path from the parking lot to the bright pink front door was blanketed with hundreds of pointsettias. *Tis the season,* I thought, but the spirit of Christmas had barely touched my life this holiday. It seemed I was dealing with the ghost of Christmas past instead.

I found Digby at his counter, on the telephone. He waved enthusiastically at me and beckoned me over to where he stood. When he ended the conversation a few seconds later, he came around the counter and gave me a big hug.

"Darling. Where have you been? I haven't talked to you in days," he said. He indicated a pair of chairs in the corner of the shop, which was about the size of Pitt's dressing room.

We sat.

"Digby," I said, "I have a couple of things to tell you. And I need some help."

"Sweetie, you know you can count on me." He worked his arms up and down as if he were lifting weights. "Need another body moved? I've been working out."

"Please. I've seen enough bodies for one Christmas season. But...it's a tiny bit on the sneaky side. Oh, who am I kidding. It's downright illegal." *What the hell*, I thought. You don't really know what your ethics are until someone tests them, and I had found out in the last couple of weeks that what I thought were rock solid ethical boundaries for me were instead giant oil slicks.

Here goes. "Well, let me give you a little background," I said. "It's about Raymond."

"Ray?" he said. He coiled up, as if expecting a blow. "What about Ray?"

"He...uh...he's...." *Oh, crackers,* I thought. *Spit it out.*

"I found out he's seeing someone else. I wanted him to tell you himself but I need your help today and you need to know why. I...I'm sorry."

He looked stunned and then hurt. If I didn't know how much he was hurting, I might have laughed at the sight of his face, a fair, strong face, worthy of the big screen, with eyes and nose all squinched up like a four-year-old whose favorite toy has been taken away.

He blinked, a lot and fast, to keep the tears back. Then he leaned over with his elbows on his knees and put his face in his hands.

After a couple of minutes like that, he sat back up and sighed, deeply and long. Finally, he said, "I guess I knew. I just didn't want to admit it. You know, you hope it will just go away and things will be the same. But they never are."

No, I thought, *things are never the same. Things have a way of changing, minute by minute. They never, ever, stay the same.*

"Are you okay?" I asked. I dug compassion out of my emotional grab bag more readily than a couple of weeks ago, maybe because I had exercised so many of my own emotions lately.

"I will be," he said through a husky throat. "I really will."

I wasn't sure who he was trying to convince, me or him, but it didn't matter. "Now I need to tell you something else," I said. "Maybe this will make it easier."

He laughed. "You couldn't tell me that first?"

"Fraid not," I said. "Ray is not being blackmailed. I found out that he and Artie—" I stopped when I realized I hadn't mentioned that part.

Digby stiffened for a second. "Go on," he said.

"Ray and Artie were blackmailing Booth," I said. "Ray found out Booth was underreporting income on his tax return and threatened to go to the IRS. Booth was paying him off."

"Wally?" Digby said, wrinkling his brow. "Do you think Ray had anything to do with Booth's death?"

I shook my head and shrugged. "I don't think so, because why would they kill off the golden goose? But who knows?"

"I just don't think Ray could kill anyone," he said.

People surprise you, I thought. "I bet you didn't think he'd blackmail anyone, either."

"No," he admitted, "I didn't."

"Can you leave the shop?" I asked.

"Sure. Just a sec." He went through a doorway into the back room and I heard him talking to someone—an assistant, I assumed. Then he came back out. "Where are we going?"

"Follow me," I said, and led him out to where my car was parked. We got in and I waited until we were crossing the Flagler Bridge before I said anything more.

"We're breaking into LaLa's house," I said.

"What?"

"You heard me. Here's why." I told him what Ray had said and he nodded.

"Got it," he said. "But wouldn't it be easier if LaLa just helped us?"

I told him about her—unreasonable, I thought—objection.

He nodded again. "Got it," he repeated.

He was quiet for a minute. "How will we get in?" he said.

"I have a key. We all have keys to each other's houses...exchanged them years ago." I motioned with my head towards my key ring, on which hung keys to LaLa's and Peep's private quarters.

As we pulled into LaLa's driveway, I got a twinge of guilt as I realized that in more than thirty years of friendship, this was the first time I had ever misused the privilege.

After we parked the car, we walked up to the front door and I rang the bell a couple of times. There was no answer, so I opened the door with the key. I knew, of course, where Booth's study was located. I led the way up the stairs and into the family quarters.

"I never thought I would be breaking into my best friend's house," I said to Digby as we stood in the doorway of Booth's study, a leather-encrusted emporium with the heads of large animals on the wall—I don't think Booth ever hunted game a day in his life—and pipe racks on the desk. The pipes had never been smoked.

"I never thought I'd move dead bodies and search for evidence my lover is a blackmailer," he said. "What's your point?"

I looked around for a minute. I didn't think I had one.

"I'll take the desk," I said. "You take the filing cabinet."

He headed across the room. "What if they're locked?" he said. Then he pulled on a file drawer. It wasn't. "Holy Hydrangea," he said. "So this is how a life of crime begins..."

I opened a desk drawer and started rummaging. "Let's just hope this isn't how ours ends."

For a few minutes, all you could hear in that room was papers being shuffled.

I wasn't finding financial records, but I was finding a surprising number of photographs. I had never thought of Booth as a sentimental type—I still didn't—but one desk drawer was full of nothing but photos.

I flipped through them out of curiosity. A lot of them were photos of Booth with famous people at parties. The farther back in the drawer I got, the farther back in time the photos dated.

Almost at the very back was a file folder with photos that apparently dated back to our high school years. Kids at football games and parties dressed in that neat, nerdy early-sixties fashion.

Two of the photos especially caught my eye. One of Booth at a party, obviously three sheets to the wind, his elbow crooked possessively around the neck of Noelle Neill, LaLa's best friend in high school. The other was our senior class prom photo.

Palm Beach High School was pretty much like any high school in the sixties. At the prom, teenagers would sneak drinks of alcohol in the parking lot, careful not to spill them in the old man's car. Only a few of the more insensitive or insecure island residents would flash major jewelry and designer gowns in the faces of their more economically normal West Palm Beach classmates.

Suddenly I was back there, and those faces started to move in my mind, reenacting the prom. There was LaLa, who had cried the night she told me she had decided to marry Booth. There was Noelle. And Booth. There was Eaton, standing next to Peep. Eaton looked so serious for such a young man. And there was Desdemona, a tiny, wispy blonde wearing a diamond necklace with an emerald and diamond pendant nearly as big as her fist and glasses as thick as the emerald.

I had a wave of sadness for those young people, so world-weary for our years yet totally clueless as to what life really would be about.

I felt a wave of sadness for myself. It had been more than thirty years, and I was still trying to figure out what I would be when I grew up.

"I found it," Digby said.

My head snapped up, the photo forgotten. I shoved the picture back into the file folder, replaced them in the drawer and closed it.

"Let me see." I walked over to where Digby stood and looked at the checkbook he was holding in his hand. He flipped through the stubs and sure enough, several of the stubs said Ray Way, with nothing written on the notation line.

"He said there should be four," I said. Digby pulled out one, flipped through some more stubs, pulled out another, and kept going until he had ripped four stubs out of Booth's checkbook.

"What shall I do with them?" he said. "Eat them?"

"Are you hungry?"

"No," he said, "actually I'm a little sick to my stomach."

"Me too," I said. "Let's just get out of here and we'll figure out what to do with them later."

We closed up the drawers, turned out the lights and stood in the doorway for a minute to make sure the room looked like it had when we came in.

"One more thing," I said. I ran down to the sitting room and fished the wadded up piece of paper out of the wastepaper basket where LaLa had tossed it and stuck it in the pocket of my linen pants.

Then we scurried down the stairs and back out to where my car waited in the driveway. A few minutes later, I dropped Digby off at his shop.

"Hold out your hand," he said as he got ready to get out of the car.

I did, and he deposited the check stubs, damp and crumpled from being clutched in his fist, into my open hand.

"There," he said with a sad look. "Call me the next time you need a partner in crime. Looks like I'm available."

I nodded and waved.

"Sorry to screw up your life, Digby," I said. "I seem to be doing that a lot lately."

He slammed the car door, walked around to my window and leaned down. "That's okay. Looks like yours is in the crapper, too. Cheerio."

Pitt was sitting at the kitchen table with a martini and a sour look.

I toyed with which way to go. Emotionally, I could have fallen either way over the line.

"What's your problem?" I snapped, making a leap toward the argument I knew I wanted to start.

He took a slow, maddening sip of his martini, didn't offer to fix me a drink, and sat, just staring at me. "Okay," he said. "We're fighting."

"I guess so," I said sullenly.

"May I ask why?"

"You may. And you may not like what you hear. That while looking for something you—not I—want, I got smacked about by a bunch of old newspapers. That I broke into my best friend's home. That I...had to tell a friend something that hurt him."

There was a long silence, punctuated by the click of dog nails on tile as Henry and Isabella ran to and fro between us, trying to get one of us to pay attention.

"There's something eating at you," he said. "It's been there for a while. I've felt it simmering under the surface. Why don't you just spit it out?"

I sighed and leaned on the kitchen counter, suddenly tired. He was right. It suddenly crystallized in my mind like the ice on the top of that fat-free, sugar-free ice cream that lives for decades in the back of my freezer.

"I wonder," I said, "if you married me for my money."

He put down his martini and shook his head, slowly, and sadly. "That's what's bothering you?"

I picked up the martini pitcher, pulled a chilled glass out of the freezer, and poured myself a drink. I dropped in an olive and shot Pitt a glare. "Yep."

"Wally, we've been married twenty-seven years. Isn't that a little bit ridiculous?"

I took a swig of martini and grimaced. I hate martinis, and had only poured it in the first place because I was mad at Pitt for not offering to pour it for me.

"I don't think so," I sniffed.

"Why *would* you think so?" he asked.

I thought a minute. "Because you are so damned eager for me to set you up socially by being a Breakers Baby."

He scratched his head, shook it in resignation and shrugged. "Socially, yes."

"And...," I said.

"And what?" he said. "And we had a deal when we got married that your money would carry us through until I made it. And I've done pretty well. And now I'm about to go over the top. So why now, the problem?"

"And the fact is," I said, "that for the first time, you want me to do something socially instead of financially."

"And," he said, looking as annoyed as I was at our conversational sand trap. "You seem to resent that."

I took a deep breath. "Yeah."

"Shit," he said, drained his glass, put it down, and walked out of the room.

I poured out my martini and went for what I wanted in the first place: Ben & Jerry's. In perfect symphony, I pulled out a pint of Totally Nuts.

Chapter Seventeen

TUESDAY, DECEMBER 31

When the dogs woke me by barking at seven o'clock New Year's Eve morning, the first thing I noticed was that Pitt was already up. I wasn't sure if he was mad. I wasn't sure if I cared. Emotionally exhausted, I wanted nothing more than to spend a year on a desert island, away from people trying to run my car off the road.

The slam of a car door outside my bedroom window got me out of bed, curiosity got me to the window, and the sight of Rezna coming up my front walk got me down to the front door in record time.

When I flung open the door, she waved a copy of *The Tattler* in my face, pushed past me into my home, turned right and stalked into our living room.

"Coffee," she barked at a stunned Petal, standing in the kitchen door. Pitt emerged from the kitchen and stared, but didn't say anything.

I followed.

"Get her coffee then get me a robe," I said to Petal on my way past. "And a Diet Coke. Please."

When I got into the living room, Rezna was enthroned in an arm chair, some ornately carved wooden thing that Pitt had picked out. She acted like putting her butt in it made the chair royal. I wasn't sure what was up, but I didn't like the look on her face. It was a mixture of defiance and...what?...exasperation?

I sat on the overstuffed sofa, which stretched longer than my car.

"What's wrong?" I asked. "Except for parties, you've never been here. And certainly never at this hour of the morning."

"Nonsense," she said. "This house was here before you were born, you know." She held out the paper. "Read this."

I heaved myself up, stepped over to her and took the paper from her hand. Thank heavens, just then Petal came in with a tray holding a cup of coffee and my Diet Coke.

I took the can and guzzled greedily, then put on the robe and slippers she handed me. "I don't have my glasses," I said. "I'll have to get them."

Rezna glared at Petal long enough for the poor girl to flinch and blurt out, "I'll go. Don't move, Wally. I'll go." She scuttled off.

When she returned and handed me my glasses, I thanked her and gave her a "get out while the getting is good" look. She did.

Then I looked at the paper, which Rezna had folded to her own column.

The Beach Session
by Rezna Van Daly
Society Editor, The Palm Beach Tattler

Palm Beach has always been the kind of town where the competition to run the best charity gala has been cutthroat.

Our town may be smaller than four square miles and fewer than ten thousand strong, but during the Season we raise mega-millions for charity—and we do it our way.

Ladies of our town run our charities, presiding as chairmen over the cocktail parties, luncheons and galas. And while they do so with the best intentions, let us be honest. One climbs the social pyramid in Palm Beach through fund raising, and the high ground is held by the chairmen of the most prestigious galas.

During the Season, there will be hundreds of events to fund good works. Some thirty million eagles will fly into the nests of our Palm Beach charities this year, and command of the helm of these charity boards does not come at a small price. It is not to be undertaken by the weak.

No deals struck in the penthouse offices of Manhattan have been the result of more networking, connection-pulling or influence-peddling activities than those made over cocktails in our little town.

When it comes to the good works of the charities of Palm Beach, never was iron will so sweetly wrought.

But never have we had people die to keep one of our own at the top of the pile. Given recent information, this writer has no choice but to call for the replacement of Peep Fenton as chairman of the Garden Club Charity Gala, for fifty years the town's most prestigious affair.

If she has any class, longtime resident Fenton will stay home from the Breakers Centennial Ball tonight.

It pains this writer to say, some things are not worth killing for.

My heart dropped into my stomach and took my stomach down to my toes, where they became a sodden, leaden mass of sorrow.

"Oh, no," I said to myself. Then, to Rezna. "Why on Earth would you write such a thing? You've known Peep all of her life."

My emotional history chart, if on view, would show that in moments of extreme stress, I tend to go numb. I cry at commercials, and when dogs get killed in movies, but in real life I tend to turn to concrete.

So I struggled to convey to Rezna what she had done to my friend. "She lives for this stuff," I said. "It's like she's addicted to Palm Beach. You know how dancers or jockeys hang out together because they crave to be around people who understand their passion? It's the same way here."

Rezna nodded her head, her eyes narrowed. She didn't give an inch.

"Except," I said, "instead of dance or horse racing her passion is social status. Of course, that's so shallow, it can hardly be called a passion, can it?"

Rezna shrugged. "At the risk of getting into an area we don't want to discuss, Wally, there are people in this town who would kill to stay on the A-list. That's pretty passionate."

I leaned on a big puffy pillow at the end of the mile-long sofa, put my feet up and drew myself into a fetal position. I wanted to suck my thumb.

"You know," I said. "A month ago I was ready to leave this town because it was too dull. Nothing important ever happened. I woke up one morning and I was over fifty and all I had to show for my life was a series of parties. I was ready to leave; to chuck it all."

Rezna didn't say anything.

"Well," I said. "Palm Beach isn't dull anymore. But dull is looking pretty good today. I think I'd like to go back there."

"So click your ruby slippers together and go back to Kansas, Dorothy," she said. "The rest of us will stay here and deal with the real world."

I sat up and put my feet on the floor. I looked down at the fuzzy pink bunny slippers Petal had given me for Christmas. I stood up and clicked the bunnies' butts together three times.

Nothing happened.

"I'm still here," I said.

Rezna smiled. "What can I do? Look, I had to print it, because that's what I do, but I feel bad about it—that's why I came to see you— and I'm willing to help Peep, if I can."

"You've done quite enough," I said. "You go back to the newspaper, or the coven, or whatever rafter you hang from when you are writing, and do what you have to do. I'm going to rescue my friend from thinking this is the end of her life."

I escorted Rezna to the front door and watched as her car drove away. Then I went upstairs and called Peep's house. I knew she wasn't awake at this hour, so I talked to her housekeeper.

"Hide the newspaper," I said. "Chew it up and swallow it, if you have to, but keep her from seeing it."

I showered and dressed. When I got downstairs, Pitt was still in the kitchen.

"Well," he said, taking a sip of coffee. "Where are we in our fight? Is one of us leaving?"

That hurt. You know, you learn to count on being able to fight with your spouse without somebody taking off. I think, however, the question might just have been—a teeny, weenie bit—my fault.

"Not on New Year's Eve," I said. "We have a date tonight, remember?"

He got up and walked over to me and held me in a long, long bear hug.

"I thought," I said from inside the hug, "you would know that all of my life I have felt like such an...observer...in Palm Beach. I had the house, but no history."

"I didn't know it bothered you," he said. "You always seemed so... disdainful."

I nodded into his armpit. "I don't know how else to act when I don't belong," I said. "But it hurt that you wanted me to have to dig into my parents' death. It's like you wanted me to pull off a scab and look underneath."

I closed my eyes. "I don't guess I'll be walking down that aisle with the Breakers Babies tonight," I said. "And just when I was beginning to really want to know."

"I don't care whether you are a Breakers Baby," he said. "I don't. I'm sorry. I just thought....oh, hell. You know what I thought. And I didn't think about how it might hurt your feelings. I was just so close...."

He let go and looked at me. "I'll have my bank," he said. "And I'll have you to thank for it. But you're not Doris Duke, you know. You didn't marry a fortune hunter. You married me because we fit together, and it's been a good match."

I waited for him to mention love.

"And I love you," he said.

I put my head on his shoulder. Was I missing out on something—some great, once-in-a-lifetime passion—by staying with Pitt? I wasn't sure. And I guessed I'd never be sure.

"Me, too," I said.

Then I told him about Peep, and showed him the paper.

"I've got to get over there," I said.

He nodded.

Peep and Mitch were surprised to see me. No wonder. It was seven thirty in the morning, not an hour people are out and about in Palm Beach, except maybe on the lakeside jogging trail.

They invited me into the breakfast nook, where Peep's dry wheat toast looked forlorn on her gold-leafed china. Mitch was chewing on a bagel. There was a dot of cream cheese on his chin. They both stared at me expectantly.

I opened the Diet Coke I had brought with me, took up the cook's offer of a croissant, slathered it with butter, and took a big bite to give myself time to think how to start this conversation.

"The thing about social position," I said, "is that it is earned." I stopped. Peep furrowed a brow. Mitch took another bite of bagel.

"So," I said, "no one can really take it away from you, if you have earned it, and people feel you deserve it."

"Cut the crap," Peep said, "and tell us why you are here."

"Well," I said, "it seems someone has gotten to Rezna with some dirty gossip and Rezna...overreacted...and...."

"Oh, my nerves," Peep said. "Where's the paper?"

"I couldn't find it," Mitch said.

"The housekeeper has it," I said.

They both looked at me as if I had sprouted warts on my nose. "Why would she take it?" Mitch says. "She knows better."

"I told her to," I said.

"Oh, my nerves," Peep said.

Mitch got up and walked out of the kitchen, toward the servants' quarters. In a few minutes, he came back, the paper open to Rezna's column. He was reading it silently. Then he handed it to Peep and stared at me.

"Why would she do this?" he asked.

I shook my head. "I don't know, but don't worry. We'll all stay home tonight...we'll all just skip the ball. Who...."

"The hell we will," Peep said. "I'm not hiding from anyone. I didn't kill anyone, and I'm not going to let anyone think I did. I'm not even following anyone, like some husbands I know," she said with a pointed look at Mitch.

"Huh?" he said. "What are you talking about?"

"I want you to quit following me," she said. "I know what you are up to."

He sat down. "Up to? I don't know what you mean."

"You are trying to drive me crazy," she said, pointing a finger at him. "You want to be rid of me like you got rid of Desdemona."

She stood, stretched to her full five feet, and leaned over her husband. "But it's not going to work," she said.

He reached up and grabbed her by her shoulders. "Peep," he said, "you can't be serious."

She pulled away. "I'm serious as I can be," she said. "And furthermore, I don't ever want you to ask me that question again. Just assume from now on that if I'm talking, I'm serious, okay?"

Mitch looked as if she had slapped him in the face with a trout. "Peep, Desdemona was mentally ill. You are just...." He stopped and flailed a hand, searching for a word.

Peep walked over to the kitchen counter and pulled a warm croissant out of the toaster oven. She brought it to the table, buttered it and dished two heaping spoonfuls of homemade cherry jelly onto it.

She took a big bite and stared defiantly at Mitch while she chewed. When her mouth was almost empty, she said, "And I'll gain weight if I want to, and if you don't like it, you can just leave."

"I...." He held up his hands, palms up. "Desdemona was a danger to herself. She tried to commit suicide more than once. She threw herself down the stairs twice. And she made threats...."

Peep put the croissant down. "You didn't divorce her because she got fat?"

"Hell, no!" Mitch boomed. "That's no reason to divorce anybody."

"And you didn't try to drive her crazy so you could divorce her?"

"I didn't have to drive Desdemona anywhere," he said. "She was already there. I just helped her find a place to live where she couldn't do any harm to herself."

Peep and I looked at each other.

"Well," Peep said. "She's gone."

Mitch nodded. "I know."

"You know?" Peep and I said in chorus.

"Sure," he said. "She called me when she left on her trip. She just wanted me to know she would be gone for a while."

"Trip?" I said. "What trip?"

"To California," he said. "To see her sister. Her sister is sick and Desdemona wanted to go stay with her for her last months, so she called me and told me she'd be gone, but that she would be back, and didn't want me to worry."

Peep shook her head as if clearing it. "Damn," she said.

"What?" Mitch asked.

"I had it all figured out, and it turns out I was all wrong." Peep stared at the floor as if it would disgorge the answer in a heave of Spanish tile.

"I wish you had told me earlier how you felt, baby doodles. I really was beginning to worry about you; you were acting a little strangely. But don't you worry, you'll be right here with me for as long as you like."

"Don't patronize me," she said dryly, "and, by the way, it's my house."

He smiled. "That's my girl."

"Woman," she corrected. "And we are going to that ball tonight. If those people think they can get me down with a little gossip, they have another thought coming."

"Whatever you say," he said, leaning over to give her a peck.

I hated to interrupt this little love-in—it seemed we were all kissing and making up this morning—but I did have one question.

"So great," I said. "It wasn't you. But somebody followed us, and somebody tried to run us off the road. So who was it?"

Neither one had an answer to that question, so I left. And I didn't come up with any answers on the way home. When I got there, Pitt had gone to work and Petal had taken off for the day. It was New Year's Eve. Party your brains out.

I thought I would spend the day getting myself ready for the party. It takes it. I could use a week, but it wouldn't make that much difference. My hair would still be frizzy and my skin would still flake. I don't, as do some Palm Beach women, hire people to come in and do my hair and makeup. I guess it shows.

But before I got started on the task of making myself look presentable, I went over to the pile of papers and clothes that still lay where I had dumped them when I had gotten undressed the night before. I put the pile of papers on the Louis IV table under the French window that looks out over Barton Avenue. Then, feeling guilty for just dropping my linen slacks on the floor in my fatigue, picked up the clothes. As I was putting the pants on a hanger, I felt something in the pocket. Crumpled up paper.

Puzzled, I pulled it out, remembering when I saw it that I had fished it out of LaLa's wastepaper basket. I had been curious as to why it appeared that she was trying to keep me from seeing what it was.

I was even more puzzled when I uncrumpled the paper. It was a letter. To Booth. Essentially, it was a threat.

"Unless you return the money you embezzled from me, I will turn you in to the Securities Exchange Commission, have you arrested for theft and take you to court to get the money back."

The letter ended with a familiar phrase.

"I will not be taken advantage of."

I picked up the telephone and dialed.

"Hello," Vanessa answered.

"Wally." I said curtly. "You want to tell me about your dealings with Booth Ewen?"

There was a moment of silence. "Hamburger Heaven," she said. "Meet me at Hamburger Heaven at eleven-thirty." The phone went dead.

I took a leisurely shower, decided to walk to Hamburger Heaven to avoid the parking hell that surrounds the little eatery, and dressed in jeans and Reeboks. I stuffed a twenty-dollar bill in one pocket and the letter in the other. I walked out the front door and into the kind of day that makes you glad to be alive. The sky was clear robin's egg. The sun was bright and warm, but the distance the winter solstice provided made it a benevolent warm, without the strength it holds in the summer.

Hamburger Heaven is, as its name implies, a burger joint about six blocks south of Barton Avenue and a couple of blocks north of Town Hall. Locals eat there, mostly. You'll occasionally come across some millionaire arguing about a ten-cent overcharge on his check, but it's generally a congenial place, buzzing and busy at lunch.

Vanessa was already there when I arrived and waved at me from the booth all the way against the back wall on the right side. It was right smack up against the wall which led to what has to be the world's smallest bathroom; I've feared I might get stuck and never get out.

I sat down and pulled the letter from my jeans pocket.

"Well," I said, and shoved it at her.

She didn't bother to open it.

"He stole my money," she said. "I had five hundred thousand dollars that I saved from a hundred-thousand-dollar a year salary—by living like I made half of that—and he stole it."

The Tupper Foundation, of which I am chairman, gives away ten times that amount every year. But of course I didn't suffer from the lack of money, and I didn't earn it. So I worked at empathizing.

"I'm sure that's annoying," I said. "But that's no reason to kill a person. Is it?"

She lowered her eyebrows. "I didn't kill him."

I raised mine. "How can I believe that?"

She sighed. "I wanted my money back, Wally. Killing him wouldn't get it back for me."

That made sense. "Did you get your money back?"

She shook her head. The waitress arrived. "California burger," Vanessa said.

"Make it two," I said. "And a Diet Coke." I looked back at Vanessa.

She shook her head. "No. And I guess I never will. He told me he had put it in an investment fund, but when I didn't get any confirmation in the mail, I called him and he pretended as if he didn't know what I was talking about. Then I realized how stupid I had been. I wrote the check to cash because he suggested that would make it easier for him. Ha! Did it ever! And I didn't even get a receipt."

Erma taught me to watch my money like a hawk, so I did think she'd been a little foolish. But I felt for her, now, hearing her story. "I'm sorry," I said. "I wish there was something I could do."

She shrugged. "Just don't tell anybody. If the directors of Old Money find out how stupid I was, they'll replace me as CEO. And now I need that job more than ever. I'll have to start over."

I was bummed for her. I've never wanted for money, but I've learned over the years that people who have some value it even more than people who never had a chance of accumulating wealth.

We ate our burgers in silence. When we were done, I paid for the lunch. She let me, and we said a sad good-bye. I didn't know how to make her feel better.

At home, I started on the routine of getting ready. Pitt came home about six, and we dressed in virtual silence, although I did tell him about Vanessa's loss. He nodded. He'd been telling me for years Booth was a crook, so it was no surprise to him, I suppose.

We arrived at the Breakers at nine o'clock. I automatically looked up as I walked into the Venetian Ballroom, a habit developed over nearly thirty years of visiting the hotel.

On painted ceiling panels, fluffy white clouds floated over crystal candelabra. I carried a special feeling in my heart for this ballroom, because I had first brought Pitt to Palm Beach for the New Year's Eve ball in the brand new ballroom in 1969.

"My head is in the clouds," I had told him that night.

They had just recently renovated the ballroom and added the cloud-lined ceiling. To say that it was special was an understatement. The hotel had always felt special to me, a welcoming place.

The warm feelings chilled when I saw Verity and Thornton DeVale not far away. I toyed with the idea of suggesting to Pitt we go find another party somewhere. LaLa swooped out of nowhere and grabbed me by the arm.

"We have to talk," she said. "Follow me." She took off across the room, toward the doors leading into the hotel. Her dress, a dark blue silk with stars of beads on the bodice and a diaphanous skirt of some sort of crimped pleated stuff, billowed behind her. I kept my distance.

When we got to the hallway, she kept on going until she reached the doors to the Mediterranean Courtyard in the center of the hotel. I followed her outside, grateful for the cool Florida night air. She leaned against a column.

"I can't stand it anymore," she said.

I didn't respond. She didn't seem to expect it. She was trembling, and I didn't think it was the temperature.

"I've seen a ghost," she said.

Now, for some people that might be a startling statement. For LaLa, not so very. "Anybody I know?" I asked.

The courtyard was dimly lit, and despite a bright, moonlit sky I strained to make out her face when she said, "Noelle."

"Noelle?"

She sighed. Then I heard her say softly. "Let's sit down," she said.

We perched on the concrete railing around a garden in the center of the courtyard.

"Here's the story," she said. "Remember how Noelle disappeared after our prom and didn't show up for graduation?"

I stared at her in the darkness. How could I forget? It had been our sole topic of conversation for the six months after the prom, our graduation and LaLa's wedding. "Yeah?"

She took a deep breath. "Noelle disappeared because she was pregnant."

I gasped. "How do you know this?"

"Booth told me," she said.

I was confused. "Booth? What did Booth have to do with anything."

"He's the one who got her pregnant," she said. "On the night before our wedding, he taunted me with the information that he had slept with Noelle on prom night...just as he taunted her on prom night with the information that he planned to marry me six weeks later. Unfortunately for her, she was already pregnant with his child. She was afraid and ashamed, so she ran away."

I gasped again. It was getting to be a habit.

"LaLa—" I started.

She held up her hand in a stop sign. "Don't lecture me about how you and Peep told me not to marry him, Wally. I can't take it tonight, and it wouldn't do any good."

I snapped my mouth closed. She was right. "You're right," I said. I felt for her, but it had all happened some thirty years before. "It's long past."

"If only," she said.

I remembered now what she had said when we walked outside. "What did you mean, you've seen a ghost?"

"There's more to the story," she said. "Noelle had the baby."

"What?"

"I didn't know this part until after Booth died," she said. "I didn't want you poking around in Booth's papers because I was afraid you might find something about it."

I didn't say anything while a wave of guilt crashed on my shores. Yes, I might have.

"This morning," she said, "I went through all of Booth's desk myself, and I found a letter from Noelle."

She shifted as if uncomfortable on the concrete balustrade. "The letter was written more than twenty-five years ago. She told him he had a daughter. She wanted him to know, she said, because it was not the baby's fault how she was conceived, and perhaps when she was twenty-one, Noelle said, she would tell her who her father was."

"But," I said. "She'd be thirty years old now."

LaLa nodded in the night. "I know who it is."

"How? Who?"

"You told me," she said. "Yesterday."

Suddenly, it all fell into place. The questions, the attitude, the hatred. "Verity," I said. "Verity DeVale."

LaLa nodded. "I think so."

"Then," I said, "she...must have killed him."

LaLa shrugged and stood up. "I don't know. I've been speaking all day with my spirit guide, but she has no answers. The cards won't help me. I'm at a loss what to do."

"Well," I said. "Why don't we ask her?"

I parked LaLa, ordering her to stay in the courtyard beside the fountain rimmed with little creatures who eternally spit water out of their mouths.

My mind playing fast-forwarded videos of Noelle with Verity's face overlaid, I began to see the resemblance. Nothing obvious, just a line of the jaw, the smile, the crinkle of an eye. What kept them from looking alike, I realized as I approached Verity in the ballroom, was that Noelle's face was, in my mind, the happy, relaxed face of a teenager.

As I approached Verity, her edgy, tense mask grew uglier, erasing the pictures in my mind.

Ice dripped from her voice to match the diamonds on her ears and neck. "Yes?"

"I need to speak to you," I said, and before the certain refusal, said, "It's about Noelle."

Her face morphed to the very picture of sadness.

"Okay," she mumbled.

She followed me silently through the thronging partiers, into the lobby and outside to the courtyard, where LaLa sat.

Verity went on the attack as soon as we stopped.

"Now you know why I hate you so much," she said. "Why I can barely stand the sight of you."

LaLa didn't react, but I did.

"Why would you hate us?" I asked.

Verity turned her head toward LaLa.

"My spirit guide said she was safe," LaLa said, her voice barely audible, even in the quiet night air. "I did her charts...."

"Where's Noelle?" I broke in. "Where is she?"

"Dead," Verity said, spitting the word off her tongue like the husk from a kernel of popcorn. "When I was six. I didn't know who she was or who my father was until my adopted parents died two years ago and I found my mother's letters in their things."

"Letters?" I said.

"She wrote letters to....him...," Verity said, barely able to force the word out of her throat. "They came back, unopened. She begged him to take me in, to make me part of his life."

She glared at LaLa. "But you were too selfish to allow such a thing, weren't you?"

I suddenly realized something. "You killed him," I said. "You killed him."

Verity's eyebrows went up. "I hated him," she said. "Can you imagine the ugly feeling in my stomach when I met for the first time the man who had ruined my mother's life?"

I backed up a step. Where was Tony? I wondered. I knew he should be here somewhere. "I didn't kill him," she said. "I had something more long-term in mind. I wanted to ruin him." Her eyes glistened with an evil light. "I put the turd in his coffin. He deserved it."

She looked at LaLa. "And you. I can still ruin you. I put the note in your pocket. I want people to know what kind of a person you are."

"I didn't know," LaLa said, her head moving back and forth slowly. "I didn't know."

She looked up at Verity. "I didn't know about you...until this morning. He didn't return all of her letters. He kept a few of them. I found them."

Verity shook a dismissive hand in LaLa's direction. "When I get through with you, you won't be able to hold up your head in this town. And your little friend Peep, too." She got up and started toward the door.

"Hold on just a minute." Rezna's voice came from the shadows behind us.

We all turned, as if Steven Spielberg himself were directing.

"Mrs. DeVale, here, was the one who presented to me the 'evidence' that Peep had killed her first husband," Rezna said. She was wearing a full body beaded gown and trembling so violently in her anger that the gown was sending out sparks of light like a disco dance ball.

"I don't like being used," she continued. She looked at me. "I made a mistake printing that slop about Peep, and I'll retract it."

Rezna turned to Verity. "I think you ought to think for just a moment about what your next move will be. Because if it's the wrong one, you could find yourself the topic of a very unflattering column."

Rezna nodded a head toward the partiers inside. "I don't think Thornton would be too happy with that, do you?"

Verity took a breath. "No," she said. "I don't."

"So," I said, "can we work a deal here?" All eyes were on me. "Rezna," I said. "You write a column that showers glowing tributes on both Peep and Verity. Verity, you spend some time with LaLa and learn about your mother from her best friend."

They all nodded at me.

"And you?" Rezna asked.

"Me?" I said. "Well, maybe I'm the only one who remembers that we still have a murderer loose around here."

Chapter Eighteen

IN THE HOTEL LOBBY, REGGIE Wert paced like a caged tiger. "We'll have it anyway," he groused, his anger at having his list of Breakers Babies stolen still not dissipated.

"I'm sure people will understand," I said. Did anybody really care? I wondered to myself.

"The press," Reggie mumbled. "The media. The specials. The prince."

I had forgotten. A *Palm Beach Post* story had reported that because of the Breakers Centennial year, there would be an unusual amount of publicity about this celebration. A&E wanted to do a special about the Breakers Babies. The History Channel wanted to do a special about the one hundred years of the Breakers. Without the historical information, all that was in jeopardy.

And to add to the media attention, Prince Charles had agreed to attend the ball, in spite of the rampaging Society Killer on the loose in Palm Beach. Rumor had it he was already on his way from the airport.

"I remember some of them," Reggie blurted. "Darla Dugan. Lois Davis. Al McHenry. All local. All here. Cream of the crop. We can go on."

From somewhere inside the ballroom I heard a smattering of applause. It started light, but it grew. In a matter of thirty seconds, it sounded as if the entire ballroom of people was applauding something. Reggie and I exchanged questioning glances and broke for the door to the ballroom.

Peep stood just inside the door, Mitch on her arm. The applause was for her. I'd have shed a tear if I hadn't had a few other things on my mind.

Ten feet away, Verity tried to hold back tears of a different sort. Thornton glared at her. His look said, "I told you so."

Vanessa pulled Digby along behind her. She smiled broadly; he looked grim. *Uh-oh,* I thought.

"We have such good news," she said. She was a vision in a red strapless number that did great things with her figure. I wondered where she had gotten the ruby necklace. "We've taken care of Raymond."

"Huh?" I said, trying to read Digby's eyes. "What do you mean?"

Digby, a stunner himself in his tux, smiled weakly. "It's over between me and Ray," he said. "But he's going to pay the money back to LaLa."

"Oh, good," I said. "I guess." I paused a minute. "Do we know they didn't kill Booth?"

Vanessa seemed startled by the question. Digby answered. "I don't think Ray would do that," he said. "Besides, why would he if he were getting the money from Booth, instead of the other way around?"

"Yeah," Vanessa said. "Why kill the goose, you know?"

We stopped for a moment while Reggie said something about the Breakers Babies being honored later in the evening. I saw Darla move across the room. She was wearing a most unflattering off the shoulder gown in a dark green. The gown pulled across her bust and stomach in such an unattractive line, not even the emerald and diamond necklace she wore could detract the eye's attention.

"Wally?" Digby said. "Isn't that you?"

"Don't know," I said. "No way to know. No records, no pictures. I'm still a mystery person."

He leaned down and kissed me on the cheek. "No mystery to you," he said. "You're just Wally."

I nodded mutely. I guessed I always would be just Wally.

I wandered around the ballroom, not sure what I was looking for. Something buzzed in the back of my brain. A whisper, so soft I couldn't hear it. I knew I was looking for something—but what?

Edgy, I went back outside to the courtyard to get some air. I was admiring the full moon when I heard someone breathing behind me. I turned around.

"Darla," I said. She looked keyed up, edgy. Her eyes darted around, her chest heaved with rapid breath. The moonlight made the diamonds around her emerald pendant twinkle, and suddenly I knew.

The wispy, fresh-faced high school girl with the emerald pendant. The strange, pudgy woman with the emerald pendant. One and the same.

"Desdemona," I breathed.

"Well," she said through pursed lips. "Aren't you the smart one? I've been surprised that any of my old friends would recognize me." She smiled a goofy smile. "Friends," she said. "I called you friends. But you're not really my friends, are you?"

She was right, but this didn't seem the time to agree with her. "Of course we are, Desdemona." I looked at her closely. "You've changed."

"Had to, didn't I?" she barked. "Didn't want anybody to recognize poor old Desdemona. Not invite her to your parties. Not speak to her on Worth Avenue. Not include her in your teas."

Subtlely, I thought, I scanned the courtyard to see if anyone was nearby. All those people out here earlier, but not a soul in sight now.

"Looking for someone?" she crooned in a sing-song voice. "No one's here, dearie. Just us chickens."

"Did you have some...work done on yourself?" I asked gently, giving myself time to think what to do.

"Heaps," she cackled. "Nose job. Hair. Contacts. Already gained weight." She frowned. "How did you know?"

"The necklace," I said. "You wore it to our senior prom."

"Ohhhh. Imagine you remembering that."

She knit her brows together, waiting on a thought, then smiled as it arrived. "Never mind," she said. "No matter. Let's take a walk."

I didn't like the sound of that. "Pardon?" I said.

"Come with me," she said. "Little stroll; all over. Got things to do."

I tried a ploy. "Something I can help you with?"

"Got to stop the Breakers Babies procession," she said.

"I'll be happy to speak to Reggie for you," I offered helpfully.

She took the gun out of her purse. It was tiny, with a pearl handle. Very cute. "Move it," she said. "Through the lobby and down the hall. Don't speak to anyone."

"Okey dokey," I said. "Let's take a walk."

I moved slowly through the lobby, nodding and smiling silently at people as I passed them, wishing someone would suddenly shout out, "She's got a gun!" like they do in the movies. It didn't happen, so I decided I'd better come up with another plan. I worked my way down the hall.

Suddenly the doors to the Gold Room flung open and partiers streamed forth from whatever function had been in process. They were happy, and they were pushy. They surrounded me, laughing and talking.

When I saw Desdemona being pushed along in the crowd, I took a chance. I ducked into the Gold Room, cutting a sharp left turn and trying to get as much into the crowd as I could. It worked. I managed to immerse myself in a group, inching my way toward the other door out of the room. As we got near the door, I put my arm around the waist of a tuxedoed man a foot taller than myself.

"Buddy!" I said, trying to sound a little on the inebriated side. "Walk me to the valet parking, will you, old chum? I seem to be a bit wobbly."

Being a gentleman, he agreed, and gave his friends a helpless look. Hiding behind him, I let him think he was helping me out the front entrance and to the *porte cochere*.

"Thanks ever so," I said when we got there. "Get back to your friends, now." He did, looking relieved.

I planted myself on the far side of a column and tried to catch my breath. We had come in Pitt's Mercedes, so I didn't have my car and I didn't have the valet ticket.

I concentrated on being invisible. Thank goodness I hadn't succeeded when Tony pulled up in front of the hotel in a police car. I sighed with relief and ran towards him.

"Tony, you are not going to believe this," I said.

"And I've got something you're not going to believe," he said. "Remember you told me about the prowler at Darla Dugan's house in New Smyrna Beach? Well, I called the department up there and asked them to check out the house. Guess what they found?"

It didn't take much of a leap.

"Darla Dugan," I said. "What did she say?"

"She didn't say anything," he said. "She was long, long dead."

I gasped. Of course. Why hadn't I known?

"Desdemona did it," I said.

"Who?"

I forgot Tony had been gone from Palm Beach for a long time. "Remember Desdemona from high school? She married Mitch—oh, it's a long story. But she killed Darla and assumed her identity. She's been in Palm Beach as Darla for several months now."

"Oh," he said.

"I think she wants to kill me next," I said. "Oh, and, she's got a gun."

He reached automatically to feel for his own. "Where is she?"

"Somewhere inside. She tried to take me out at gunpoint but I got away."

"Let's go," he said. "Stay near me."

He didn't have to tell me twice.

I lost sight of Tony the minute we entered the Venetian ballroom, because I saw the look on Pitt's face when he saw the two of us together. Before I realized what I had done, I made a beeline for my husband. I remembered Tony and turned around to find him gone.

As I approached Pitt, I nearly got knocked over by a waiter emerging from a door in the wall. It was one of the doors that goes into the bowels of the hotel, where the staff do their work for the functions held in the ballrooms.

I hugged my husband. "Trouble in paradise," I said.

"I know," he replied.

"Pitt, don't let's fight at the moment, because someone is trying to kill me."

"Kill you?" He looked justifiably doubtful.

"Desdemona."

"Desdemona?"

"Stop echoing me and help me look for her. She looks like Darla—I mean, she *is* Darla Dugan."

"You've lost me."

"I hope not," I said. "Look, just find LaLa for me, and Peep, tell them Darla is Desdemona, and to get the hell out of her way."

He shrugged and shook his head, bewildered. "Okay."

I turned and pulled on the little metal ring on the door in wall. It pulled open to reveal a concrete floored hallway. Stacked tables occupied almost every spare inch of space. Folded chairs filled in the rest of the space.

I made my way down the narrow passage to a swinging door. I opened one door, gingerly peeking through. Brown-paper wrapped packages tied up with string were stacked from floor to ceiling. They were stamped "laundry," so I figured they must be clean tablecloths and napkins, of which thousands are used in a week at a hotel like the Breakers.

"Why there you are," Desdemona said. She stepped out from behind a stack of laundry. The gun was in her hand. I wondered why I thought looking for her was a good idea.

"Hello again," I said. "Oh, Desdemona, I have a question for you."

"Certainly, dear. If you would just step over here." She motioned with the gun toward a two-foot laundry package. "Sit."

I did.

"What's your question?" she said, rummaging in her purse while keeping her eyes on me.

"Did you by any chance kill Booth Ewen?"

She nodded thoughtfully. "Why, yes I did," she said.

"May I ask why?"

She continued to rummage in her purse. "Sure. He knew about Eaton. He saw me push Eaton in front of the Santa sleigh. So I had to get rid of him."

"Eaton?" I said, stunned.

"He knew I was at Darla's," she said. "They were old friends, and little did I know he was one of the few people she would allow to visit her in New Smyrna Beach. God knows nobody else came to that God-forsaken place. She wouldn't even have servants. But one day Eaton arrived and there I was. So I came down last Christmas and silenced him."

She smiled a self-satisfied smile as she located whatever she was looking for in her bag. "I wouldn't have killed Booth, but he happened to see it. So he tried to blackmail me when he figured out I was masquerading as Darla."

She held up a book of matches. I waited for her to pull out a pack of cigarettes.

I was getting the major shivers.

"Taffy?" I said.

"Yep," she said, putting down the matches. She pumped an arm, working her biceps, like a weightlifter. "Those hours in the fitness center really paid off on that one. She fought."

"Why?"

She rummaged in her bag again and pulled out fingernail clippers. With them, she clipped off some of the string binding a laundry package. "She knew I was an imposter," she said. "I could tell by the look in her eyes at DeVales' that night. And she was going to tell you."

Watching me carefully, gun pointed right at me, she pulled off the twine.

I feared I knew what was on her mind. Sure enough, she came over and stood a couple of feet away. "Stand up and turn around," she said.

I did.

"Put your wrists together," she ordered. *We've all watched way too much TV,* I thought, complying with her order. She wrapped the string around my wrists. It was tight and it hurt.

"Ow," I said, pulling with my hands. The string only got tighter. Somehow she had my wrists tied to the string on the package on which I leaned.

She ignored me and walked back over to where her purse sat. She put the gun down beside it. Then she walked over to the wall and pulled out a cardboard box from behind a stack of laundry. She picked it up and brought it over next to her bag.

I stood about two feet away from a wall. Behind it, I could hear people talking and laughing, with music in the background. The wall apparently was shared with the Venetian ballroom; I was just feet away from several hundred people. But would they hear me if I yelled? A mistake could be costly. I stayed quiet.

She started pulling papers and photographs from the cardboard box and stacking them on top of the laundry package. She arranged them carefully, as if she had a certain way she wanted them to look. There were papers and photographs. She stacked them in a little circle that had a hole in the center. Then she began crumpling up papers and putting them in the center. It looked like a little bitty campfire.

My skin went cold.

Matches.

Campfire.

"Desdemona," I said sweetly. "What are you doing?"

"We can't have that processional," she said. "They'll take pictures."

"Processional?"

"The Breakers Babies," she said. "Darla was one, you know."

I hadn't until Reggie had said so earlier. "Yeah?"

"Pictures," she said as if I were some sort of idiot. "Television. People who knew Darla might see it. My cover would be blown."

I didn't think now was the time to tell her that ship had sailed. "I can talk Reggie out of it if you'll let me," I said, thinking myself quite the clever one.

"You'd just run," she said. "You already did."

"Why don't you just leave?" I said. "Don't be in it."

"They'll come after me for the television show," she said. "They'll run after me with cameras."

"You'll hurt people," I said. "Innocent people."

"They're not so innocent," she said. "They all conspire to keep people out." She dropped her shoulders and looked at me with eyes I remembered from thirty years ago. "It hurts, you know."

Guilt pinched tighter than the string on my wrists. "I thought you said I was one of the nice ones."

She looked thoughtful. "You still excluded me," she said. "I tried so hard to please Mitch. He wanted to go to your parties."

My parties. Even I didn't want to go to my parties.

"Did you follow Peep?" I asked.

"Yep. I wanted to learn what it was about her that makes people like her and accept her—I mean, she's invited everywhere. Why?"

I couldn't answer that one myself, but I was getting the answers to a lot of questions from the last few weeks.

"And you followed me?"

"When you were all in Peep's Jaguar, I thought I could get rid of all of you. Almost did, too." She struck a match.

"People have already recognized you," I pointed out. "You know it will happen again."

"I don't think I'll stay in Palm Beach," she said. "I think I'll go to Paris. Nobody will know there. Or care. And if I do this right, no one here will be able to talk."

She held the match to a laundry pile. It caught. Like Queen Elizabeth anointing nobility, she walked around the room, touching a burning match to each laundry package. First the paper would catch, then the string, then finally the cloth inside.

It was my luck that genuine royalty decided to arrive just as Desdemona decided to make stairs out of several laundry packages and climb up to reach a taller stack.

Apparently, Prince Charles arrived at the ball, because just on the other side of the wall hundreds of people broke out simultaneously in thunderous applause.

It startled Desdemona, causing her to lose her footing. Horrified, I watched her struggle to keep her balance, then pitch off the ten-foot stack. She landed on one knee. *That had to hurt*, I thought, though I couldn't hear anything but applause.

Unfortunately, the applause hid my screams. As the flames began to crack around me, I pulled at the strings binding my wrists. They wouldn't break, but I was able to pull the laundry stack, inch by inch, along behind me.

I lumbered across the room, pulling my burden behind me. When I reached her purse, I knocked it over with my chin and pulled at it with my teeth until the clippers fell out. I picked them up in my teeth, turned around and dropped them onto my shadow laundry package. Then I leaned backward and picked them up in my hands. I clipped the string around the laundry package until those that bound my wrists to the package were cut. Then I concentrated on clipping the ones on my wrists.

Finally, I succeeded. Like a madwoman, I unwrapped the laundry and pulled a tablecloth from the package. I threw it over the burning paper, extinguishing the fire and wrapping the smoldering papers and ashes in the cloth. I pulled the corner together and carried my gerryrigged bag over to where Desdemona lay, clutching an obviously broken leg.

"Let me help you," I shouted. "I'll get us out of here."

She grabbed me around the neck and pulled. I almost tumbled on top of her, but I grabbed her arm and pulled her to her good foot. Together, her arm around my neck, we hobbled toward the exit into the ballroom.

While we were struggling with this maneuver, the applause in the ballroom changed to screams as the crowd began to smell the smoke. I could hear the pandemonium. I detoured to a wall and set off a fire alarm, no mean feat with Desdemona hanging on to me.

As we reached the door into the ballroom, she suddenly gave a huge lunge and pushed me down to the floor. The portfolio fell and Reggie's papers flew everywhere, and as I scrambled to collect what I could, she limped back into the laundry room, disappearing behind a stack of tablecloths.

My bag of scorched history once again clutched to my breast, I stumbled out the door and into the hysterical crowd in the ballroom. With a rush, the sprinklers came on and as Breakers staff ushered the guests out the exits, we all got soaked.

I emerged from the hotel, sopping wet, to find Pitt looking anxiously for me. He grabbed me and wrapped me in a hug. I turned around to see Reggie, trying against the restraining arms of several Palm Beach firefighters, to go back inside the building. I ran over and grabbed Reggie by the arm and pulled at him. "I've got your papers, Reggie."

I pointed at the tablecloth bag in my arms. He understood, and a big smile broke out on his face.

While hundreds of guests sat, soaking wet, on the lawns and beach while the firemen worked, the hotel staff went solicitously around, doing what they could to make the guests comfortable.

Reggie picked through the ashes to see what survived of his precious records. "She wouldn't burn, you know," he said. "The Breakers wouldn't burn. She was built not to."

I had to admit he was right. It appeared that except for the laundry and some decoration, not much had actually caught fire. The firemen didn't appear to be in panic mode; they squirted smoldering areas, watchful. They said no one had been hurt, except for being jostled as the crowd left the building.

Pitt wrapped me in a blanket, and I leaned against him as we sat on a wall.

"Wally?" Reggie said.

I looked at him. He handed me a photograph, burned at the edges. I looked at it. "Women holding babies?" I said.

"The Breakers Babies," he said.

Rezna came up behind us, wrapped in a Breakers blanket.

"Let me see that," she said. I held up the photo to the light from the beach patio. She leaned in. "There she is," she said.

"My mother?" I said. I scrutinized the photo. "Which one?"

"That one," she said, pointing.

A dark-haired young woman stood among a dozen others in front of the barebreasted women of the fountain at the front entrance to the Breakers. She held a baby in each arm.

I flipped over the photo. The ink was faded to a light sepia, but the names were readable. Second row left: Cay Calvert Tupper. While babies names were not given, I had to assume I was one of them. It appeared I belonged in Palm Beach, after all. I realized I had been living in fear of this moment—of opening the Pandora's box of my past. But all I felt was relief at not fighting it anymore. Whatever it was, it was part of me.

Tony came out of the building and walked toward us as if his feet weighed a hundred pounds each.

"We found her," he said. "We found Desdemona." He shook his head, slowly. "She didn't make it out of the laundry room."

Sorrow burst up in me like the flames from which I just escaped. I clutched the photo so tightly I could feel the glass straining under my grip. The Breakers Hotel had stood a hundred years, and had a hundred times a hundred secrets to divulge. One of them had surfaced tonight, answering my questions about my birth.

But, I realized, the Breakers had confirmed one thing I knew already, something that is a secret only to those who most need to know: Money can't buy happiness, and don't let anyone tell you it can.